Lily
AND
DUNKIN

Also by Donna Gephart

As If Being 12¾ Isn't Bad Enough,
My Mother Is Running for President!

How to Survive Middle School

Olivia Bean, Trivia Queen

Death by Toilet Paper

DONNA GEPHART

Lily

AND

DUNKIN

Delacorte Press

30776 6098

G

Text copyright © 2016 by Donna Gephart
Jacket art copyright © 2016 by Mary Kate McDevitt

All rights reserved. Published in the United States by Delacorte Press,
an imprint of Random House Children's Books,
a division of Penguin Random House LLC, New York.

Delacorte Press is a registered trademark and the colophon
is a trademark of Penguin Random House LLC.

Visit us on the Web! randomhousekids.com

Educators and librarians, for a variety of teaching tools,
visit us at RHTeachersLibrarians.com

Library of Congress Cataloging-in-Publication Data
Gephart, Donna.
Lily and Dunkin / Donna Gephart. — First edition.
pages cm
ISBN 978-0-553-53674-4 (hc) — ISBN 978-0-553-53675-1 (glb) —
ISBN 978-0-553-53676-8 (ebook)
[1. Friendship—Fiction. 2. Transgender people—Fiction. 3. Manic-depressive
illness—Fiction. 4. Mental illness—Fiction. 5. Middle schools—Fiction.
6. Schools—Fiction. 7. Florida—Fiction.] I. Title.
PZ7.G293463Li 2016
[Fic]—dc23
2015017801

The text of this book is set in 13-point Granjon.
Jacket design by Sarah Hokanson
Interior design by Trish Parcell

Printed in the United States of America
10 9 8 7 6 5 4 3 2 1
First Edition

In memory of Leelah Alcorn

(11/15/97–12/28/14),

whose life and death

show us the urgent need for empathy,

understanding and kindness.

And to our son, Andrew . . .

because I promised.

You cannot do a kindness too soon,

for you never know how soon it will be too late.

—RALPH WALDO EMERSON

Lily's Family Tree

Bob McGrother

Ruth McGrother

Gary McGrother

Ellie McGrother

Sarah McGrother

Lily Jo McGrother
(Timothy James McGrother)

Meatball McGrother *(dog)*

DUNKIN'S FAMILY TREE

Bubbie Bernice

Doug Dorfman

Gail Dorfman

Dunkin Dorfman *(born Norbert Dorfman)*

Girl

Lily Jo is not my name. Yet.

But I'm working on that.

That's why I'm in the closet. Literally in my mom's walk-in closet, with Meatball at my heels.

I scratch under Meatball's chin, and his tiny pink tongue pokes out the side of his mouth. He's adorable like that.

"Practice," I tell Meatball. "Only six days until school starts." *I have to do this. I can't. Have to. Can't.* I almost feel my best friend (okay, my only friend), Dare, push me toward the dresses.

Thinking about my plan for the first day of eighth grade makes my stomach drop, like I plunged over the crest of a roller coaster at Universal Studios. I'm sure not one other person going to Gator Lake Middle is dealing with what I am, probably not one other person in the entire state of Florida. Statistically, I know that's not true, because I looked up a lot of information on the Internet, but it feels that way sometimes.

Meatball's wagging his stubby tail so hard his whole body shakes. I wish the world were made of dogs. They love you one hundred percent of the time, no matter what.

"I've got one for you," I tell Meatball as I pull a hanger from the rack. "The past, the present and the future all walk into a bar."

I examine the summery red fabric. The tiny white flower print. I remember being with Mom when she bought this dress.

"Ready for the punch line?"

Meatball looks up at me with his big brown eyes, dark fur falling into them.

"It was tense."

Silence.

Holding the dress to my chest, I say, "The past, the present and the future all walk into a bar. It was tense. Get it?"

Meatball tilts his head, as though he's trying hard to understand. I scratch under his chin to let him know he's such a good dog and I'm a total dork for telling a grammar joke to an animal.

Then I focus on the dress.

"These are lilies of the valley," Mom said, pointing to the flowers when we were in the store. She held the dress to her cheek for a moment. "Those were my favorite flowers when I was growing up in Burlington, New Jersey. We had them in the garden in front of our house, near the pink azalea bushes. They smelled so good!"

I sniff the flowers now, as though the tiny, bell-shaped blossoms will smell like anything other than a dress. "I'm glad Dad's at Publix," I tell Meatball. "And Mom's at her studio. Gives me time to put the first part of my plan into action. The practicing part."

Half of me is so excited I could explode. It feels good to finally be doing this. The other half—where other people's voices jam together in my brain—is terrified. Excited. Terrified. Yup, those are the right words.

I take off my pajamas and let the dress slide over my head and body. The silky lining feels smooth and soft against my skin. It's hard to get the zipper up in the back. I consider going to Sarah's room and asking for help, but decide to do it myself, even though I know she'd help me.

When I was little, I tried on one of Sarah's old dresses and loved how it felt. How *I* felt in it. When Mom came home from work that day, she laughed and made me whirl and twirl. Even Dad laughed. Back then.

"What do you think?" I ask Meatball while I twirl, feeling the skirt of the dress drift up, then back down against my legs.

Meatball barks.

"I'll take that as an approval."

He barks again.

"Or you might have to pee."

I slip into Mom's sandals, barely believing my feet have now grown as large as hers, but they have.

In her full-length mirror, I see how the top of the dress bags out. If only I had something up there to fill it out, like Mom and Sarah do. I consider grabbing one of Mom's bras and stuffing it with socks, to see how it would look. How it would feel.

A blaring car horn shatters my thoughts.

Meatball barks.

Scooping him under my arm, I put my face up close to his. "Come on. Let's help Dad carry in the groceries."

He licks my nose.

"Oh, Meatball, your breath is so bad."

He nuzzles into my arm.

"But your heart is so good." I kiss the top of his head. "Hope Dad remembered Pop-Tarts. Breakfast of champions."

As we rush down the stairs, I hear Sarah's bedroom door open behind me. When we reach the bottom, I let Meatball down, then hurry to the front door and fling it open.

Dad's bent over, grabbing bags from the trunk of his car. I walk down the path to help. It's so bright and sunny, I have to shield my eyes with my forearm, but I can make out the back of Dad's T-shirt: *The King Pines*. I laugh out loud, realizing it was probably supposed to read *The King Pins* for one of the local bowling teams. Dad and his mom, Grandmom Ruth, run a T-shirt screen-printing business—We've Got You Covered—and sometimes orders get messed up.

Because Dad hates to waste anything, we all end up

wearing his mistakes. My favorite was when a group of senior citizens asked Dad to make matching shirts for their upcoming vacation with the words *The Bus Trippers*. Dad goofed on the spacing, and the shirts ended up as *The Bu Strippers*. He had to redo the whole order. Those shirts got tossed, though, because Dad said there was no way any of us were wearing those rejects. It's funny how one little letter can make such a big difference to the meaning.

Grandpop Bob, who started the business with Grandmom Ruth about a million years ago, used to say, "Words have the power to change the world. Use them carefully."

After two years without him, I still miss him and his wise words.

I'm reaching my hand out to help when Dad turns toward me, each of his hands loaded with grocery bags.

I hold my breath, hoping Dad understands how much this means to me. Hoping that this time will be different, that—

"Timothy! What the hell are you doing?"

I deflate like a week-old balloon. *Practicing, Dad. I'm practicing being me.*

"You know the rule," he says, letting out a huge breath. "You can't be outside the house dressed like that." Dad shifts the bags in his hands. "Where's your mother?"

I let my arms fall slack to my sides. I wouldn't have the energy to carry in the groceries now, if I wanted to. And I certainly don't have the energy to answer Dad. He should know Mom's at her yoga studio. It's not my job to remind him of her schedule.

"Go back in the house, Tim." Dad sounds like the air has leaked out of him, too. I hate that I caused it. "What if one of your classmates sees you? Imagine how they'd make fun of you when school starts. Get in now. Go."

They already make fun of me, Dad.

He looks around. "Someone's coming. Hurry."

I glance along the sidewalk. Someone *is* coming. A boy, carrying a Dunkin' Donuts bag and grooving to some music only he can hear. I love the way he doesn't seem to care how he looks, dance-walking outside like that. He could be in a commercial for Dunkin' Donuts: "happy-looking, doughnut-carrying boy." I wish I felt that happy. I wish—

"Go!" Dad says.

I should walk back inside. Make it easier for Dad. Make it easier for myself.

But I don't.

The boy gets closer to our house. He's about my age. Tall. Curly, dark hair, kind of like Meatball's fur. Pants too heavy for this summer heat.

Dad's face is bright red now. He's breathing hard through his nostrils, like a bull. I wish *he'd* go inside and leave me alone, but he's standing there, sweat drenching the pits of his reject T-shirt.

Every molecule in my body tells me to move, but I force myself to wait a few more seconds. Dare would be so proud, but she's not here. I look back and see Sarah in the doorway—slender, graceful, with her shoulders back and her red hair, long and loose—Meatball, his stumpy tail wagging, at her feet. I can tell by the look in Sarah's eyes that she's rooting for me, waiting to see what I'll do. To see what Dad will do. *Practice,* I tell myself. *This is practice.* And I pull my shoulders back, too.

"Timothy McGrother," Dad says quietly. "If you want to wear *that*"—he juts his chin toward Mom's beautiful dress with disgust—"you'll do it inside our house. Not out here." He looks at the tall boy with the heavy pants, who is much closer now. "Do . . . you . . . understand?"

My heart stampedes.

Sarah steps outside, wearing a skirt, tank top and sandals. No one yells at her to go back inside. No alarm bells clang when she comes outside wearing a skirt. No one's worried the neighbors in perfectly posh Beckford Palms Estates will see her. No one's ashamed . . . of her.

"Now!" Dad explodes, straining from the grocery bags he's carrying and from his frustration with me.

"I'm going," I say. "It's just—"

"Hurry, Tim!"

Dad sounds more panicked than angry, so I turn. But then I swivel back because that boy, who I've never seen around here before, is on the sidewalk, passing right in front of our house. I can almost hear my friend Dare screaming inside my head, *Say hello to him, idiot!*

7

Practice, I tell myself. *Say hello, Idiot. Practice. Hello, Idiot.*

I lift my arm and wave, entirely aware that I'm wearing my mom's red dress and white sandals. *Hello, Idiot.*

From the corner of my eye, I see the vein in Dad's temple pulse.

The boy notices me waving. He stops grooving and looks my way, surprised. *What does he see? A girl stuck in a boy's body or a boy stuck in a girl's dress? Probably the latter.* I expect his features to twist into pure revulsion. My mind shuffles through every way this can go horribly wrong. In front of Dad. *What was I thinking?*

But the boy smiles. At me. Outside in bright daylight, while I'm wearing my mom's dress and sandals. Maybe he thinks I'm a girl. *I am a girl.* Unfortunately, not everyone understands that yet.

Then the boy waves back, with the hand holding the Dunkin' bag. I officially love that bag. And if I'm not mistaken, he walks with more bounce in his step as he continues on. *Could that be because of me or is it the music he's listening to?*

"Happy now?" Dad asks. His voice sounds defeated. "Please move. These bags are breaking my arms."

I sashay back up the path to our house, to my sister, who I know saw the whole thing and is smiling, too. "Don't worry," Sarah whispers into my ear. "I'll get the rest of the bags." Then she adds, "He's cute. Isn't he?" And my heart flutters.

I love my sister.

And I can't keep the smile from my face, even though I know Dad is sad and mad and disappointed. Because of that Dunkin' Donuts boy, I feel my first practice went pretty well.

Dad drops the grocery bags onto the kitchen counter so hard, I worry the glass jars I hear smack against the countertop might break. But I don't stick around to find out if they do, not even to check and see if he remembered Pop-Tarts.

Upstairs in my room, lying on my side atop the ugly brown comforter with Meatball curled behind my knees, I smooth over the tiny flowers on Mom's dress again and again.

The Dunkin' Donuts boy smiled when he saw me.
Me.
Lily Jo McGrother.
Girl.

BOY

Norbert is not a normal name. I would do anything to change it to something less make-fun-able.

But Dad named me after his father and his grandfather. *Dad. Don't think about him.*

As if I could ever put the brakes on my brain. My mind is like a multilevel racetrack with dozens of cars zipping in different directions. To stop that much mental activity, it would take something drastic, like getting run over by a Mack truck.

I cross the street out of Beckford Palms Estates, where we're staying with Bubbie, into the real world of smaller homes and strip malls with Publix grocery stores. And heat. Wet, sticky heat. No Mack trucks, though. In fact, hardly any traffic at all. In New Jersey, where I'm from, you took your life in your hands when you crossed a street this big.

Safely on the opposite side, I try to remember which way to the Dunkin' Donuts. It's been a long time since I've been here, visiting Bubbie Bernice, and back then Mom drove us to the Dunkin', so I didn't pay attention to which way she went. *What would I change my name to? Thaddeus? Pretentious. Mark? Boring. Phineas? Already taken.* This makes me smile. Good old Phineas. I can't believe I had to leave him behind when we moved to Florida. Leaving my friend Phineas was one of the toughest things about leaving New Jersey and moving here.

But not *the* toughest thing.

Don't think about it!

No one here knows me as Norbert. Maybe I could change my name before school starts. I'll ask Mom.

I can't believe school starts in only six days. I'll have to get clothes. I wish they required uniforms so at least I'd know what everyone would be wearing. Are the styles the same here in Florida as they are in New Jersey? I wish

Phin were here. He'd know what I should wear. He's so good at knowing stuff like that—what's cool and what's lame.

Even without Phin telling me, it's obvious what I'm wearing now is super lame. It's about a million degrees, and I'm sweating in places I didn't know you could sweat— like the backs of my knees—because I'm wearing corduroy pants. What sane person wears corduroy pants in August in South Florida? But when I realized how flippin' hot it was, I didn't want to go back into the house to change. Mom was crying when I left, and Bubbie was patting her hand and making her tea. When Mom cries this hard, it makes me worry about Dad, and I think maybe he's not going to be okay. I can't think negatively, so I had to get out. And stay out for a while, corduroy pants melting my legs and all.

Before I left New Jersey, Phin told me I needed to be relentlessly positive. So that's what I'm going to do. Dad's going to be okay. Dad's going to be okay. Dad's going to be—

Stop. Thinking. About. It.

To quiet my brain as I walk, I stick in earbuds and turn the volume way up on the music Phineas had chosen for me the last time we hung out. He said he picked all upbeat songs because he knew I'd need them. And here I am, in hotter-than-Hades South Florida, needing them.

I hope I find someone to sit with during lunch at Gator

Lake Middle—my new school. We drove by it yesterday. There's a track and basketball courts behind the one-story building and a small lake. I wonder if there are alligators in the lake. Probably. That might be why it's called Gator Lake Middle.

Bubbie told me alligators could be in any body of water other than a swimming pool or the ocean. I didn't believe her, so I looked up some stuff about Florida. She's right about the alligators. But I'll bet she didn't know it's estimated that there are 1.3 million alligators in Florida.

If you think about it—and I have—there are at least six ways to die in South Florida: being eaten by an alligator, poisonous snakebite (there are six varieties of poisonous snakes in Florida), lightning strike (South Florida is the lightning-strike capital of the United States), hurricane, flood, even fire-ant bites, if there are enough of them.

I wish we hadn't moved to South Florida. There are too many ways to die here.

I don't want to die. I don't want—

Stop! You're not going to die here in South Florida.

But it could happen. It could happen anywhere.

Sometimes, I wish there were an off switch for my race-car thoughts.

I walk faster with extra-long strides to match my thrumming heartbeat, even though I don't know where I'm going.

I'm sure if I walk long enough, though, I'll find a Dunkin' Donuts. They're everywhere.

I go up one street and down the next, wiping sweat from my forehead and upper lip, wishing I were wearing shorts instead of long corduroy pants, wishing Phin were here, wishing—

Stop!

When I see the Dunkin' Donuts sign, a wave of relief washes over me. I need an iced coffee and a doughnut before I pass out. Caffeine and sugar. Breakfast of champions. Maybe two doughnuts and a really large iced coffee. Maybe two iced coffees.

I have enough money for only one iced coffee, though, and two doughnuts, so that's what I buy.

After adding several packets of sugar to my coffee and guzzling it, I decide to save the doughnuts till I get back. I'll need something to get me through this day.

The caffeine gives me a nice buzz, and I feel good. Really good. I'm half dancing, half walking back to Beckford Palms Estates, which is crazy if you think about all the things wrong with my life.

When I pass the grand entrance fountain and walk through the pedestrian gate at Beckford Palms Estates, I think it's weird that no one's outside. I dance-walk past one perfectly cut lawn after the next and don't see a single person. Nor a married person, for that matter. Ha. Ha. Phineas would have appreciated that one.

It feels like I'm on the set of a reality TV show. Maybe I am. What if there are cameras everywhere and none of this is real? What if people are watching us all the time? I stop dance-walking just in case. Of course, smart people are probably in the air-conditioning, working or watching TV or being bitten by a battalion of fire ants or whatever people in South Florida do when it's a million degrees outside. I realize I'm most likely not on a reality TV show, which is a big relief. So I go back to grooving to the upbeat music that's flooding my brain with happiness through my earbuds.

I glance ahead and see a guy pulling groceries from the trunk of his car.

Life! There is actual life here at Beckford Palms Estates.

A girl rushes down the path toward him. He's probably her dad. I wish he were my dad. I know that's dumb, but if he were my dad, my life would definitely be different. Easier. Infinitely better.

Stop thinking.

But he's not. He's her dad, and she probably doesn't realize how lucky she is. Which kind of makes me not like her, even though I don't know her.

The girl waves. At me! She's wearing this cute red dress. And suddenly, my opinion changes, and I like her.

I can't help but smile.

I'm sure I look like a complete idiot, wearing heavy pants in summer and sweating like Niagara Falls, but she doesn't seem to mind. She's got the prettiest blue eyes. Amazing eyes, like a shimmering swimming pool I want to dive into.

WWPD? What would Phineas do?

He'd wave back, of course. Simple. Perfect. Obvious. *Just wave back, dummy.*

So I do. Only I wave with the hand holding the Dunkin' bag because that's how smooth I am.

But the girl smiles. The blue-eyed girl with the pretty red dress smiles. At me.

I make a mental note of her house number—1205 Lilac Lane—and keep going.

Maybe Beckford Palms won't be the worst place in the world.

Then I remember why we're here. I remember where Dad is. Why Mom was crying when I left the house.

And I know for sure it will be the worst.

THE TWO OF US

The moment I cross the foyer into Bubbie Bernice's house, my sweat turns to ice crystals, even on the backs of my knees. It feels like an igloo in here—a gigantic, five-bedroom, six-bathroom igloo with a huge workout room. I wrap my arms across my chest and shiver.

Mom's in the kitchen sitting at the round table, near the sliding glass doors that lead to the pool. Her eyelids are pink and puffy, but at least she's not crying anymore. I worry about her. She's been entirely too sad lately. I hope she snaps out of it soon.

Mom glances at the Dunkin' bag.

"Breakfast of champions," I offer lamely, as I slide into a seat near her.

She tilts her head, and her long brown curls fall to one side. "How are you, Norbert?" She gives my hand a squeeze. "Really?"

How am I? I do a quick inventory of my brain. I feel exhausted from what's been going on. But I still have butterflies in my stomach because that girl smiled at me. *Exhausted. Excited. Exhausted. Excited.* Part of me wants to leap up and do something. Another part wants to take a long nap in a cool, dark room. *How do I explain all this to Mom?*

I shrug. "Where's Bubbie Bernice?"

"She went for a quick six-mile run."

A quick six-mile run? I look down at myself. My belly bulges a little—maybe more than a little—but I'm tall, so it's no big deal. Right? "It's like a million degrees outside." I bite into one of my two Boston Kreme doughnuts. "Is she going to be all right running out there?"

Mom taps the table with her chewed fingernails and laughs. "Norbert, your bubbie could run a marathon across Death Valley and be fine."

I take another sweet, creamy bite and lick the chocolate icing off my upper lip. "That's prob'ly true."

Mom nods at my doughnut. "Give me a bite."

I pass Mom the doughnut, and she takes a huge bite from the side I didn't eat from. "Mmm." She closes her eyes for a moment. "Sorry. Didn't mean to take so much."

I think about what Mom's been through, where she had to leave Dad before we came to Bubbie's house, how far she had to drive to get us here—1,200 miserable, mind-numbing miles—and I hand her my other doughnut.

"You sure?"

I nod. It feels good to do something nice for Mom.

She points at me with the doughnut clutched in her fingers. "Don't tell your bubbie I ate this. She'll probably make me do a hundred sit-ups or something to make up for it."

We both laugh.

"Bubbie is hard-core when it comes to exercise," I say.

"Mhmm," Mom says, her mouth full of doughnut.

I wish Dad were here. He loves Boston Kreme doughnuts, too. I doubt they have doughnuts where he is. When Dad was in a good mood, he could chow down half a dozen doughnuts in one sitting. Sometimes a whole dozen, except for the couple Mom and I would eat. And Dad wouldn't even get big from eating all those doughnuts, except that one time when they changed his meds and he ballooned like the Goodyear Blimp.

That was a rough time.

Mom taps the table again. "Norbert, why don't we get you some new clothes for school?" She swipes a napkin across her lips. "We can stop for lunch, too. It'll be nice; just the two of us."

Her words "just the two of us" should be happy, together words, but all I hear is the one of us who's missing. *Dad.*

"Unless you want to wait for Bubbie to join us," Mom says, finishing off her doughnut and licking each finger.

"Mom?"

"Yeah, Norb?"

"Do you think we could . . ." I'm not sure how to say this. "Could we change my name before I go to this new school?"

Mom bursts out laughing.

"It's not funny," I say.

Mom covers her mouth with her hand. "Of course not. I'm sorry. I know kids have made fun of your name in the past."

"And teachers," I say.

"Really? I didn't know that."

I nod.

"And you want to keep that from happening here, huh?"

I nod again.

Mom rubs her left cheek with her knuckles. "You know your dad named you Norbert. He picked that name because it meant a lot to him."

With those words, all the happy air leaks out of the room. And it's me and Mom and the weight of what's happened to Dad between us.

She sniffs hard and dabs at the corners of her eyes with a napkin.

I don't feel like going out for new clothes or lunch or anything. "Maybe we can go later."

Mom reaches toward me, but I don't have the energy to grab her hand, so she gives up and drops it onto the table. I notice chocolate icing on her thumbnail.

I drag my heavy, doughnut-filled, coffee-filled body upstairs to one of the guest bedrooms, where I'm now staying. I push the frilly pillows out of the way and flop onto the big bed. Atop the girlie white comforter, I curl into myself, sweat pooling behind my knees and back and neck, despite the freezing air in the house. I shiver and stare at the mirrored door. I almost expect to see someone else in the reflection. Phineas? Dad?

But all I see is me, curled into a big doughnut shape.

I look sad, like Mom did earlier on.

I want to look happy, like the girl I saw today at 1205 Lilac Lane. The one with the bluest eyes and the pretty red dress.

One Word

Reluctantly, I drag my body from bed, go into Mom and Dad's room and put Mom's dress and sandals back into her closet. On my way out, I touch some of her business suits and remember when Mom used to work as a lawyer. She'd come home late every night and flop into a chair, exhausted. We had a family meeting when Mom decided to give up the law practice and open her own yoga studio—Peaceful Poses.

Mom looked very serious when she told Sarah and me that her parents pushed her into becoming a lawyer, but opening a yoga studio is what she's always really wanted to do.

We were behind her one hundred percent.

It's been nice having Mom home more . . . relaxed and energetic.

I change into the baggy cargo shorts Dad bought me and one of his T-shirt company rejects I like: *Congratulations, Beckford Palms Baseball Camps!*

Practice is over for today. I wish it felt like a relief to change back into boy clothes. I prefer wearing girl clothes, but the rest of the world doesn't. *Dad doesn't.* I wish he were more accepting of me, like Mom and Sarah. Like Dare. If it's so hard to be myself at home with Dad's critical eye, how will I ever be able to do it at school this year?

Downstairs, Dad's sipping a beer and watching TV.

It's way too early for a beer . . . and TV. He's usually at the T-shirt shop this time of day.

"Dad?" I say tentatively.

"What's up?" He takes an extra-long swig and doesn't turn his gaze from the screen.

I wish Sarah were here with me instead of up in her room, probably working on one of her cool knitting projects and chatting with her friends online. If Sarah were here, she'd know the right things to say. But I have to figure it out myself. "Can I sit with you?"

Dad moves some newspapers out of the way, but still doesn't look at me. I want to run back upstairs, hide under my ugly brown comforter. But instead, I sit. "So . . ."

Dad jams his thumb on the mute button, silencing the TV, and turns toward me. "I have to go into the shop soon," he says, as though he can't wait to get away from me, like when the kids at school used to play keep-away from the kid who they labeled with cooties. When it comes to Dad, I feel like I'm always that kid with cooties. The more I try to be who I really am, the more he pushes away. And it feels like it's been getting worse the past couple of years, especially since Grandpop Bob died.

Dad notices my T-shirt and his face relaxes. "How ya doin', Camp?" He playfully punches my shoulder.

I rub it, like he hurt me.

"Sorry, I didn't mean to—"

"Seriously, Dad? You think *that* would hurt me?"

He shrugs.

I drop my hands into my lap and shake my head. "You didn't hurt me." *At least, not in the way you think.*

"Good," Dad says, and reaches for the remote, as though our conversation—brief as it was—is over.

"Dad?"

He drops his hand and looks toward his lap. "Hmm?"

I wish I could talk fast, blurt the whole thing out. Make him understand. I have a thousand words roiling in my head, but can't seem to pick the right ones, the ones I need him to hear. "I want to talk about the dress. And . . . something else."

He inhales sharply.

I exhale slowly, the way Mom taught me. *It's all in the breath. You can get through almost anything with the breath.* "I'd like to buy new clothes for when school starts, maybe some dresses and—"

Dad springs up, knocking the newspapers and remote control to the floor. "I don't want to talk about this now, Tim. I've got to get to the shop. Can't leave Grandma alone there too long."

The word "Tim" hurts. You'd think I'd be used to it by now, after hearing it for thirteen years, but I will never get used to that name. "But Dad." I stand. My heart hammers so hard, it feels like all the slow exhales in the world won't be able to calm it. "I need to talk about this and—"

"Can't this wait till your mom gets home?" Dad runs his fingers through his wiry red hair.

Very gently, I say, "I need to talk to *you,* Dad."

He sits again, so I do, too, but he's farther away.

"Okay," Dad says, holding out his palms, then clenching them into fists. Open, clench. Open, clench.

It feels like he'll bolt if I say one wrong word. I move a millimeter closer to him. I always feel like I'm trying to get closer, and he keeps moving away. *What words can I use to keep him here and say what I need to?* I've had this conversation in my head so many times, but now, when I need the

22

words to come, they're bunched together like bumper cars in a massive pileup in my brain. And I can't seem to pull the right ones loose.

"Dad," I say softly, willing the words to find their way to my mouth in time.

His knee bounces like he's waiting for the starting pistol so he can take off.

"I've dressed like a boy all the way through seventh grade."

Dad nods. "That's right."

I test the water. "For you."

"For me?" He shakes his head. "You mean for you, Tim."

I hold my collision of words back and let Dad talk.

"Did you get beaten up? Attacked?"

I don't tell Dad how much I'm made fun of, teased, bullied. I don't tell him it's a small torture every time I have to dress and act like someone I'm not, like playing a role in a movie I don't want to be in. A role I wasn't born to fill. I simply shake my head side to side.

"See," Dad says. "Then you did it for yourself, Timothy, to keep yourself safe." Dad's words are tight and thin. Dad's words are the wrong ones. They are full of untruths.

"Look," I say. "I know I was born with boy parts. I get that. And it makes people comfortable if I dress and act like a boy. It's what they've learned to expect. But remember when I was little and wore Sarah's dresses?"

Dad nods. "But you outgrew that phase, Tim."

"No," I say quietly, my fingernails digging into the flesh of my palms. *It was never a phase. You only choose to believe that, even when the truth is staring you in the face.*

Dad lowers his head and runs a hand through his hair again. "You can't do that, Tim. You can't go out of this house like that. It's not right. You'll get . . ."

I'm silent and give Dad a chance to finish, but he doesn't. "I'll get what?" I can't imagine anything harder than going out every day as someone I'm not.

Dad presses his palms on his thighs and looks straight ahead. "You'll just have to try harder, son."

His words crush me. *I'm not your son!* I want to shout. *Try harder for what? For whom?* "I have tried," I say, my throat constricting, voice sounding pinched. "I have and I have and I have." *For you.* "But it's not who I am. Every day, *every single minute of every single day,* I know that I . . . am . . . a . . . girl."

He turns so I can see only the back of his head. "I've, um, got to—"

"Dad." I reach out and gently touch his shoulder.

He flinches.

"I need to talk to you about something else." I gulp down the lump in my throat. "The hormone blockers. Remember I told you about them? I have to get started on them now or else—"

"Goddamn it, Timothy!" Dad turns, his face filled with fury and something else. Pain? "Your mother gave birth to a boy. We had a boy. What am I supposed to do? Just let go of that? Am I supposed to let him die?"

The last word lingers in the air between us as the front door opens and Mom walks in, oblivious to the disaster she's entering into.

"How's my happy family?" she asks, her yoga mat carrier slung over one shoulder, flip-flops hitting the tile floor as she approaches. *Whap. Whap. Whap.*

Neither of us answers.

Dad rockets up and kisses Mom on the cheek, talking directly to her, as though I've left the room. "I've got to get to work, honey."

"But, Dad . . ."

He's already gone. The front door slams, and Mom turns to face me. One look at me is all she needs to understand.

Mom plops down on the couch next to me and puts her bare arm around my shoulders. She leans her head into mine. And without knowing what was said, somehow she knows. "I'm sorry."

"Why?" I ask, leaning my head against hers. "Why won't he let me be . . . me? Am I so bad? He wouldn't even let me *talk* about the hormone blockers. I need them, Mom!"

"Shhh." She strokes my hair. "It's hard for your dad, sweetheart. His mom is so . . . so . . ."

"It's hard for me." *Dad doesn't have to deal with the Neanderthals at my school.*

Mom kisses the top of my head. "I know. Your dad's

worried about you. That's all." I hear Mom's slow exhale, and I want to tell her it doesn't work. When dealing with Dad, the slow breathing thing is totally ineffective.

"He's making it impossible for me," I say. "I can't go on like this. I can't turn into—"

"Shhh." Mom presses her head even closer to mine.

I want to cry, because it feels like Mom really does understand. I don't know what I'd do without her and Sarah on my side. And of course, Dare, who's ready to fight the whole world on my behalf, or at least the kids at school. I'm lucky to have each of them.

But I need Dad, too.

"He'll come around," Mom says. "It'll just take some more time for him to get used to it."

"I don't have more time." I pull away from Mom. "I'm beginning to change. And it's making me crazy. I need to start hormone blockers right now or things are going to happen that can't be reversed. I can't wait any more, and I need one of you to sign the form so I can get them."

"I'll talk to him," Mom says. "Again. Please be patient a little longer. I want your dad to be on board before we take this next step."

I stand, feeling light-headed. "It's so unfair."

As I walk away on wobbly legs, trying not to think about what will happen to my body without hormone blockers— the deeper voice, bulging Adam's apple, facial hair and hair down there—what's already beginning to happen—Mom says one word that cracks through the hurt. One word that manages to make the muscles of my mouth form into a weak smile.

One word that matters.

I drag my traitorous body up to my room and lie on the ugly brown comforter. Tears trickle out, but I know I'd completely lose it if Mom's tiny, two-syllable word weren't ping-ponging through my brain, releasing bits of hope each time, reassuring me of who I am.

Lily.

She called me Lily—my chosen name—for the first time. *Why now? Does she understand how much I need her to? Does she realize how much her complete acceptance of me matters?* Maybe she'll keep calling me Lily. I hope so. Now maybe Sarah will call me Lily, too. And someday, Dad might even . . .

Lily.

Lily.

Lily.

Me.

Lily.

Hope.

Meatball charges into my room—tags jangling—and leaps onto my bed. He nuzzles close and licks my cheeks again and again with his tiny pink tongue. He must like the taste of salt.

Lily.

THOSE EYES

When Bubbie knocks on my door, I bolt upright. I must have fallen asleep.

"Hi, bubela," she says, marching in. "Did the heat wear you out?"

Her *Bodies by Bubbie* T-shirt, which is supposed to be light gray, is now a dark gray because it's drenched in sweat.

I lift my arm in a lame wave. "Nope. I'm good." But really, I'm beat. The heat definitely wore me out.

Bubbie makes guns with her biceps, then shakes her short, curly hair. "Since I'm warmed up from my run, want to do a little weight lifting with me?"

A little weight lifting? There's no such thing as *a little* weight lifting with Bubbie Bernice of the famous Bodies by Bubbie franchise. My bubbie is an exercise guru/maniac/freak.

"Maybe later," I lie. There will be no later. If I wanted every muscle in my body to hurt, I'd go ahead and get run over by that Mack truck. It would be quicker than working out with Bubbie and much less painful. Besides, my ego would be crushed if I were bested by a short woman with tattoos of the words "You are stronger than you think" running down her left forearm and "Get out of your own way" running down her right.

"I'll hold you to that," Bubbie says, coming over and kissing me on the forehead. "You're stronger than you think."

I glance at her tattoo. "I know."

"Well," Bubbie says, clapping her hands twice. I almost expect the lights to switch on and off, but they don't. "If my favorite grandson in the whole world won't lift weights with his old bubbie, I'll lift them by myself. Those things aren't going to lift themselves, you know." She makes guns with her biceps again. "Then I need to get ready for my date with Mr. Matthesen. We're going to the early bird special at the Golden Trough. I'd rather have a nice piece of fish somewhere, but he likes to strap on the feedbags at that place. Well, I'd better continue my workout and hop in the shower."

"Bubbie, maybe you'd better stand in the shower. Wouldn't want you to slip from hopping." I raise my eyebrows so she knows I'm joking. I can't believe Bubbie has a date. She's got a better social life than I do. Maybe if I were super strong like her, I'd have a better social life, too. I secretly glance at my right bicep muscle and flex it. It looks exactly the same as before I flexed.

"Nonsense," Bubbie says, wiping her forehead with the back of her hand. "I'll burn more calories if I hop in the shower."

She winks and jogs down the hall.

Being around Bubbie makes me feel happy. She's one of the few good things about coming to Florida.

Don't think about the bad things.

When I was younger and we'd visit Bubbie Bernice, she'd

be out front playing catch with me and some of the boys in the neighborhood. Bubbie would be the first one leaping into the pool when we were having a barbeque. And she'd always make popcorn and cuddle with me to watch movies at night. I got to choose which movies we watched every time.

Maybe being here won't be so bad.

Yes, it will. You know it will.

Stop. Thinking.

It's hard to sit still with all the energy Bubbie brought into the room, so I get up and finally change into shorts. My legs are too long. And hairy. How can I have legs this hairy and be going into eighth grade? *Everything* developed early on my body—like in fifth grade—including the mutant extra hair, my protruding Adam's apple and a deeper voice.

I put the corduroys back on. Better to be hot and sweaty than be mistaken for a gorilla recently escaped from the Palm Beach Zoo. Bubbie took me to the zoo once. I loved the naked mole rats. She let me stand there and watch them burrow in and out of their dark tunnels for nearly an hour. They seemed frantic as they raced here and there, often running over on top of each other. That's what my thoughts feel like at times. Frantic. And other times it feels like they're making their way through sludge.

I head downstairs to find Mom reading the newspaper at the same table where we had eaten our doughnuts. "Hey,

Norb." She smooths the paper out. "Want to go shopping for school clothes now? Only six more days till you're a big eighth grader."

"I wish I weren't so big." I hate being taller than everyone. I shake my head, feeling like I'm disappointing her. "Heading out to explore," I tell her. I don't tell her the particular address I plan to visit.

Mom stands on her toes, but I still have to bend down for her to kiss my forehead. "Don't get overheated, Norb. Remember to drink lots of water. And eat something substantial." Then she stuffs a few dollar bills into my palm.

"Whew," I say. "I'm tired just thinking about all those things." I hold up the money. "Thanks."

Mom reaches up and ruffles my already ruffled hair.

She's always reminding me about the heat and drinking enough water, even when we lived in New Jersey. Even when it wasn't that hot outside. Possible dehydration is a risk from one of the medicines I take—my mood stabilizer. My antipsychotic medicine has other possible side effects— worse ones—but I try not to think about them because I have to take it. I've been taking those two medicines for a couple years now—ever since my diagnosis. But the good thing is that Mom made a deal with me. She promised that when we came to Florida, I'd be in charge of taking my medicine myself. Mom said I could keep the medicine in my room instead of in the kitchen, and she wouldn't nag me about taking it, like she used to do in New Jersey. She said I've been doing a great job and she trusts me. I won't let her down. I won't pull a Dad.

"I'll be careful," I say, but I don't promise to drink water, because honestly, I hate the taste of water. I'd much rather drink soda or sweetened iced coffee or juice.

Mom kisses me again. On my cheek this time, which she can reach when standing on her toes, without my assistance. "Take care of yourself, Norbert. Call if you need anything."

"Thanks, Mom. I will." And I go to the sink and drink some lousy-tasting water because I know it will make her happy.

The minute I step outside, a wave of heat whacks me in the face. I inhale it into my unsuspecting lungs and feel sweat prickling in my hairy pits. "Terrific," I say to no one as I walk along our block, turn the corner and head down Lilac Lane. There's a dog in the window at 1205, but no blue-eyed girl in a red dress. For a moment, I wonder if she was real. I think of her smiling at me, of her waving. I remember her blue eyes. She was real.

I consider going back to Bubbie's and letting Mom take me clothes shopping, but I'm not ready to be cooped up in the car with her, then dragged through a bunch of stores. School clothes shopping would remind me of Dad and the time he bought me about ten times as much stuff as I actually needed and Mom had to return most of it the next day. And that will remind me of—

Stop thinking about him!

I walk out of Beckford Palms Estates and down a few blocks, all the while trying out different names for myself, to see which one might fit. *Bernie. No. Mitch. No. Julian. No. Jacob. Maybe. Andrew. Maybe. Kyle. Perhaps. Nicholas. Possibly. Charlie. I'm not a Charlie. But then again, anything's better than Norbert. A girl will never say, "Hey, I want you to meet my boyfriend, Norbert. We're going to make out now." Not. Going. To. Happen.*

I see the Beckford Palms Public Library ahead and think I'll go inside to cool off. Maybe I'll even take a sip from the water fountain, because if Mom were here, she'd want me to. And I really appreciate that she's finally trusting me and letting me handle my own medicine every day.

"Hey!"

As I look up into the twisty branches of an enormous tree, a bunch of leaves rain down on me. At first I think it's birds swooping and I make embarrassing jerking motions to swipe them away from my head, but then I realize it's only a bunch of stupid leaves.

"Hey!" someone calls again from one of the lower branches. Legs dangling, long hair obscuring the face. I feel like I know the boy, but that's crazy because I don't know anyone here, except Bubbie and Mom. Maybe I met him during one of my visits to Bubbie a long time ago. Maybe he was one of the boys I played ball with in the street back then.

The boy in the tree pulls his hair away from his face and

I see them—blue eyes. "Want to climb up here or are you heading to Dunkin' Donuts again?"

What? Is it the girl I saw earlier today? It looks like a boy. But how would this boy in this tree know I might be going to Dunkin' Donuts . . . again? I'm totally confused and probably being a jerk because I'm staring, trying to figure it out. Maybe the dosages of my meds need a little tweaking. Mom said we'd find a good psychiatrist down here to make sure I stay on track.

"Hello? Can you hear me?"

Sounds like a boy, but not real deep, not like my voice. I shield my eyes. Maybe it's the sun playing tricks. *Say something, Norbert.* "I, um, don't climb trees."

"Come on," he says in this warm, welcoming way.

I shake my head.

The boy shoulders a backpack and climbs down the wide trunk, landing on the ground in front of me with a thud.

Now I can get a good look. Definitely the same blue eyes as the girl this morning. Maybe it's her twin brother or something. Maybe . . . "Aren't you—"

"Where you headed?" he asks, cutting me off.

I stare at those blue eyes and tilt my head. "I just thought—"

"I need a drink," he says.

"Me too." My throat is sandpaper dry.

* * *

34

Inside the cool, oily, doughnut-smelling air, I reach into my pocket and touch the money Mom gave me. Another iced coffee would be great now. And some answers.

Those would be nice, too.

The Question

"Heading out," I call to Mom.

"You okay, hon?"

No. "Yes!"

"Spending time with Bob?" she asks.

I love that Mom knows me so well. "That's the plan."

"Be careful up there, sweetheart."

"Always am."

Before I visit Bob, I step into the chilly air of the Beckford Palms Public Library. The automatic doors make a whooshing sound as they open, and I shiver. After signing up for a computer, I research hormone blockers again—I need to be certain about the right time to start them. There's something called Tanner Stage II. That's when my boy parts start growing, when hair starts growing down there, when all the things I don't want to happen start happening. That's when I'm supposed to start the hormone blockers. That means I should be starting them *now.* It's not like I'm asking for estrogen or surgery. Yet. I just don't want to grow hair down there or get a deep voice or a bulging Adam's apple or . . . *Why can't Dad support me on this?*

I log off the computer and head to the children's section. Memories flood back. Grandpop Bob helping me cut out a picture of an elephant during story time with Miss Carol. Grandpop Bob smiling while I signed my name for my first library card. Grandpop Bob reading *The Lorax* to me while we sat under the shade of our banyan tree next door to the library. Him rapping his gnarled knuckles against the trunk, saying, "See. It's old like me, but it's still sturdy and good." I remember hugging Grandpop Bob then, feeling like I was hugging the trunk of our tree, feeling safe and protected.

I didn't realize that feeling would end. I didn't realize Grandpop Bob wouldn't be around forever. I didn't realize how hard things would become.

I borrow *The Lorax* and head outside.

Slipping the book into my backpack, I stand under the banyan tree's twisty branches. "Hey, Bob," I say, patting his trunk and feeling closer to my grandpop.

With a heave, I grab the lowest branch and hoist myself up, until I'm sitting in a solid crook, looking down on the world. I pluck some leaves and make a pile in my lap. Up here, I feel like I'm part of the tree—strong and solid, too.

Carefully, I pull out the book and read about the little creature who speaks for the trees, remembering Grandpop Bob reading this to me so many times. Hugging me. Telling me how much he loves me.

I try to recall the last time Dad hugged me like that.

An ache fills my chest.

I need this book today. I need my tree.

I've read the book three times when I take a break and look down.

I'm surprised by who is walking by.

I'm excited to see the boy again and forget I'm dressed very differently from when I saw him this morning. I should have kept my stupid mouth shut, because if I hadn't yelled "Hey!" he wouldn't have looked up.

People forget to look up. They forget about the treetops and the sky. They forget about the clouds and the birds and the sun and the moon. People are so focused on their small, skull-sized kingdoms and their dumb smartphones, they forget about the glorious world around them, especially the big, beautiful world above them.

As soon as the boy looks up, his eyebrows raise. I can almost see his mind flood with questions, or at least one specific question that I don't feel like answering. I make sure my long hair obscures my face. *What was I thinking, calling down to him? Stupid!*

It would have been so much easier to stay in Bob's branches and not have yelled down to this new, mysterious boy. To go back to my book as though I never saw him approach. But with Dare at horse camp in Pennsylvania and my family working so much and Sarah being so busy with her Knit Wits group and other high school friends, this entire summer has been one long exercise in lonely.

And apparently, the subconscious part of me has had quite enough of lonely.

So after the boy looks up, startled, I send down my lapful of leaves—an avalanche of nature, a gift to rain over him. At first he jerks so awkwardly it looks like he's having a seizure or something. Then I realize he might be afraid. Of leaves. *Who in the world is afraid of leaves?*

This tall, awkward boy intrigues me enough to pack *The Lorax* into my backpack and climb down. Enough to face him and deal with the inevitable question.

Naming Things

Inside the cool, sweet, oily-smelling air of the Dunkin' Donuts, the boy buys two iced coffees and hands me one. I don't usually drink coffee, but I'm happy to have something to do with my hands. He also buys himself a jelly doughnut, but I shake my head when he points at the racks of doughnuts behind the counter.

At our little table, he takes a loud slurp of coffee. "Ahh," he says, "liquid energy."

He sounds so confident and genuine. I sip my coffee. It needs sugar, but I don't get up to get any.

"So?" he says.

"So?" I say, but understand what he really wants to know. *Ask him his name. What school he goes to. Anything to avoid the question.*

"Did I . . . ? Weren't you . . . ?" He ducks his head, like he's embarrassed.

I wait for a full question that doesn't come.

People walk into the store.

"You want to go somewhere else?" I ask, feeling my cheeks get warm just thinking about telling him in such a crowded space.

"Definitely," he says, sliding out of the seat, holding his Dunkin' bag with his doughnut and his sweaty cup of iced coffee. "I always want to go somewhere else."

I try to figure out what he means as we venture back outside. Heat rushes over me like an ocean wave.

"Is it always this hot here?" he asks as we walk.

I slurp the bitter coffee. "Only until November fifteenth."

"That's incredibly specific," he says. "Does God, like, have a calendar or something and on November fifteenth, He turns on the cosmic air conditioner down here?"

I like the image of God turning on a cosmic air conditioner. "Something like that."

The boy takes a long swig of coffee and swipes the back of his mouth with his hand, the one holding the Dunkin' bag. "Because, really, I don't know how I'll survive this heat until . . . November fifteenth?"

"For starters," I say, motioning toward his legs. "You might want to rethink your choice of pants. Shorts work better." *Though a skirt or dress works best.*

A flash of hurt crosses his face, and I want to apologize

even though I don't know what I said wrong. Maybe there's something the matter with his legs. Maybe he has scars from burns or something. I sip my bitter coffee to keep from saying anything else.

We end up back where we started, where I first dumped a pile of terrifying leaves on his head. I open my arms wide and announce, "This is Bob."

The boy looks around. "Where?"

I touch the bark of my banyan tree. "*This* is Bob."

"You named a tree?"

I rap my knuckles on Bob's sturdy trunk. "Named him after my grandfather."

The boy nods. "That's cool. Did your grandfather work with trees or something?"

I laugh. "Nope. He started a T-shirt shop—We've Got You Covered. My dad helps run it now with my grandmom." Just mentioning Dad makes my stomach tighten. Maybe I'll print him out information about hormone blockers from the Internet. Again.

"That's different," the boy says. "Cute name."

I sit on the sparse grass near Bob's trunk. The boy sits beside me, stretches out his long, corduroy-covered legs and runs his hand over the grass. "You know, the grass here is tougher than where I'm from."

"St. Augustine."

"No, I'm from New Jersey. Where's St. Augustine?"

I laugh. "The grass is called St. Augustine." I run my

hand over it. "Built to be hardy and withstand our crazy heat. St. Augustine is also an old city in Florida, a few hours north of here."

The boy raises his eyebrows. "Is there anything you don't know?"

I feel myself blush. "Your name."

An emotion flashes across his face. Hurt? Disappointment? I said something wrong again, but what?

"I . . . don't like my name."

Neither do I.

"It's . . ." He runs a hand through his dark, curly hair. The gesture reminds me of Dad.

I won't make fun of it. Promise.

"My name's—"

He sounds like he's in pain. I glance at the bag in his hand and blurt, "Dunkin."

"Huh?"

"Your name. It's Dunkin." I point to the bag. "Right?" I ask, hoping he'll play along.

"Now I know you don't know everything," he says. "It's definitely not Dunkin. It's—"

"It can be Dunkin." And suddenly, I don't want to know the name he doesn't like. "Or at least, I can call you Dunkin if you don't like your actual name." *I understand not liking your actual name.*

"I like the name Dunkin," he says, holding up his Dunkin' bag. "I really like it. A whole lot. Get it? Like the

41

hole from a doughnut. Ha!" His voice gets quicker and clipped, probably from drinking all that coffee. "Dunkin's cool. It's really cool. I've got to tell my mom. I'll bet Phineas will like it, too."

My brain feels like it's working through a swamp, trying to keep up with Dunkin's wild rush of words. *Who's Phineas?*

Dunkin takes his doughnut from the bag and holds it with the square of wax paper. "Can I ask you something?"

I take a deep breath. *Be brave, Lily. Be brave.*

"You want a bite of my doughnut?"

I laugh and nod, feeling my hair fall back onto my shoulders. It's so hot. I wish I'd put it up in a ponytail. "That's what you wanted to ask?"

"Nope. This is: What's *your* name?"

"It's complicated." I surprise myself with my answer. Usually, I say "Tim" or "Timothy" but think *Lily*. I guess I'm tired of thinking the truth but saying a lie.

"It's Complicated," he says, tapping his chin, which I notice has some stubble on it. He must already be shaving. I touch my own chin, panicked because I feel a new hair. *I have to get hormone blockers!* "It's Complicated is an unusual name," he quips.

Who is this tall, funny guy? And why did he have to wait until the last six days of summer to walk past my house? He's expecting me to tell him my name. A perfectly reasonable request. "My name's Timothy." *Fail.* "Tim. But I don't really

42

like it." *Better. Tell him why.* "It's just . . . a dumb name. It doesn't suit me. I don't know." *You do know!*

Dunkin nods like I've said something meaningful, but I know I've told him nothing that matters.

"Look, I know I don't know you," he says. His right knee is bobbing, which reminds me of my talk with Dad this morning, of his impatience with me. "But I have to ask you something. And it might sound crazy. Okay?"

I hold my breath, squeezing my hands into fists, and barely nod.

"Weren't you, um . . ." He takes a big bite of doughnut and talks with his mouth full. "Wearing a dress this morning?"

The Lie

I seize up, sure I'll never breathe again. Maybe if I don't breathe, I'll faint. And if I faint, I'll bang my head on Bob's hard trunk and knock myself out. And if I get knocked out, I won't have to answer Dunkin's question.

Unfortunately, none of these things happen. It's just Bob, me, Dunkin and his impossible question hanging in the humid air between us.

"Yes," I say, feeling both terrified and brave at the same time. "I was wearing my mom's dress when you saw me this morning." *Good girl, Lily. Now tell him why.*

Dunkin's eyelids open wider, and he holds the mostly

eaten doughnut without taking another bite, so I know I've shocked him. I don't like his reaction. It feels like he's judging me, and it doesn't feel good. *Could this boy be dangerous? What made me think he was different from everyone else?*

I blink a few times, praying the right words will come. True words. But what actually happens is the real part of me closes down. Walls spring up. Doors clang shut. Mental alarms are set.

I hate this feeling.

"Okay," Dunkin says, I guess to encourage me to explain further.

But the way he says it doesn't imply that anything is okay. There's so much judgment in that one word, I know he'll never understand. I was stupid to hope he might.

Words flow from me like pollution into a stream: "My sister, Sarah, dared me." I check his eyes to see if they're little lie-detector machines going off, but nothing in them changes. "This morning, she dared me to wear my mom's dress and sandals and go outside. Can you believe it?" The lies taste like dirt in my mouth.

"Wow," he says, letting out a breath, like the lie I told was a relief.

My shoulders slump.

"I don't know if I'd be brave enough to do that." He pops the last piece of doughnut into his mouth. "Why'd your sister dare you?"

44

"Thought it was funny, I guess. It's been a boring summer."

He coughs as though that last bit of doughnut got caught in his throat. "That must have been really embarrassing when I walked up then. Huh?"

I swallow hard, as though something's caught in *my* throat. "Oh yeah," I say, "completely embarrassing." Each lie I utter hollows me out a little more.

Dunkin leans back on his elbows on the pointy St. Augustine grass, as though he doesn't have a care in the world. I envy him. Why can't I be relaxed like him? Why can't things be easy for me, like they must be for him?

I lean back against Bob, hoping he'll give me strength. But all he gives me is a sharp scratch on my left shoulder from a jagged piece of bark.

For a second, I'm mad at Bob. But deep inside, I know I deserve it.

THE WEIGHT OF SECRETS

I can't believe I asked this guy if he was wearing a dress. *Who does that? People who want to get beaten up. People who never want to have a friend.*

My sister, Sarah, dared me, he'd said.

The first thing that pops into my mind is how lucky he is to have a sister, especially one who's fun enough to dare him to do stupid stuff. I always wanted a sister or a brother . . . but there's only messed-up me.

The second thing is how embarrassed I feel because I thought he was a girl, with pretty blue eyes and long blond hair. I had hoped . . .

My cheeks get warmer from thinking about it.

He's so cool and confident. And smart. I'll bet he's one of the popular kids at school. All the guys probably wear their hair long, like he does.

How can I tell him the truth about me? The truth about where my dad is now and why we moved here. The truth about Phineas. The truth about why I have to take two different medicines every day to keep my bipolar disorder under control. How can I tell him any of it without scaring him away?

He seems so at ease, the way he leans back on that tree. So comfortable with exactly who he is.

So, while a million thoughts collide inside my brain, I say nothing. I lean back, the weight of my secrets heavy on my chest. The prickly St. Augustine grass poking the backs of my arms, like small fire ant bites.

I ache because I want to go home—not to Bubbie's house in Beckford Palms Estates, but my real home back in New Jersey. I wish I could go back to the way things used to be with Mom and Dad and me. And even Phineas.

Eavesdropping

At dinner, since no one's talking, other sounds become more pronounced: forks scraping plates, Meatball's huffing, his tags jingling as he settles under the table, Dad's breathing.

"The funniest thing happened on the way home," I say, trying to lighten the mood. "There were plastic pink flamingos stuck in a bunch of lawns around the neighborhood. One of the flamingos wore a knit cap with a pom-pom and another wore a knit flamingo hat." I hold a bite of pasta in my cheek. "A flamingo wearing a flamingo hat. Hilarious. Right?"

Sarah and Mom look at me, but no one laughs.

"What are those flamingos about?" Dad grouses.

"I don't know." The pasta goes down hard. "The Beckford golf cart dudes came around and put them in the back of their cart." I put my fork down. "Then they asked me and Dunkin—this new kid I met—if we knew who did it, like it was the crime of the century or something."

Sarah looks down, but I see her smile. I knew she'd think it was funny.

Dad grunts. "Probably a couple bored troublemakers. School should start earlier."

Sarah shakes her head.

Mom pokes at her eggplant Parmesan with her fork. "So, who's this Dunkin?"

I look at Dad and realize I don't want to say that he was

the boy who walked by while I was wearing Mom's dress this morning. "A new boy." Dad doesn't react. "He just moved to the neighborhood."

"Is he going to Gator Lake Middle?" Sarah asks.

"Not sure." I never asked Dunkin about school. I'll have to find out next time we get together. If we get together.

My family's quiet again. What's with them tonight?

Sarah winks at me, and I try to wink back, but both my eyelids close at the same time. This makes her crack up, and I can't help but laugh. A burst of laughter comes from Mom, too, and a piece of eggplant shoots from her mouth.

"Ew!" Sarah says, and we laugh even harder.

"Knock it off." Dad grimaces, and we finish dinner in silence, except for Meatball, who shakes his hindquarters near Sarah's chair, which makes his tags jingle like crazy.

"Don't feed him," Dad says.

Why is he so grumpy? Because of what we talked about earlier today?

Meatball keeps wagging and wiggling and jingling because he knows that even though she's not supposed to, Sarah will sneak him bits of food throughout the meal.

I wish I had the guts to break the rules like Sarah does.

I'm drying off after my shower when I hear Mom and Dad talking in their bedroom. Their room is on the other side of the wall from the bathroom, so I pull the thick towel tightly around myself and press my ear to the warm, wet tiles. I know I shouldn't be eavesdropping, but they're talking loud enough that I can hear through the wall, and I can't help but listen.

Maybe I do break the rules sometimes.

"We have to give her the hormone blockers," Mom says. "I know you don't like the idea of them, Gary. But . . ."

I focus as hard as I can, willing my breathing and heartbeat to quiet so I can hear them more clearly, but my pulse pounds in my ears and I miss the rest of what Mom says.

"He'll be better off without them, Ellie. Let nature take its course. When Tim becomes more boy-like, it'll be good for him." I picture Dad running his hand through his wiry red hair. "Besides, those things cost as much as a mortgage. Did you read the papers Tim gave us about them? They sound like a rip-off."

"Gary, if *Lily* becomes more boy-like, it'll be the worst thing that could happen to her. I think it would kill her. And I don't give a flying fig how much they cost. Lily needs them."

Go, Mom!

"Stop calling him that!"

I shiver, even though I'm wrapped in a thick towel.

"It won't kill him, Ellie. Stop being so dramatic. You're not in court, you know."

"Then stop making me feel like I have to defend my daughter!"

There's a long pause. I imagine Mom pacing, taking a few calming breaths. And I picture the vein along Dad's temple pulsing.

"Remember that time I caught Lily with the nail clippers after her bath?"

Dad's quiet.

"She told me she wanted to cut her penis off, Gary. That it didn't belong." An unbearable silence, then Mom's voice: "She was five years old, Gar. She knew when she was five."

I knew before I was five. And I remember holding those nail clippers that Mom had left on the counter. But back then, I didn't think about the possibility of bleeding to death. I just wanted it gone. And I still do.

"That night ..." Mom sniffs hard. "I promised myself I'd do whatever she needed to feel okay. To keep her safe."

Dad's voice booms: "If you want to keep *him* safe, Ellie, you'll let him stay the way he is. Middle school kids can be rotten. The world can be rotten. Letting this go on is what's dangerous to Tim."

Silence.

"Gary, even your dad knew."

"What?"

"Your dad knew," Mom says.

My breath catches as I remember the time Grandpop Bob brushed my hair with Sarah's pink princess comb that I'd handed him. I remember twirling in Sarah's old dress, and Grandpop saying, "You're beautiful, sweetheart. You're perfect."

I shake the memory from my head because it's too painful, and I press my ear harder against the warm shower tiles.

"Told you what?" Dad asks, and I realize I missed some of their conversation.

"Your dad told me something was different about Tim. That he was more girl-like."

"What does that even mean?" Dad asks way too loudly.

"It means your dad knew," Mom says. "Bob knew. And he was okay with it. He loved Lily just as she was. And so do I."

"My mom's sure not okay with it," Dad counters.

Thinking of Grandmom Ruth sours my stomach.

"Ruth," Mom says, laughing in a way that's not funny. "The devoted grandmother who avoids visiting our home like we have the plague or something."

"That's just since the incident last year," Dad says.

My heartbeat feels like it's slamming against my ribs. I had no idea that's why Grandma Ruth hadn't visited. I wondered why we hadn't seen her much. I didn't know it was my fault.

"Ah, the *incident*," Mom says, as though the word is acid on her tongue.

"Ellie, she saw Tim skipping down the stairs wearing a dress. What was she supposed to do?"

"Not drop a glass jar of strawberry jam all over our tile floor!"

"She was shocked," Dad says.

"She's small-minded, Gary."

"Ellie!"

"It's true."

I wonder how Grandpop Bob was so accepting and Grandmom Ruth so closed-minded and yet they were married for a really long time. I also wonder which one my dad's more like. I think I know.

"Honey," Dad says. He doesn't sound angry, just matter-of-fact. "The way my mom thinks is the way most of the world thinks. That's why we have to protect Tim, keep him from dressing like a girl outside this house. Let him turn into the boy he's supposed to be. That's the best thing for him."

"You can't really think that, Gary. You can't truly believe—"

"Ellie!" Dad snaps. "People are cruel. They do horrible things. We have to keep Tim safe."

"Well, I'm glad we agree on that," Mom says. "Just not on the best way to do it. Lily has to get those hormone blockers."

I think they're done talking, then Mom bursts out with one word: "Soon!"

I shouldn't have eavesdropped on Mom and Dad's conversation, because falling asleep is now impossible. After trying for hours, I climb out of bed and turn on the little lamp over my desk. I pull out a piece of stationery and my favorite purple pen and write a letter to one of my heroes. Sometimes, I write letters to people I admire because it makes me feel like I'm talking to someone who understands. I have a stash of them in my desk drawer. I've never had the courage to send them. Or even known how to find out where my heroes live. Just writing them has been enough for now.

Dear Jenna Talackova,

My name is ~~Timothy~~ Lily. I think I'm a lot like you, only not as pretty.

How did you do it? How did you stand in front of all those people and be your true self? I know you got hate mail and some people wrote mean things about you. But you did it anyway. You're so strong. You showed the world exactly who you are—a beautiful woman, inside and out.

I want to do that, too, Ms. Talackova. I realize starting eighth grade isn't as big a deal as being in the Miss Universe Pageant, but still, it feels so hard. Maybe too hard.

Someday . . . I hope I'll be able to inspire someone, too, like you have, Ms. Talackova. (But first I have to get through the eighth grade!)

Wish me luck!

Your friend and fan,
Lily Jo McGrother

A TRICK

When I wake, I take my two pills with a glass of orange juice, then go online to look up magic tricks. I haven't learned a new one in a while. It would be fun to get back into my hobby. I'd gotten pretty good at them in Jersey.

In fact, I was great at entertaining Mom on those days when Dad couldn't quite manage to get out of bed. The dark days he was on the down side of his bipolar disorder, Mom and I hung out. It sucked that Dad was so depressed, but at least Mom and I had each other for company. Dad's crazy highs weren't much better. It was best when Dad took his meds and was right in the middle—good old Dad—telling dumb jokes, eating too many doughnuts and loving my mom and me more than anything else in the world.

Those thoughts open up a gaping hole in my heart, so I shake my head to dislodge them and focus on the screen. I scroll through a bunch of tricks I already know until I find a new one. But I'll need a couple supplies.

Downstairs in the kitchen, I find what I need.

"Nu?" Bubbie asks. "What are those for?"

I shake a cloth napkin out and mysteriously drape it over a pepper shaker. "Wouldn't you like to know?"

Bubbie laughs. "Maybe I wouldn't."

"It's for a magic trick."

Bubbie holds up her arm and pinches a tiny bit of skin

underneath, between her elbow and shoulder. "Maybe you can figure out how to make this disappear."

I shake my head. "Do you have a coin?"

"Who wants to know?"

I give Bubbie *the look*, and she finds her purse and fishes out a penny. "Don't spend it all in one place," she says, and hands it to me.

"Cheapskate," I joke as I cradle my items and head toward the stairs.

"Good luck, Merlin," she calls.

"Who?"

"Never mind!"

I spend the next hour practicing the new trick. Again and again. It's the only way to get it perfect. "This is my coolest trick ever," I say to no one.

Then I realize that besides Mom and Bubbie, I don't have anyone to try the trick out on. That's a depressing thought. I realize my number one priority when I start at Gator Lake Middle should be making friends. Maybe I'll have better luck there than I did at my school in Jersey.

Maybe at Gator Lake Middle, they'll appear like magic.

Dare's Back!

A familiar melody threads itself through my dream. It sounds like our doorbell, but I'm dreaming, so I know it can't be real and I stay asleep. Deeply asleep.

"Tim!"

I pull my head off the pillow and realize I'm drooling. *Gross.*

"Wake up!" Sarah yells from downstairs. "Someone's here for you."

Tumbling out of bed, I stumble to the bureau and yank out shorts and my *Ultimate Frisee* reject T-shirt. Sometimes, I wonder if Dad ever makes T-shirts right the first time. Then I smoosh some toothpaste across my teeth with my finger and am ready to go.

I'm so tired I trip down the first couple stairs. But when I see who's in the foyer, I immediately wake fully and run the rest of the way down. I tackle my best friend in a bone-crunching hug. She smells like sunscreen and chlorine. A whole summer of horse camp hasn't changed that smell. I pull back and look at her face. Thinner. She looks older, more mature. *Do I?* "Dare!" I squeeze her again, not believing I made it through the whole summer without her.

Everything will be better now.

"Nice to have you back," Sarah says.

Dare gives Sarah a fist bump, and Sarah heads upstairs.

"Notice anything?" Dare asks, turning in a slow circle, then holding her brown arms up, like she's filled with fabulous.

"Um, your boobs got bigger?"

Dare shoves me. "I lost like fifteen pounds. Fifteen pounds! I kept up my swimming and worked out every morning, plus all the riding and long walks. It was soooooo pretty up there. And they fed us really healthy foods, like kale, carrot and quinoa salad." Dare strikes a pose that reminds me of Jenna Talackova. "Now I'm totally awesome and ready to start eighth grade," she says. "No one at Gator Lake Middle will be able to resist this package."

We crack up.

"I've missed you," I say, sitting on the bottom step.

Dare sits next to me and shoves her shoulder into mine. "Me too." She looks at my clothes and says, "But I see you're still playing the Tim game." Then she raises one eyebrow. *How does she do that?*

"I tried."

"What do you mean you *tried*?" she says way too loudly.

I speak softly. "Yesterday, I went outside in my mom's dress."

"No way." Dare smacks my shoulder.

I nod. "Yup. The pretty one she has with the lily of the valley flowers on it and a pair of white sandals."

Dare pulls a bag of carrots out of her pocket and starts munching away. "So what happened?"

I don't tell her about Dad's scary reaction. I skip to the part I know she'll be most interested in: "I met a boy."

"What?" She stops chewing.

"Mmhmm."

"No way!" Dare smacks me on the back of the head with the heel of her hand that's holding a carrot, but it doesn't bother me because I know she's just excited for me. And then I remember to think of Dare. "Did you meet any boys at camp?"

Something changes on Dare's face. Then she's herself again. "Nah. It was the All Girls Channel at camp, except when we had a dance with the boys' camp next door on the last night." She waves her carrot nub. "Bunch o' dorks."

For some reason this makes us laugh again.

"It's really good to have you back," I say, leaning closer to her.

"That's because I'm filled with awesome sauce, son!"

Everything feels easy and light with Dare . . . until she says, "So, where should we go today to practice? The mall? That coffee place I like? Oh, how about the thrift shop on Ronald Doss Road? I can get myself some funky clothes for school while we're there."

My throat tightens, like I'm allergic to her words. "I didn't mention this, but yesterday when I wore Mom's dress, my dad—"

"Oh, here we go again. Your dad doesn't accept who you really are, so you can't be that person, blah, blah, blah." Then Dare becomes quiet and levels me with a stare. "I guess some things didn't change over the summer."

And suddenly, I'm not one hundred percent thrilled to have Dare back.

DUNK YOUR DOUGHNUTS

The only way Bubbie gets me to join her for a jog is because our destination is Dunkin' Donuts and she's promised to buy me a large iced coffee—my life force. Once we get there, I'll talk her into buying me a doughnut, too. Bubbie—unlike the girls my own age—can't resist my wily charm.

"Sure you don't want to come?" Bubbie asks Mom. "We're going to Dunk Your Doughnuts."

Mom and I laugh.

"I think it's Dunkin' Donuts," Mom says. "And I'll pass on the jog. Still sore from working out with you last night."

"Moving around is the best cure for soreness," Bubbie says, touching her toes a few times. "Besides, exercise will keep you alive longer."

Mom shakes her head.

"Come on, Bubs," I say. "Let's get this torture over with." I take off out of the house, keenly aware that my shorts showcase my hairy gorilla legs in the worst possible way. I make sure *not* to jog down Lilac Lane on our way out of Beckford Palms Estates. I need to minimize my embarrassing moments as much as possible.

I'm hyperventilating like I need CPR, my leg muscles are on fire and I'm already wishing I were back at the house, showered and wearing a pair of nice, leg-hair-covering jeans. And we've only gotten to the edge of Beckford Palms Estates.

"Come on, Norbert!" Bubbie says, pounding me on the back and sprinting ahead.

"Com . . . ing!" I gasp. The thought of an iced coffee is the only thing that propels my legs forward as I chase a small, gray-haired woman through the streets of Beckford Palms.

That's how I end up at "Dunk Your Doughnuts," sweating like a human lawn sprinkler and bumping into the *one* person—other than my family—who I know in Beckford Palms.

"Dunkin!" Tim yells.

He's sitting with a girl, who's taller than he is and has a great smile with insanely deep dimples. *His girlfriend?*

"Why did that meshuga—crazy—boy call you Duncan?" Bubbie asks.

Tim is not meshuga. And I like the nickname.

"And why is his hair so long? Makes him look like a girl, if you ask me." Bubbie stands on her toes and stretches. "Not that anyone has."

I think of Tim wearing a dress on a dare and how I thought he *was* a girl. A good-looking girl, and I feel my face get even hotter than it already is from our ridiculously long jog.

"I'm going to order for us," Bubbie says as I head toward their little table by the window.

Tim and I high-five. "This is—"

"Dare." She looks me up and down. "And who is this guy high-fivin' my best friend?"

She's got this expression like she's not joking around, like she's . . . protecting Tim or something. I'm not sure if I should tell her my real name or the one Tim made up for me.

"That's Dunkin," Tim says, like he read my mind. "He just moved here from . . ." Tim looks at me with those seriously blue eyes, then ducks his head, so his hair falls in front of them. "Sorry. I forget."

"I'm from New Jersey," I say.

"A Jersey boy," Dare says, and I'm not sure how I should respond.

My legs are killing me from jogging, so I join them at their table. I hope that's okay. Right then, Bubbie calls from the counter, "Norbert, do you want a whole wheat bagel or sesame?"

"Jelly doughnut, please."

"Sesame it is," Bubbie says.

"Norbert?" Dare asks.

Tim's looking down, but I can tell he's smiling. Or is he laughing at me?

"Whatever," Dare says. "It's not like my parents gave me a normal name."

Tim and Dare laugh.

"We'll still call you Dunkin, if you want," Tim says.

"Dunkin is good," I say.

They nod, which I guess makes my new nickname official. I've been in Beckford Palms only a few days and already, I have a cool nickname. *Score!*

61

"My dad's like that." Dare nods toward Bubbie. "No junk food. Except for the occasional box of Pop-Tarts." She winks at Tim. "My dad even sent me to a summer camp that was the All Healthy Foods Channel." She sips on an artificially red, slushy drink. It looks so good, I think of asking Bubbie for that, but know she'll never buy it for me. "He's practically forcing me to binge on junk once in a while outside the house." Dare shakes her head and looks at Tim. "Parents. They have no clue how much they mess us up."

My stomach clenches. Thoughts of Dad leak under the steel, reinforced door in my head, but I shove some towels down there and stave the flow.

"Amen to that," Tim says. "Parents."

Memories of things I don't want to remember start flashing through my mind. *The dark night. The knock at the door.* "Hey, do either of you have a coin?"

Tim reaches into his pocket and slams a penny on the table.

"Saltshaker," I say to Dare, and she passes it.

"Napkin," I say to Tim.

He gives me a few from the dispenser.

I feel like a surgeon, about to perform an operation. "Okay," I say, covering the penny with the saltshaker and covering the saltshaker with a napkin. "Keep your eyes on the penny at all times. I'm going to make it disappear."

"Mhmm," Dare says, taking a loud slurp of her drink. "I doubt it."

Tim seems riveted.

I grab the saltshaker through the napkin and bring it back past the table's edge. Then I let it drop into my other hand beneath the table, all the while maintaining eye contact with Tim and Dare. The empty napkin is still in the shape of the saltshaker in my hand above the table.

"Ha!" Dare says. "The penny is still on the table. You, good sir, are a lousy magician."

"Dare!"

"What?" Dare asks. "He is. The dumb penny's sitting right there."

"Well, look at that. It certainly is," I say, because being a showman is part of being a good magician. "I don't know why that didn't work. Hmm. Let me try one more time."

I position the saltshaker-shaped napkin over the penny. And as I bang the saltshaker on the underside of the table, I smash down the empty napkin. Then I lift the napkin. Only the penny remains.

Tim's head jerks back. "How'd you do that? That's amazing."

"You made the saltshaker disappear," Dare says. "Wasn't expecting that one."

I pray neither of them thinks to look under the table, where I'm holding the saltshaker.

"Come on," Bubbie says, swinging the Dunkin' bag. "Let's go, Norbert."

"Bye, Dunkin," Tim says. "Cool magic trick."

"Thanks," I say, squeezing the saltshaker in my sweaty palm.

"Bye, *Norbert*," Dare says. But she smiles in a nice way, and her dimples go Grand Canyon deep.

Bubbie shoots out the door and starts running.

Luckily, Tim and Dare watch her through the window, which gives me an opportunity to get up and slip the saltshaker onto a counter behind a canister of straws.

Pumping my arms and willing my legs to move faster, I shout, "Hey, Bubbie, wait up! I thought we were going to stop and eat. Wait! You're going to spill my coffee!"

THE DENTURE DEBACLE

Mom makes me go with her to buy school clothes in the afternoon, which turns out to be significantly less miserable than I had imagined.

I get a couple pairs of jeans, three pairs of khaki pants, a bunch of short-sleeved, collared shirts and a pair of sneakers and shoes. When we're done shopping, we eat grilled cheese sandwiches and ice cream sundaes at Friendly's.

Mom actually looks happy, which is really nice.

I don't ask where the money for all this stuff is coming from. Ever since Dad's denture debacle, things have been pretty tight in the money department for us. Maybe Bubbie's paying for everything. She's loaded. Mom says her Bodies by Bubbie franchise—videos, products, private classes—is a phenomenon. By the size of Bubbie's house, I'll take Mom's word for it.

I wonder how much money we had before Dad and the denture debacle, which happened just before we left New Jersey.

Dad came home, beaming. He was dressed in a wrinkled business suit that smelled like he'd pulled it from the bottom of a hamper loaded with dirty socks. Dad was whistling, like it was the best day of his life. His mood was contagious, and I got all excited, even though I didn't know what we were excited about. I even remember what Dad was whistling: the "Happy Birthday" song, which was odd because it wasn't any of our birthdays.

Mom's face looked concerned, her mouth pinched and her eyelids narrowed, like she was trying to figure out what was wrong with this picture. An itch of worry spread over me, too.

"I've got it," Dad said. And he swept Mom into a huge hug, twirling her twice. "We're going to be rich," he said. "Rich. Rich. Rich. Rich. Rich. Rich. Rich." His eyelids were open way too wide.

Instead of sharing in his excitement, Mom sank onto the couch and put her palm over her mouth.

I wasn't sure why Mom was being such a party pooper, but I was interested to see what Dad was so jazzed about. Maybe we would get rich from whatever this thing was. And maybe I could get a new phone, and we'd even move to a mansion instead of our little row house.

"Picture this," Dad said, making a wide arc with his right arm. "Doug Dorfman, Denture King of South Jersey. I'll sell dentures to everyone in the country. The world. Maybe even on other planets." Dad laughed, but nothing was funny. He stood in his rumpled suit, as though waiting for me and Mom to cheer or something, but he didn't say anything that sounded like a million-dollar idea. In fact, he wasn't making sense. How would Dad sell dentures to everyone in the world? He wasn't even a dentist. Sometimes, he didn't even like to brush his own teeth and had stinky breath.

Mom shook her head slowly from side to side, but Dad didn't seem to notice.

"There's money to be made in this," he said, leaping from one part of the room to the other. Leap. Leap. "Big, big money. And I'm going to make it. Whoa!" Leap. "Whoa!" Leap. "Whoa! Whoa! Whoa!" Leap. Leap. Leap.

Dad looked like the frog on that old video game, Frogger, avoiding cars in the road.

"Sit down, Doug," Mom said. "Your jumping around is making me nauseated."

"It's going to be amazing," Dad said. "I'm going to sell more dentures than anyone in the history of dentures. Isn't that right?" he asked me, holding up his palm. So I high-fived him, even though I knew it probably irritated Mom that I did. I wasn't trying to encourage Dad by high-fiving him, just trying to keep him from nose-diving in the other direction.

"I bought a billboard!" Dad shouted. "Right on the side of the highway, for everyone to see."

"What?" Mom screeched. "You did what?"

I gave Mom a little space on the couch, in case she planned on totally freaking out.

"How much?" Mom asked in a quiet voice.

Dad waved her away. "It doesn't matter, Gail. That's not important. Don't you see? We'll make a thousand times what that billboard ad cost as soon as the orders start rolling in. Ten thousand times that amount when I expand to other states." Dad twisted his hands together in a weird way in front of Mom's face. I pressed my back into the couch. "Plus," Dad said, "doesn't Dorfman's Dentures sound terrific? Absolutely terrific! Can you hear the beautiful alliteration? Doug Dorfman's Dentures. It's a winner, Gail. A wildly wonderful winner. Am I right or am I right?" He looked at each of us, his eyes bulging. "I'm right!"

Mom spoke softly, as though she barely had any energy left. "You have zero experience with dentistry, dentures, all of it, Doug. What made you think . . . what . . . how much did the billboard cost?"

Dad looked like someone had stuck a pin in his balloon. "You always do that, Gail. I've got this great idea . . . this brilliant idea and you . . . you always ruin everything."

"Yup, that's me," Mom whispered from her corner of the couch. "The Official Ruiner of Everything."

Then Mom went into the kitchen and made herself a tuna salad sandwich, while Dad continued to pace and talk to himself about his great new business idea.

I went straight to my room and played music loudly.

Now I wish I had stayed downstairs with Dad. Maybe I could have helped him.

Turned out buying an ad on a billboard cost everything we had. All of Mom's savings from her years of working at the bakery were wiped out in one fell swoop. My small college fund vanished—poof! Mom said their retirement fund—what little there was—was drained, too. And Mom couldn't get the money back no matter how hard she fought with the billboard people. Nonrefundable. No exceptions. Mom said she wished she'd taken Dad off of all their joint accounts years ago, but she hadn't.

So, when Mom and I packed up our lives and drove out of New Jersey heading toward South Florida and passed Dad's billboard on the highway—DOUG DORFMAN, DEN-TURE KING—with Dad wearing the crumply business suit and a hokey crown that must have been Photoshopped in and a huge, fake white smile—Mom gave the billboard her middle finger.

That's how we left New Jersey: broke and with Mom's middle finger standing at attention.

I know Mom was cursing the billboard people for not returning their money, not Dad. Mom knew he couldn't help it.

But she looked so sad and angry that I reached into our bag of snacks, unwrapped a Jelly Krimpet Tastykake—her favorite kind—and handed it to her. Those things could always make Mom smile.

Well, almost always.

You, Being You!

The day before school starts, we are in Dare's bedroom, trying on every single piece of clothing she owns. Dresses. Skirts. Blouses. Shoes. (Even though her foot is a size and a half smaller than mine.) Dare even borrowed a couple of her mom's flowing scarves for us to glam it up with.

Once, when we were little, and did this during a sleepover, Dare's mom, Ophelia, looked at me strangely for a few moments, then came into the room and joined us. And when I asked her to put makeup on my face like she was doing for Dare, she did but said, "Don't you tell your parents I did this. Okay?"

Even back then I knew it would be okay to tell Mom but not Dad. But I didn't mention it to either of them. Just in case. It made me feel so good that Ophelia accepted me for who I was. That she didn't think there was anything wrong with my wanting to wear makeup, too.

Now I'm wrapped in a fabulous purple scarf and wearing a long black skirt and silky navy top with a plunging neckline that shows exactly how flat my stupid boy chest is. A pang of jealousy hits me as I look at Dare's new and improved boobs. She's so lucky her body made them over the summer. She didn't even have to do a single thing to make it happen. I'll need to take estrogen hormones if I want my body to make boobs someday. But before I can do that, I need hormone blockers to stop my body from betraying me and developing male characteristics. I've got to make Dad understand how important the blockers are, how they can buy me time before permanent, irreversible changes take place. All the wrong changes.

But I don't need to think about that right now. For the moment, I can take a break from worrying.

Dare is wearing pink sweatpants and a purple T-shirt with fake gems in the shape of a heart on it.

"So," Dare says, trying on a rainbow-colored scarf. "Are you gonna finally do it?"

"Do what?" I ask, even though I know exactly what she means. I'm stalling.

Dare rummages through the mess of clothes we piled on her floor. "Do this," she says, depositing a pink skirt and my favorite light blue blouse on the bed. "First day of school. You, being you."

I touch the silky fabric of the blouse—so much softer than the boy clothes Dad buys me. I rub it against my cheek, and it feels just right against my skin. Dare has no idea how much I want to do this. But I think of Dad and how he hates when I dress like a girl. Then I think of the kids at school who already make fun of me. I think of Dunkin. I look at Dare and say, "Maybe it would be better if I wait a year and do it when we start high school. The kids will be more mature then. Right?"

"Ugh!" Dare throws her beautiful brown arms up in total despair. "What am I going to do with you, Lily Jo McGrother?"

I clutch Dare's soft pillow to my chest. "Be my friend."

Dare plops down onto the bed. "I can do that. But at least take these home with you. Think about it."

I love that Dare calls me Lily when we're not in school. Mom calls me Lily now, too, even though Dad doesn't like it. And Sarah told me she'd call me Lily when I'm ready to fully *be* Lily.

"Okay," I say. And with that one word, I make a promise to myself.

I will try again.

Sisterly Words of Wisdom

I wake forty-five minutes before my alarm is set to go off.

It gives me enough time to lie in bed and allow my stomach to twist and roil. The other kids at Gator Lake starting eighth grade don't have to deal with this. They worry about normal things like zits, what they'll wear and who likes them.

My bedroom door creaks open. Sarah's head appears. Her warm smile makes everything feel better. "Wanted to wish you good luck today."

"Come in," I say, sitting up in bed and patting the space beside me.

Sarah's wearing a long skirt, brown boots and this sheer top with a tank under it.

"I wish I looked like you." I can't believe I say what I'm thinking, but it's true. Sarah is beautiful, and it seems so easy for her. A part of me has envied Sarah for as long as I can remember, but I've never actually said it out loud.

She locks eyes with me. "You're great just the way you are." Then she lifts my chin, so I have to hold my head up high. "What are you wearing today?" She eyes the skirt and blouse I borrowed from Dare that are hanging on my closet door.

I take a deep breath. "If I wear boy clothes, I think Dare will kill me."

"She's a good friend," Sarah says.

"Yeah, but if I wear girl clothes, I think Dad will kill me."

"Well, who's scarier, Dad or Dare?"

"Dare," we both say at the same time, and crack up.

I love my sister.

Sarah touches my arm. "Maybe it would be a good idea to wait on the girl clothes, you know." She looks right in my eyes. "Middle school can be kind of . . . hard. Kids aren't very accepting . . . of themselves, much less anyone else."

"Tell me about it," I say, thinking of the Neanderthals I'll have to face today.

"Maybe wait a little," Sarah says quietly. "Be you at home, but . . ."

"You're starting to sound like Dad."

She wrinkles her nose. "Sorry."

"It's okay," I say, but I'm sad that my own sister doesn't think it's a good idea to be who I truly am right now.

"Hey," Sarah says. "The Knit Wits will be meeting here after school."

"What are you guys working on today?"

Sarah pulls two tiny pieces of yarn from her pocket—one is light blue, the other soft pink. "We're knitting cute little hats for the preemie babies at Beckford Palms Hospital."

"That's cool," I say. But all I can think about is how the whole boy/girl color code is determined right from birth. The moment a baby comes into the world, someone decides whether the baby gets a pink hat or a blue hat, based on the baby's body. Not brain. Why can't they put a neutral color hat on the baby and wait to see what happens?

With a silly British accent, Sarah says, "Must be off. Bad form to be late the first day and all. Cheerio, matey!" She wraps her arms around me, hugging me tight enough to give me the strength I need to get through the next few hours.

"Thanks, Sar. Love you."

"Love you, too," she says, and touches the tip of my nose. She glances at the girl clothes. "No matter what."

*　*　*

I'm halfway through my Pop-Tart (I shared a bit of the edge with Meatball) when Dad joins me in the kitchen, the newspaper folded under his armpit. He smells of the strong peppermint soap Mom buys.

"Hey, Tim. Ready for your first big day as an eighth grader?"

I can tell Dad's happy I'm dressed in boy clothes.

"I guess," I say, but I have zero enthusiasm in my voice. Dad should notice this, but doesn't seem to.

He pours water into the coffeemaker. "Want some?" he asks.

"No thanks," I say. "Well, I'd better get this over with."

Mom bounds down the stairs, yoga mat carrier slung over her shoulder. "You ready, sweetheart?" She grabs my cheeks with her warm palms and looks into my eyes.

That's when hot tears leak out.

Angrily, I swipe them away with the back of my hand. I nod toward Dad, even though he didn't really do anything except make coffee.

"I know," Mom says, and holds me.

But I don't know if she does. How could she? She was born into the right body. Nine hundred ninety-nine out of a thousand people are born into the right body. *Lucky them.*

"Be patient with him," Mom whispers. "It'll happen."

Maybe she does understand.

I take a deep breath, inhaling what little courage I can for the beginning of eighth grade.

Through the window beside the door, I watch Dare walk up the path to our house, smiling her awesome, deep-dimpled smile.

When she sees what I'm wearing, that smile won't last.

I look at Dad bent over the newspaper, then at Dare approaching our door, and I feel like no matter what I do, I can't win.

a Sign

"Hey, sweetheart," Mom says, pulling Dare into the foyer and giving her a big squeeze.

But while Mom is hugging Dare, Dare is glaring at me, saying how deeply disappointed she is with her eyes.

"You ready for the first day of eighth grade?" Mom asks.

"*I* am," Dare says, making a dig only I understand.

"Well, let me take a photo of you two." Mom runs off to get her camera.

Dare slaps a hand on her hip and looks at me.

"I know," I say, feeling like a failure.

Dad glances up from his newspaper and gives Dare a quick wave.

Mom returns, fiddling with the camera. "Come on," she says, signaling us to move closer. "Pretend you've been, you know, best friends since preschool."

Which we have, ever since Ms. Christy's class at Klever Kids. *It would have been clever if they spelled it correctly.*

I first met Dare while she was reading a Berenstain Bears book. I plopped down next to her and watched as she ran her finger under the sentences and listened as she quietly read the story "Too Much TV." The rest of that day and many days following, Dare and I played Berenstain Bears together. We pretended Ms. Christy was Mama Bear and Papa Bear was off to work. Dare was perfect as Brother Bear, and I, of course, was Sister Bear.

Now I slide closer to Dare so we can get this whole paparazzi thing over with.

Dare, I notice, does not move one millimeter closer. In fact, she leans a tiny bit in the other direction. It makes my heart ache.

"Smile," Mom says.

I force a tight-lipped, lopsided excuse for a smile.

Dare doesn't even bother.

"Wait," Mom says, and runs off again.

Dare shakes her head. *At Mom? At me?*

"Stop looking at me in that tone of voice," I whisper, hoping it will crack through Dare's anger, but she doesn't respond.

"Here," Mom says. "Hold this."

Mom hands us a sign she made. It reads: *Lily and Dare— 1st day of 8th grade.*

This—finally—makes Dare smile.

I smile, too. A real smile. Last year's sign read: *Tim and Dare—1st day of 7th grade.* And each year before that was the same, except for the grade. I guess the sign changed because Mom changed. She's really embracing the new me. The true me.

Love you, Mom, I mouth. It feels like she wrapped my raw heart in a tender hug.

"You're too cool, Mrs. McGrother," Dare says, and gives my mom a fist bump.

When Mom takes the photo, I know I look genuinely happy, because that's how I feel. I peek over, and Dare looks happy, too. Maybe she's even done being disappointed in me for dressing like a boy.

Dad looks up and nods. "Have a good first day."

"Thanks, Mr. McGrother," Dare says.

"Bye, Dad."

Mom puts her camera down and shoos us out the door, only I can tell she wants us to leave because she's getting misty-eyed and probably doesn't want to blubber all over us.

Dare pushes open the screen door and I follow.

As I walk down the path away from our house, Dare bumps her hip into mine. I act like I'm going to do the same, really hard, but instead I nudge my shoulder into hers.

I peek back to see if Mom's watching. She's standing outside the door, one hand over her heart. The other is holding the sign.

A Hopeful Feeling

"You said you were going to do it." Dare shoves me again, and I lose my balance and fall off the sidewalk.

"It could still happen," I say, getting back in step with her. "The year's just starting." I hope she'll quit being disappointed. I'm disappointed in myself enough for the both of us.

"It's not going to happen if *you* don't make it happen." Dare stops walking. "Nobody can do this for you, Lily. Did you ever consider there could be someone like you—hiding—at our school, and if you're brave, it could make it easier for that person?"

I doubt anyone else at our school is like me. But the thought gives me a spark of hope.

"When you're brave and honest, you make it easier for the next person. Like Rosa Parks. Jackie Robinson. Thurgood Marshall. Ruby Bridges. Like—"

"Jenna Talackova. Janet Mock. Laverne Cox. Jenny Boylan."

"Exactly." Dare nods. "I'm not saying it's easy. I'm saying it's important, not only for you but for the next person."

"I know," I whisper, my head down. And I do know, but I can't think about the next person right now. I can barely keep myself together. In addition to four new mustache hairs, which I plucked, I found another couple wiry hairs down there this morning, and I'm going to lose it if Dad doesn't let me get hormone blockers soon.

"I'm not sure you do," Dare says loud and clear, never knowing when to let something go.

Sweat drips down the sides of my face, and I just want to get to school before I'm a gross, sweaty mess for the first day.

Dare points her finger right under my nose. "If you can't be comfortable with who you really are, then how do you expect anyone else to be?"

She's right. She's always right, but I don't want to talk about it anymore. I want to get my head in the right place for school. "Could we please talk about something else?"

Dare looks me in the eye, squeezes my shoulders and says, "Sorry. Sometimes there's no off switch to my mouth."

And like that, we're okay again, bumping shoulders and moving forward.

The Neanderthals

I get my schedule and rush over to Dare to compare. When we see we have lunch together, we high-five. We also have the same social studies and PE classes. Two fist bumps. I wish we were together in every class, but Dare's better at math and science than I am, so she's in the advanced classes. We both have honors Language Arts, but different teachers and at different times.

Our homerooms are at opposite ends of the school, so when we escape the noisy, smelly cafeteria, we quickly hug, then separate.

I don't get far when I see Dunkin heading toward me. I smile.

Just then, John Vasquez and a couple of his Neanderthal friends, like Bobby Birch, who have grown taller and bulkier over the summer, step in front of me. Testosterone at its finest. The good feeling from seeing Dunkin evaporates.

My heart pounds. My legs want to run. But where would I go?

I don't want this to be how I start my first day of eighth grade.

It irritates me that I have to look up to the Neanderthals because of their growth spurts.

I should be in homeroom now. The bell's going to ring soon. I think of saying that's why I need to go, but I don't, because no one cares about being on time the first day. Returning students are too busy catching up, and new kids are too busy getting lost.

"Hey, fag!"

With that one word, all the hope about this year being different leaks out of me.

Nothing has changed from last year, except the size of the Neanderthals.

I can't believe Vasquez says it just like that. Right in the hallway with tons of kids around. He says it like the words are maggots in his mouth. Says it like it's a true thing. It isn't. It's an ugly thing, the way he says it. It's not the right word, even if he'd used the correct word, the inoffensive word. Still, it makes my stomach squeeze into a tight, sick ball.

"Fag!" Vasquez says again. "Nice hair."

I'm instantly self-conscious about my blond hair. The hair I had to fight Dad to keep long. The hair that looks just like Mom's. The hair I love.

Vasquez wears a crew cut. He reaches over and yanks my hair. "Fag."

"Yeah, friggin' fag," Bobby Birch echoes, clenching and unclenching his fat fists.

If it's this bad when I'm dressed in stupid boy clothes, I don't want to imagine what this reunion would have been like if I came to school wearing Dare's skirt and silky blouse. I've heard that Vasquez and his buddies have done some awful things to kids outside of school. I imagine if I dressed how I wanted to, in clothing people label for girls only, I'd probably be on the floor in a puddle of my own blood, their hard fists pounding my body.

I pull into myself, wishing they'd leave. Hiding in my boy-appropriate clothes was a good idea this morning. I hate to admit it, but Dad was right.

Vasquez shakes his head at me. "Why are you such a fag, McGrother?"

I assume that's a rhetorical question.

The Neanderthals saunter off, probably to harass someone else, like a kid with crutches or in a wheelchair. These guys clearly emerged from the shallow end of the gene pool.

I wish I could go home and curl up under my ugly brown comforter with Meatball nestled behind my knees. Or climb into the welcoming branches of Bob, with a good book. But I can't do any of those things. I've got to get to homeroom and meet my new teachers and classmates.

I pull my shoulders back.

I won't let the Neanderthals ruin my first day of eighth grade.

Marching toward homeroom, I shake off that ugly word and let it fall to the scuffed hallway floor, along with a lone tear that slips out.

COWARD

At the end of the wide, crowded hallway, I spot the long hair.

Tim looks up, and I see his deep blue eyes, like the ocean. When he sees me, he smiles, and I instantly feel great. It's nice to know at least one person in this huge new school. One person I can talk to. One person I can—I hope—eat lunch with, if we're lucky enough to have our schedules match up. I can't believe I never asked him where he went to school.

I walk through the crowd of kids toward Tim, so we can compare schedules, and maybe he can show me where my homeroom is because I have no idea and I really don't want to ask anyone.

My moment of relief is instantly replaced by a tightening of my stomach.

A few tall guys stand in front of Tim, their backs to me. I can hardly see Tim anymore between their big bodies. Usually, I can see over people's heads, but these guys are nearly as tall as I am.

I inch closer, though, so I can get a sense of what's going on, but not too close.

It looks like one of the guys says something to Tim and pulls his hair. *Who does that? Is this second grade?*

I'm near enough to hear the word one of them uses. An image pops into my mind—*that bright day less than a week ago when I saw Tim standing in front of his house, wearing a red dress. Tim, with his long, blond hair and blue eyes.*

I hear the word again, thrown out in the hallway in a threatening way.

Alarm bells go off in my head, so I stop moving and clutch my schedule so tightly it crumples.

I should rush over to help. It would be the right thing to do. It would be the thing Dad would have done, when he was having a good day. He loved helping people, fixing their problems.

But rushing into this situation that I don't know anything about would be a terrible way to start at a new school. What if the guys turn from Tim to me? What if they call me a fag?

I take a step back. And another step, as kids crowd around them.

One of the guys shifts enough for me to see Tim's eyes, pleading for it to end. I know that feeling so well from the kids who picked on me at my school in New Jersey.

Without realizing I've made my decision, I duck my head and swivel around. I rush back toward the library, away from Tim and the ugly words that are flying at him and the hate coming from the kids encircling them.

I find a stairway and head up, up and away from being a halfway decent human.

Coward.

I push open a door that leads to a less crowded hallway and walk forward.

Coward. Coward. Coward.

It's not until a sharp sound pierces my thoughts that I realize I'm supposed to be in homeroom. And I have no idea where it is.

TWO WORDS

Some teacher smooths out my schedule, squints at it and points toward my homeroom. I find the classroom and slip into an open seat along the back row. I'm late, but a couple kids walk in after me, so I guess it's no big deal.

I'm still thinking about what happened to Tim and how I was a giant chicken when the homeroom teacher calls roll. Of course, I'm lost in my thoughts and the teacher has to say my name twice. My stupid, make-fun-able name is awful enough the first time.

Some girl a couple rows ahead of me leans toward another girl and giggles. "Norbert Dorfman? That's an unfortunate name."

I slink way down in my seat—which is awkward because I'm freakishly tall. I realize this roll-call humiliation will be repeated in every class.

My next class is Language Arts. I find it right away and take a seat in the back. Tim walks into the class, and my immediate response is happiness, but it's replaced by guilt. I walked away when those guys were hassling him in the hallway. *What kind of person does that? The kind of person who wants to survive eighth grade.*

When Tim looks up the rows and his blue eyes settle on mine, I duck my head, because what I did—or more accurately, what I didn't do—was cowardly. I would have wanted someone to stick up for me if I were in that situation. I shouldn't have ducked my head, though, because I realize too late that Tim gave me a friendly wave, and now too much time has passed to wave back without it being awkward.

I ache for my friend Phineas, so I wouldn't feel lonely, but I know that's stupid and crazy.

Mr. Creighton tells us about his teaching career and his dogs and his nerdy love of books. I like him.

But then he calls roll. Why didn't he do it at the beginning of class like other teachers do? I got all comfortable with his stories, then this.

When he says, "Norbert Dorfman," I'm paying attention and raise my hand fast, so he can go on to the next name.

Not fast enough, apparently. Someone nearby whispers, "Norbert Dorfman. Seriously?"

I startle when the kid beside me taps my elbow. He slips a folded piece of paper into my hand. I wonder if it's for someone else and I'm supposed to pass it along, but the kid signals that it's meant for me.

Me?

That's when worry floods my mind. I'm afraid someone's written something mean about my name or . . . maybe it's a note about someone threatening to fight the new kid after school or . . .

Under my desk, I unfold the paper and glance down while Mr. Creighton writes a funny quote on the board about a book and a dog. I don't care about the quote; I care about the note.

There are two words on it that tell me the kid who wrote it is a better person than I am.

Two words (and a punctuation mark) that make me feel happy for the first time since I walked into Gator Lake Middle School.

Hi, Dunkin!

What's In a Name?

I'm happy to see Dunkin in my class. I hope he didn't stick around to witness what those idiots said to me before homeroom. I don't want anything to mess up my chance to be friends with him.

Someone makes fun of Dunkin's real name when roll is called, so I slip him a note with his nickname. I'm so glad to see it makes him smile.

I hate having to answer to Timothy McGrother, even though every fiber of my being wants to shout: *I'm Lily Jo McGrother!*

When I raise my hand, Mr. Creighton looks at me—really looks at me—like he's trying to get to know who I am. He seems like someone who doesn't need to put people into certain boxes to feel more comfortable with the world. I have a feeling Mr. Creighton would like me just fine as Lily.

Where I Don't Belong

We don't have to change into PE clothes because it's the first day, but the coaches give tours of the locker rooms, like they did at the start of sixth and seventh grade. And they go over the same rules they give us every year, about being prepared and about respecting other people and their property. *Yeah, right!*

The sixth graders look small and terrified. I feel sorry for them, but am glad not to be in their shoes. It's hard enough being an eighth grader, especially with the three Neanderthals from this morning in my class. They still make me feel small and terrified.

There's nothing exciting in the locker room for Coach Ochoa to show us—just old benches in front of the lockers, in which people have carved their initials, their girlfriends' initials and other things that make my cheeks warm. There are already a couple wads of toilet paper stuck to the ceiling. And urinals with cakes in them, like the one that Joey Reese thought was hilarious to put in Matthew Greene's locker last year.

I'm relieved when the tour and lecture are over and we're standing in the gym, outside the locker room.

Coach Ochoa drones on about changing quickly and not being late for class. I tune him out and watch Coach Outlaw walk the girls into the locker room on the other side of the gym. Dare's in that group, and I should be, too.

SOMETHING IN MATH CLASS (AND THE CAFETERIA) DOESN'T ADD UP

The guys who bothered Tim are in my math class. It's hard to tell for sure it's them, because there are a lot of kids at this school and they look kind of similar, and I only saw those three for a few seconds, mostly from the back. But I paid attention because of what they were doing.

So I glare at the guys on Tim's behalf, but I'm in the back row, so they can't see me. If one of them turned around, I know I'd look down because I'm a coward.

One of the guys turns around. And waves.

Surprised, I wave back.

He nods and faces front.

What just happened?

As I stare at the back of the guy's head—at his very short hair—and think of Tim's long hair, I feel like a traitor for being friendly to one of the guys who was so mean to Tim this morning. But then again, how well do I know Tim? He could have started something. Unlikely, but possible.

I'm shocked when the guy who waved punches the guy next to him and gestures toward the back, toward me. He whispers something behind his hand, then that guy turns and nods at me.

I nod back.

Are they being friendly or planning to do something mean to me later on? This doesn't feel mean. It feels . . . nice. I take a breath and wonder: *Is this what being popular feels like?*

I sit taller and actually pay attention to what the math teacher says.

"I'm sure you'll all be thrilled to know we'll be expanding your knowledge of algebra and learning some geometry postulates and theorems, too. Oh yes, I can tell you're exploding with excitement." He pauses. "On the inside."

Most of the kids laugh a little. I do, too, because I feel like I'm one of them. And it feels good.

Different.

* * *

At lunch, I hold the orange plastic tray in a death grip, wishing again that Phineas were here. Mom wouldn't like it if she knew I were thinking that, but I hate navigating this loud, crowded, foul-smelling cafeteria alone. The good energy of feeling a part of everything in math class has completely evaporated.

"Dunkin. Over here."

I head toward the table where Tim and Dare are sitting. They're smiling at me, and Tim pats the seat beside him. I'm so glad I have someone to sit with that I relax the grip on my tray.

When I'm almost at their table, I hear, "Yo, Dorfman!"

I hunch forward, expecting those words to be followed by a hurtling chocolate milk carton, like what might have happened at my school in New Jersey. But nothing comes.

"Over here, buddy."

A bunch of tall guys are sitting at the table one row away from Tim and Dare's. I recognize three of them from math class . . . and from earlier this morning. One is waving me over, like he's signaling a plane to land. I actually do that stupid thing and look behind me to make sure he's not signaling someone back there.

No one behind me.

Tim and Dare watch.

I feel like this is a test I didn't study for.

"Right here," the biggest guy calls, patting the seat beside him. "We have to ask you something, dude."

The other guys are shoving white bread sandwiches into their faces and nodding.

I glance at Tim and Dare, as though they might tell me what to do in this unexpected situation. Tim's biting his bottom lip, his hair hiding his eyes, so it's hard to read him. Dare looks pissed off, but I'm beginning to think that might be her natural look.

I offer a weak smile and say to Tim and Dare, "Catch you guys next time."

This table full of guys might be my key to fitting in. I can't give that up to sit with Tim and Dare. Even though Tim did slip me that note in Language Arts class. Even though those guys said something terrible to Tim. I think it was those guys. Maybe I'm wrong.

I walk toward that table feeling like this might be my year. I'll bet these are the most popular guys at school. I get a pinch in my gut, though, just before I get to their table, a worry that the question they need to ask me might be something rude or embarrassing. *What will I do then? Try to sit with Tim and Dare after all? Awkward!*

I shake the thought from my head and decide to be positive, like Phin was always telling me I should be. They want me to sit with them because they think I'm cool. Maybe I am cool here in Florida; I don't know much about life here yet.

I put my orange tray on their table and slide onto the bench.

The biggest guy—the one who had waved to me in math class—jerks his thumb toward Tim and Dare's table. "You're not friends with *them*." He makes a disgusted face. "Are you?"

Am I? Is there something about Tim and Dare I don't understand? They seem nice. I focus on the shriveled hot dog on my tray.

"Well, are you?" another guy asks. He's got ketchup smeared on the side of his mouth, but I don't tell him.

Everyone at the table has stopped eating, food squirreled in their cheeks, and is looking at me.

I feel Tim looking at me, too. And Dare, I'm sure, is glaring at me with her death rays.

Even though I'm perfectly still, my heart thunders. *WWPD? What Would Phineas Do?*

I make sure my back is to Tim and Dare's table. "Of course not."

The big guy pounds me on the shoulder, and everyone nods and goes back to eating.

I shove a giant piece of hot dog into my mouth. It barely fits with the lie taking up so much room, and I feel like I might choke on them both.

Defector . . . and Pop-Tarts

Lunch sucks.

Well, it was perfectly okay sitting with Dare until the new kid—my potential new friend from New Jersey, Dunkin—

took one look at us and chose to defect. He marched right over to enemy territory and set up camp.

I didn't see that coming.

I never do.

If eighth grade continues like this, I might have to spend it perched in the branches of Bob. Heck, if Julia Butterfly Hill—one of my heroes—could live in a redwood for two years, then surely I can manage eighth grade in a banyan tree. Mom and Dad would understand. At least Mom would. And Sarah would probably bring me food and a bucket to poop in.

When I look over at Dunkin sitting with the enemy, I wish I were wedged in the branches of Bob right now, instead of in this noisy, stinky cafeteria, filled with Neanderthals and a defector from New Jersey.

"Another one's gone over to the dark side," I say to Dare.

She responds by reaching into her bag and pulling out a razzleberry Pop-Tart. With icing! "This should make you feel better," she says, handing it to me.

It smells of sweet, delicious razzleberries, and I don't even think that's a real kind of fruit, but it should be. I lick the icing. It tastes real enough for me.

I decide that even though Dunkin chose to sit in enemy territory, the world cannot be in total disarray when there are razzleberry Pop-Tarts in it.

"There is hope," I tell Dare, holding up my Pop-Tart like a talisman against evil.

She glances at something or someone just beyond my shoulder, then back at me. "Indeed there is," she says.

SWEET . . .

The question contains only four words.

But those words seem loaded with importance, and I have a feeling they may change my life.

"Do you play basketball?"

That was the question the guys had wanted to ask me?

The pieces click into place. They are unusually tall. I am unusually tall. Do I play basketball? Of course I don't. I don't play any sport that requires the smallest amount of athleticism or ability to stay upright for any length of time.

How does one answer this question when a whole group of guys are staring and expecting an obvious yes?

One lies.

"Hells yeah, I play b-ball." At first I wonder who said that because I don't talk like that, but I must have heard it somewhere since those are the words that fly from my mouth.

It must have been the right answer because the guys nod and a couple of them pound me on the back, even though I'm not choking to death on my hot dog.

Despite the fact that I'm being pummeled (in a nice way) and I just lied, I feel pretty terrific.

That is, until I look over at Tim and Dare's table.

Tim looks genuinely sad—well, what I can see of him from behind his hair. Then Dare pulls something out from her bag and Tim looks happier. For some dumb reason, I wish I were the one to make Tim happier.

"We've got to start practicing," the guy everyone calls Vasquez says.

He seems like the one in charge.

"Yeah, tryouts are next month," a guy across from me chimes in.

"Tryouts?" I say, choking on my own saliva.

"Yeah," Vasquez answers. "You'll be our secret weapon. It will be sooooo sweet."

I glance over and see that Dare has given Tim a Pop-Tart, and he's actually taking a bite with his eyes closed. He must love Pop-Tarts like I love doughnuts. The best way to take the first bite is always with your eyes closed.

"Yeah," I say, my stomach in knots. I don't want to practice basketball with these guys. They're probably amazing. They'll find out how much I stink. I've never intentionally played basketball. I mean, in PE in New Jersey, we had to learn some basics, but I was lousy.

I look over at Tim again quickly so he and Dare don't notice. Tim's so happy eating his Pop-Tart that it makes me smile.

"Yeah," I say again. "Sweet."

After School, Part 1

Before Dare heads home, she and I do the handshake we created in fourth grade. I can't believe she still wants to do it, but I'm glad. Even when I'm an old lady, I'll remember our handshake. *Slap. Slap. Clap. Clap. Snap. Snap. Shake, lock thumbs and wiggle our fingers.* It's dumb, but fun.

Vasquez and his buddies head toward the bus loop—losers!

I don't see Dunkin anywhere. Not that I care. *Traitor!*

I walk to the Beckford Palms Library and borrow *A Crooked Kind of Perfect*. It seems like the right book for today, plus I'll be able to finish it in one sitting, because it's pretty slim and I've already read it twice before.

Tucked safely in the branches of Bob, I get lost in Zoe Elias's world and her dream for a piano, only to have her dad return with a "wood-grained, vinyl-seated, wheeze-bag organ. The Perfectone D-60." I sigh. Dads can be frustrating like that sometimes. In the book, Zoe's dad can't be what she needs him to be, but eventually she accepts him for who he is and it all works out.

I'm not sure it's going to all work out with Dad and me. *Will he let me get hormone blockers before it's too late? Will he ever love the real me?*

AFTER SCHOOL, PART II

I'm walking toward the exit when Vasquez wallops me on the shoulder. "Glad you'll be playing ball with us this year."

"Yeah, me too," I say, even though I'm not.

"We'll get together soon and practice, but I gotta catch the bus." And he jogs off.

He looks so effortlessly cool. I guess Tim wasn't one of the cool kids after all, but Vasquez definitely is. He's got tons of people who eat lunch with him and come up to talk with him. I can't believe he wants to be friends with me. *Me!* I'll just have to figure out the basketball thing.

I use the bathroom, then stroll out of the building into the bright sunlight with my shoulders back, feeling pretty good about my first day. Except my head's been throbbing since last period. Caffeine withdrawal. So instead of going to Bubbie's, I head toward Dunkin' Donuts to get an iced coffee.

That tree—the one where Tim dumped a bunch of leaves on me—is on the way to Dunkin' Donuts. When I'm directly beneath it, something makes me look up. This time no leaves rain down, but I do see the bottoms of sneakers and someone up there with long blond hair.

"Hey," I say, shielding my eyes from the sun.

Tim lowers the book he's reading and looks down. His face is pinched and angry. Then he goes right back to reading, like I'm invisible or something.

"Hey," I say again, irritated.

"Hey what?" Tim asks.

"You, um, want to hang out?" I figure I'm on a roll with making friends, so I might as well try to work things out with Tim.

"No, um, I do not want to hang out."

He sounds really pissed. "Why not? What's your problem?"

"Are you serious? What's *my* problem? It's not okay to dump me and my friend in the cafeteria, then act like we're best buds outside of school."

"I wasn't—"

"Save it for someone who cares," Tim says.

"Cold," I mutter, even though it's a million degrees outside.

But the truth is, Tim's right. That's exactly what I did. I was about to sit with him and Dare when a better offer came along, and I took it. And I'm glad I did, because it was worth it to get a whole bunch of new friends. Popular friends. Friends who don't sit in trees . . . named Bob.

I scowl at Tim, but he's already got the book in front of his face again.

I'm beginning to understand why Vasquez and the guys make fun of him.

* * *

When I get to Bubbie's, Mom's at the kitchen table, stuffing *Bodies by Bubbie* DVDs into padded mailers. I shiver as the cold air in the house freezes the sweat on my body.

"What's up?" I ask, my head in the fridge, then the pantry, then the fridge. I end up eating a sawdust and raisin muffin (aka bran muffin) because there isn't any good food in the house— another reminder we're not home in New Jersey. We had tons of junk food there, especially when Dad did the grocery shopping. And when Mom worked at the bakery, there were always cakes that someone had messed up or a few smooshed cupcakes that didn't look perfect, but still tasted great.

"What's up with you? I'm just helping Bubbie with her business. It's the least I can do since she's letting us live here for a while." Mom sighs and puts the mailer down. "You know I'm going to get myself together. Right?"

I focus on Mom and nod. I didn't realize she wasn't together. Just thought she was sad, which is perfectly normal considering what's happened.

"I'm going to get a job," she says. "Maybe at a bakery. And we're going to get our own place, too. It won't be big like this house, but . . ."

I don't want to hear any of this. I don't want to think about what it all means. I don't want to think.

"So anyway, how was your first day?" Mom asks.

I'm glad she changes the subject, so I can focus on something else. I shrug like it was no big deal, but I'm dying to tell Mom what happened.

She picks up another mailer. "You go through an entire day of school in a new state and all I get is a shrug?"

"I made some friends."

Mom's face lights up.

I realize all the guilt and grief I felt from dumping Tim and Dare in the cafeteria were worth it to see Mom looking so happy.

"So, who are these new friends?" she asks.

"They're basketball guys," I say, and I tell her all about them, at least the good parts.

A Flamingo Kind of Guy

I don't want to climb out of Bob's strong branches, but the sun's going down, so I'd better get home before Mom sends out a search party. Some night I'd love to sleep in Bob's branches. I might have to strap myself in so I don't fall, but it would be so cool to sleep up high in my favorite tree.

"Where were you?" Mom asks the minute I walk into the kitchen. "Your sister came home hours ago."

"High school gets out way before middle school."

"Oh yeah, I forgot."

"Plus I spent some time in Bob after school."

"Aha! I figured that's where you were. How was your first day? Was it hard going in dressed like that?"

I love how Mom's so open and real when she talks to me. She's always been pretty accepting, but she's been amazing lately.

"To be honest," I say, munching on some mini-pretzels, "it was probably easier. A couple Neanderthals bothered me already."

"What? Are those stupid boys still harassing you?"

I nod. "And they got taller over the summer. But don't worry. It's okay."

"It most certainly is not okay," Mom says. She's a lot like Dare in that way. "How did they bother you?"

I shove in a mouthful of mini-pretzels.

"Not too many," Mom warns. "Making dinner soon."

"Sorry," I say. "But really, it's no big deal. I shouldn't have said anything."

"Tim—I mean, Lily, will you tell me if it ever becomes a problem?"

"Of course." *Not.*

I watch Mom sip her stay-healthy tea concoction that she drinks before dinner. What those stupid boys said definitely bothered me, but not as much as Dunkin snubbing me and Dare at lunch so he could sit with them. I know he's too new to know that they're jerks, but still . . . we'd asked him to join us first.

"Hey, you know what?" I ask.

"What?"

"There were more flamingos outside on the lawns when I came home. The guys in the golf cart were plucking them out again before I walked into the house."

"Hmm," Mom says. "What's that all about?"

"No clue," I say. "But it's pretty funny." I wonder if

Dunkin is behind the flamingos. They started appearing when he did. But he doesn't strike me as the kind of guy who would sneak around planting pink plastic flamingos in random lawns. Of course, he doesn't strike me as a basketball-playing kind of guy who hangs out with Neanderthals, either.

I guess everyone has secrets.

TOMORROW?

Day two in school, the guys meet me at my locker. Vasquez slops his arm over my shoulders. "Practice at the courts behind school tomorrow."

He's smiling, so I smile, but inside I'm not smiling. *Maybe there's a seventh way to die in South Florida—by humiliation on the basketball court.*

"Tomorrow?" I ask in a voice that's way too high-pitched for a guy my size.

His arm slips off. "You busy tomorrow? 'Cause we've gotta practice."

"Not busy."

"Great," Vasquez says, and squeezes me around the neck way too hard. *Eighth way to die?*

Then he and the guys walk off. They don't get too far down the hall when I see Vasquez push Tim's notebook out of his arms. I shake my head because that was a dumb thing to do, but at least he didn't hit Tim or anything.

Besides, I can't worry about that now. I've got to figure out how to play basketball.

By tomorrow!

A Very Bad Sign

The only bad thing that happens today is Vasquez knocking my notebook out of my arms. No words are said. He doesn't even push me. It could have been much worse.

I take this as a good sign.

In PE, we watch a film about proper nutrition and don't have to change into PE clothes, which is another good sign. I wish we could watch a film in PE every day. My life sans having to go into a boys' locker room would be infinitely easier. Imagine walking into the wrong public restroom and having to stay there. That's how I feel all the time.

Mr. Creighton's Language Arts class is amazing! He tells us we're going to write a short story, and the art students are going to illustrate it. Then we're going to have a party with the authors and illustrators signing their creations. He's going to provide the cookies, juice, music and prizes and make it like a real publishing party at a bookstore.

I have no idea what I'll write about, but it will be fun to read my classmates' stories, especially Dunkin's. Even though he's been kind of a jerk since school started, I'd still like to get to know him better, maybe give him another chance. I have a feeling there are interesting things going on in that head of his. I feel like he might be a kindred spirit. But he sat with the Neanderthals at lunch again. Any buddy of the Neanderthals can't be a friend of mine, which is a shame because I could use another friend. Dare's been so busy lately with her other buds, practicing lacrosse and stuff.

After school as I walk toward Bob, I think about all the great things that happened today—especially the publishing party we'll have in Mr. Creighton's class—and I'm in such a good mood I almost don't notice the sign.

Almost.

But then I see it on a wooden post, jammed into the ground several yards in front of Bob. I let the words settle into my soul. Then I rush into a stall in the library restroom and heave. Only a little bit comes out—an acidy, vile version of the Pop-Tart I ate at lunch.

After standing in the stall and catching my breath, I gain the courage to go back outside and reread the sign. Just to be sure.

I read the words I want to un-know the moment I know them.

Then I'm sure.

This is very bad.

A REQUEST

"Bubbie, I need your help," I say during dinner.

She sits up taller, which is sort of a lost cause since she's so short. "How can I help, bubela?"

I force down a bite of salmon, hoping the tiny bones don't poke my throat. "I need to get good at basketball. Fast."

Mom grins.

"I want to try out for the school team."

"That's terrific, Norbert!" Mom says too loudly.

Bubbie looks me up and down, then shakes her head. "I'll do what I can. But don't expect to be the next Michael Jordache."

"Jordan," Mom corrects.

"Jordan Jordache." Bubbie waves her hand dismissively. "Whatever." Then Bubbie points her fork at me. "Meet me out back after dinner and we'll do drills." She sizes me up. "Lots and lots of drills."

"What kind of drills?" I ask, feeling the tiny bones poking me in the throat. *Way #9 to die in South Florida?*

"Oy vey," Bubbie says. "Just be grateful your old bubbie has a basketball and meet me out back."

As I shovel sautéed spinach with garlic into my mouth, I realize I am grateful . . . because if I don't get good at basketball in a hurry, Vasquez and the guys probably won't want to hang out with me anymore.

Then I'll be right back where I started when I arrived in South Florida.

Nowhere.

With no one to hang out with.

DISASTROUS DRILLS

I'm wearing jeans, a T-shirt and sneakers when I join Bubbie out back, after our disgusting dinner of salmon and garlic spinach. (Mom snuck me three chocolate chunk, butterscotch macadamia cookies as soon as Bubbie went out back, and I'm thankful she kept me from starving.)

There's a grassy area and a cement area to the side of Bubbie's pool, but no basketball court.

"How are we going to practice without a hoop?" I ask.

"Don't worry about that, Jordan Jordache," Bubbie says, and surprises me by throwing the basketball—hard—like a cannon shot. Bubbie might be short, but she's got some serious strength.

The basketball slams into my chest before I can react.

"Why'd you do that?" I rub my chest.

Bubbie grabs the ball from the grass, puts it in the crook of her arm and walks so close we're practically nose to belly button. She looks up and opens her mouth, and the smell of garlic and fish on her breath makes me gag. "Norbert Dorfman," she says, reaching up and poking me in my already sore chest. "Rule number one of basketball: When someone passes you the ball, catch it. And not with your chest."

106

I stop rubbing my chest, even though it still hurts.

"And don't you have a pair of athletic shorts to wear? It's too hot for jeans."

"I'm good," I say, even though my legs are sweating so much the fabric is sticking to my skin.

Bubbie squints at me and walks over to the section of cement. "Let's try something safer."

She demonstrates how to dribble back and forth between her right and left hands.

When I try it, I can't get the rhythm right and fumble the ball. Wait. Fumbling is football. I'm hopeless.

Bubbie throws me some easy passes.

I miss at least 60 percent of them.

Then she tells me to throw the ball against the wall and catch it fifty times in a row without missing.

I make it three times before I miss the ball. Then five times. Then two. Then seven. *Fifty in a row without missing?*

My arms are sore. My chest still hurts. My head throbs. I need more caffeine. "I quit!"

"You can't quit, Norbert. We're just getting started."

"Thanks, Bubbie." I drop the ball. "But I'm done."

I go into the house and up to the guest room, knowing I've got to find a way to get out of basketball practice tomorrow.

About a half hour later, Bubbie comes in. I worry she'll be mad at me for quitting drills.

"Hi, bubela," she says, sitting on the edge of the bed.

She doesn't sound mad, so I get up and show her my newest magic trick with the pepper shaker.

"Now, that's a good one," Bubbie says. "And don't worry, Norbert. You'll get the basketball thing. It'll just take time. And practice. Do you think Jordan Jordache got famous overnight?"

I sneak the pepper shaker into the trash basket for now, get up and give Bubbie a big hug.

"Want to join your mother and me at the movies?" she asks.

"What's it about?"

"It's a beautiful story about a woman who reconnects with the love of her life fifty years after she first met him."

"Um, no. Thanks anyway."

"Suit yourself," Bubbie says, and strolls out.

I'm glad she's getting Mom to go with her, but maybe they should have chosen a comedy. Mom needs something to cheer herself up; she still seems pretty sad most of the time.

While they're at the movie, I practice magic tricks, like the levitating pencil and the disappearing scarf. I'm pretty good at them now. And I try to come up with a way to get out of basketball practice with the guys tomorrow. I'm not so good at that.

FUTURE SITE OF THE
BECKFORD PALMS COMMUNITY PARK.
YOUR TAX DOLLARS AT WORK.
THIS SITE WILL BE CLEARED
AND CONSTRUCTION WILL BEGIN
ON A NEW PLAYGROUND.
"THE COMMUNITY THAT PLAYS TOGETHER . . .
STAYS TOGETHER!"
—MAYOR HIGGINBOTHAM

I climb into Bob's branches and hold on tight, but it's no use.

I can't relax when the sign's words keep bouncing around in my mind: *This site will be cleared . . .* Bob is the only thing on the lot. What else could *"be cleared"* refer to? How could anyone want to get rid of Bob? People love this tree. Little kids climb it. I climb it. People stop under it for shade when they're walking their dogs. I've even seen people picnic beneath it. Mom and I have picnicked beneath it.

Beckford Palms *needs* Bob. Not some dumb park.

I need Bob.

He's a perfectly healthy tree. It doesn't make sense to get rid of him. And the worst part is that he has no idea what's going to happen to him. Or maybe somehow he does, because a strong wind whooshes past, and Bob sheds a few leaves on me—as though he's crying.

The only thing that makes the walk home bearable is

the flamingos stuck into a couple of the lawns at Beckford Palms Estates. I'm growing to love those unexpected plastic birds.

One of the flamingos has a tiny hat with a peace sign on it. Another has a rainbow-colored scarf wrapped around its skinny neck. And a third has a small Elmo doll taped to its beak. Elmo was my favorite character from *Sesame Street* when I was little. (Sarah told me I learned to read from watching *Sesame Street*.)

A Beckford Palms golf cart pulls up, and some guy angrily plucks the funny flamingos from the lawns, tosses them into the back of the cart and drives away, taking the one bit of pizzazz from this boring, bland neighborhood with him.

Terrific.

Every good thing gets taken away.

SHOULD I BE SAD?

I can't fall asleep because I keep worrying about basketball, so I'm awake when Mom and Bubbie come home from the movies.

Mom comes into my room and sits on the edge of my bed. She runs her fingers through my hair. Then she sighs. "Norb?"

"Mhmm?" I sit up. "How was the movie?"

"It was good, honey. Listen, Norb, we haven't really

talked about this, but I think we should. I'm wondering how you're feeling about . . . your dad."

I shrug. *Why does Mom want to talk about Dad now? It's late and I have so many other things on my mind keeping me up.* "I'm all right. I mean, I'm not happy for him, but you know." *He'll be fine. It'll just take some time like before and then he'll be okay again.*

"I'm a little worried, Norb," Mom says, "because, well . . ." She twists a lock of her hair. "I haven't seen you cry. And that concerns me a little. I mean, you've seen me crying buckets. Right?"

Mom has cried buckets—enough for the both of us. She cried before we came here, during the drive and a bunch since we've arrived. "Why does it worry you that I haven't cried?"

Mom's eyebrows shoot up. "Well, he's . . . I thought you'd . . . I'm not sure. I just feel like it should be affecting you way more than it seems to be."

"I haven't felt like crying about it. That's all. Is that wrong?"

Mom pats my knee. "No, honey, it's not wrong. Everyone deals with things in his or her own way." Mom taps her chin. "But you're not even feeling a little sad, Norbert? I could try to find you a therapist you can talk to down here. I know you didn't like the ones you went to in New Jersey, but maybe it will be different here."

I shake my head. "I don't need a therapist, Mom. I'm

doing great. Really." *Why would Mom want me to be sad? Getting too sad is a bad thing. It's a terrible thing.*

Isn't it?

BLOOD, SWEAT AND FRUSTRATION

I wake way before my alarm goes off. It's still dark, but I know I won't be able to fall back to sleep. I have too much energy.

I feel terrific, like it's going to be the greatest day of my life, which is really weird because nothing has changed since yesterday. I slept only a couple of hours, since I had so much on my mind. You'd think I'd feel exhausted, but I'm just the opposite. Supercharged!

And I'm feeling optimistic about Dad for some reason. Things will definitely get better for him, then maybe we'll be able to move back to Jersey and things can return to the way they were. Not that I liked school that much in Jersey, but at least Mom, Dad and I were together there. I don't know why Mom's talking about staying here, about getting a job and our own place.

This morning, I'm feeling way more positive about the whole basketball thing, too. Maybe while I slept for those couple hours, my brain figured out what my body needs to do to be the best basketball player in the history of Gator Lake Middle. And then Vasquez and the guys will totally worship me. I'll single-handedly bring our team to victory.

I push off the girlie white comforter and leap out of bed. I wish basketball tryouts were today. I'd probably out-perform everyone. I feel invincible.

I do some arm raises and deep knee bends, like Bubbie does when she's waiting for someone. My legs are a little sore, but I don't care. I pretend to dunk an imaginary bas-ketball to the cheers of an adoring crowd. They chant the number on the back of my jersey. What will the number on my jersey be? Jersey, just like the shirt, or Jersey, the state. That's a good sign. Right? Jersey. Jersey. I dribble around the bed with my nonexistent basketball and to the window and back, avoiding imaginary players on the other team, until I get to the basket and slam it in. "Whoa!" The crowd goes wild. Cheerleaders jump and shake their pom-poms and scream my new name. "Dunkin, Dunkin, Dunkin!" Teammates slap me on the back, then lift me up onto their shoulders. We fall into a celebratory heap.

It's amazing.

I'm amazing.

I do so many pretend basketball moves in the guest room I wear my body out, but my mind's still on super speed. I'm ready to *GO*!

When the sun finally wakes, all pink and soft clouds, I rush out back and find the basketball. Dew covers its pim-ply rubber surface. I bounce the ball in place a few times on the cement area near the pool. I'm able to control it, and it doesn't fall into the pool, which I take as an excellent sign of my vast improvement since last night. I'm going to practice before Bubbie wakes. And by the time she comes out, I'll be able to show off my awesome skills.

Fifty times, I tell myself. *Throw the ball against the wall and catch it fifty times.* Maybe when Bubbie comes out, I'll be up to a hundred times with no misses. Maybe a thousand times!

You've got this! It's almost like I hear Phineas's relentlessly positive voice in my head. *You've so got this, Dunkin!*

But how would Phineas know that my nickname from Tim is Dunkin? I shake the thought from my head and bounce the ball several times.

"I've got this," I say confidently to no one.

Positioning myself a few feet from the wall, I hold the basketball with both hands.

I throw the ball as hard as I can against the wall, intending to catch it and throw it again and again like a superstar basketball player. Like Jordan Jordache! Ha!

The ball, apparently, has other ideas. It rockets back at me so fast I don't have time to react. It smashes into my face. Blam! Right into my nose.

I drop like a sack of oranges onto the spiky St. Augustine grass. "Don't got this, Phin," I mumble through my hand, which is catching the sticky blood now leaking everywhere.

Leaning my head back, I squeeze my nose shut, but that only makes it harder to breathe. The coppery taste of blood clogs my throat. My nose and cheekbones and eye sockets pulse with pain.

As if that's not bad enough, I'm sweating, because even though the sun recently came up, it's about a million humid degrees outside. I punch the top of the stupid basketball, which serves only to hurt my knuckles.

On the prickly grass, I'm covered in blood, sweat and frustration. I feel entirely deflated. *EnTIRELy deflated. A deflated tire. Yup, that's me.* I'm glad Phineas isn't here to see me like this, although he'd appreciate my clever wordplay. Even Phin couldn't be relentlessly positive in this situation. He'd probably tell me to get up and brush myself off, but I don't. I lie on the grass, feeling increasingly irritated at everything (the stupid basketball) and everyone (Phineas). A friend shouldn't stop communicating with a friend because he moves to another state. It wasn't my fault. None of it was my fault.

Right, Phineas?

I hate basketball. I hate Gator Lake Middle School. I hate that I had to choose between Vasquez and Tim. I hate the sun, which is shaped suspiciously like a basketball. I hate every single thing about South Florida. And I hate Phineas Charlton Winkle most of all.

I feel instantly bad about that last one. I could never hate Phin. He's been with me during the worst of times. I'm sure he'll come around. That's the way it is with him. He always shows up when I need him most.

For now, I close my eyelids against the blazing sun and realize I didn't turn into a superstar basketball player overnight. I'm still a super klutz.

Nothing has changed.

And I've still got to find a way to get out of practice today.

THE INVITATION

At school, Vasquez seems genuinely happy to see me.

"Dorfman!" he calls as he approaches my locker. I like the name Dunkin better than Dorfman, but anything is better than Norbert or some of the other things I've been called.

Vasquez punches me in the shoulder. "Hey, what happened to your nose? And why do you have black circles under your eyes?" He reaches out and presses the area under my right eye.

"Ow." I slap his hand away.

"Sorry, man."

"It's okay," I say, even though it isn't. I slam my locker closed and lie: "I walked into a door. Wasn't paying attention."

Vasquez laughs, even though it's not funny. "You sure your dad didn't do it?"

The question catches me off guard, like something heavy slammed onto my chest. I wish everyone would stop talking about Dad.

Vasquez must sense something's off in my reaction because he gives me a little shove. "Hey, just kidding."

I force a fake smile. "Yeah. Sure."

"You can still practice with us after school," Vasquez

says. "Right? I mean, you're going to be our secret weapon, Dorfman."

This makes me feel good. Even though I know I'm still absolutely lousy at basketball, I love that Vasquez thinks of me as their secret weapon. I'd like to keep him thinking that for as long as possible, which means he can't see me play. "Actually," I say, "I'm not supposed to play sports for a couple days." I point to my face, like that explains everything.

"Oh," Vasquez says. "That sucks." He taps me in the chest with the back of his hand. "You'll be better by Saturday. Right? We have a pickup game on Saturday at noon. Everyone goes to that."

My stomach plunges while my mind races to find an excuse. Meanwhile, my stupid mouth blurts, "Sure. I'll definitely be better by Saturday." I want to punch myself in the mouth so I don't say anything else, but my face has had enough pain for one day.

"Great," Vasquez says. "Can't wait to see what kind of game you've got, Dorfman. Our team's going to be awesome this year!" And he pumps a fist into the air.

I do, too, even though I know that if I'm on the team, it will be anything but awesome.

As Vasquez struts away, I realize I still have a couple days before Saturday to practice. There are worse things than being asked to play basketball by a new friend.

Much worse.

Saturday, Part 1

I should spend as much time visiting Bob as I can, since the city is going to cut him down. But I'm not sure I'll be able to bear sitting in Bob today, with the knowledge of what's to come. But I feel like I need to, so I pack Pop-Tarts and water in my backpack and my iPod with music by Yo-Yo Ma on it.

Sarah's out by the pool with her Knit Wits friends, so I head out to say hi to everyone before I leave.

"Hey, Tim," one of them says.

"How's it going?" another asks, barely glancing up from her knitting.

"Good," I say. "What are you guys making this time?"

I love the Knit Wits. Their club's mission is to make the world suck less through knitting projects. It's an international group, and Sarah's started a local chapter.

"We're making scarves," Justin says. "To mail somewhere up north, where it gets really cold. Then Knit Wits up there will tie the scarves around trees and include a note that says, 'If you're cold and need a scarf, take one. It's free.' "

"That's incredibly cool," I say.

Justin continues, "At the next meeting, we'll make blankets for a camp for kids with cancer. Right, Sar?"

"Yup," my sister says. "We'll need bright orange and white yarn for that project."

"You guys are rock stars," I tell them. I tried knitting a

couple times and was hopeless at it, or I'd definitely be a Knit Wit, too. "Well, happy knitting. I'm heading out to Bob."

"Have fun," Sarah says. "Want me to make Bob a scarf?"

The thought makes me sad, because I know he won't be around to wear it. "Nah," I say. "Save it for the people up north who really need it." I'd tell Sarah and the Knit Wits what's going to happen to Bob, but I'm afraid if I say anything about it right now, I'll start crying.

"Bye, sis," Sarah says in front of her Knit Wits friends.

And not one of them even looks up.

Inside the house, Dad's on a stool at the kitchen counter, hunched over the newspaper, gripping his "World's Best Dad" coffee mug that Grandmom Ruth bought him one year for Father's Day. Dad's so focused on what he's reading, his lips are moving. This makes me smile.

"Bye, Dad," I say, but he must not have heard me.

I ache for him to turn around and look at me.

But he doesn't.

So I shoulder my backpack and head out into the heat, toward Bob.

SATURDAY, PART II

I've been awake for hours. Most of the night, really, trying to figure out how to get out of this stupid pickup basketball game.

Yesterday evening, I squeezed in one more practice session with Bubbie. There wasn't much improvement from the first time Bubbie tried to help me, but at least I didn't smash myself in the face.

I look in the mirror and gently press my nose. Still tender.

I'm not ready to get on a basketball court with other people watching me, judging me. Probably crashing into me. Even with Bubbie's help, I don't know if I'll ever be ready.

But the guys have been really nice to me at school this week. They included me in their conversations at lunch (mostly about girls and basketball) and offered me stuff from their lunch trays and lunch bags that they weren't going to eat.

I can't disappoint them today.

So I pull on shorts, even though they show my gorilla legs, and I yank a T-shirt over my head. Then I give Mom and Bubbie kisses on their cheeks and say "No thanks" to Bubbie's offer of a sawdust and raisin muffin.

Of course I forget to bring water, and it's a sauna outside. I've got to remember important things, like water, on boiling hot days. It's not till I'm near school—my stomach a nervous mess from worrying about the guys seeing me attempt to play—that I realize I forgot something else: taking my medicine. Yesterday, too.

Oh well, too late now. It probably won't make a difference. I'll just have to be more careful from now on.

My head feels fuzzy, though, and I have a pulsing head-ache. Caffeine. I need coffee. And maybe a doughnut.

There's a five-dollar bill in my pocket that Bubbie handed me last night after what she deemed "a determined effort" during drills. (I think "determined" was a euphemism for "pathetic" and the five dollars was pity money, but I've got no shame since I'm perpetually broke. I took the cash.)

I'm really close to school and can actually hear the ball bouncing on the court behind the building. Someone calls, "I'm open! Pass it!"

The guys must be sweating and laughing and throw-ing the ball to each other, blocking shots and running for rebounds. (Bubbie made me watch basketball videos last night, while she explained what the players were doing and why. She taught me terminology, too. My bubbie is like a walking basketball Wiki. I should have paid *her* five bucks for all her help.)

I imagine Vasquez passing the ball to me, fast and hard, and it hitting me square in my tender, bruised nose. I see myself crumpling onto the court, blood squirting from my nostrils while the guys stand around in a circle of shame. In my mind, they point at me while I lie curled on the court, gushing blood, and Vasquez shakes his head. "Why did we think *he* could play basketball with us?"

My thoughts make my heart pound, as though these awful things are actually happening.

I touch my nose—still sore. Then I decide to do the only

sensible thing—turn around and walk away as fast as possible.

Toward salvation.

Toward Dunkin' Donuts.

I'll bet Vasquez and the guys won't even notice I didn't show.

Too Many Butterflies

I thought visiting Bob might make me feel less lonely.

But while I'm perched in his sturdy branches, listening to Yo-Yo Ma's beautiful cello music through my earbuds, a chasm the size of the Beckford Palms Public Library opens in my chest. I think about how Dad didn't turn and look at me before I left the house. He had to have heard me. I was right there. I think about how Dunkin sat at the Neanderthals' lunch table all week. I think about how Dare's been busier than ever, with hardly any time for me. After school and on weekends, she's got riding lessons and piano practice and lacrosse practice, and unlike me, she has plenty of other friends to hang out with. Maybe Dare's even making new friends this year, while all I'm doing is sitting in the branches of a doomed banyan tree.

Why would anyone want to be friends with me anyway?

If only I could get started on hormone blockers, I know I'd feel better about myself. I'd stop worrying so much about changing in ways I don't want to. And if I felt better about myself, maybe I'd act more confident and then other people would like me more. Maybe . . .

I turn the sound up on my iPod to block out my thoughts, but it doesn't help. I still feel miserable.

A memory of my eighth birthday party floats into my mind. *Mom said I should give out invitations to everyone in my class, so no one would feel left out. I made a party favor for each person. It took forever to fill twenty-one plastic butterfly container party favors with different-colored sand. The day of my party, I waited, wearing a silly birthday hat, and the only person who showed up was Dare.* Dare, with her gift of a tiny bonsai tree, which I still have. Dare, who always showed. At the time, it didn't feel like enough, though, but now it makes me love her even more. My self-assured friend who tolerates my lack of self-assuredness.

I wish Dare were here with me now.

I wish *someone* were here now.

The remaining twenty sand-filled butterflies looked so pretty sitting on my bureau, but they were a constant reminder of my no-show party, of my feeling unwanted.

Tipping my head back, I look through Bob's leaves to the cloud-filled sky. Then I break off bits of strawberry Pop-Tart and attempt to fill the empty space inside myself, bite after bite. Unfortunately, it's like trying to fill the Grand Canyon with breadcrumbs.

After two Pop-Tarts, I feel stuffed and empty at the same time.

Then I see someone who gives me a tiny ray of hope.

And I sit tall in Bob's strong branches.

Norbert and Tim, Sitting in a Tree

By the time I've walked only a few blocks, my headache has intensified.

I. Need. Coffee.

Also, I feel kind of bad for ditching the guys at the court.

Part of me wants to turn and go back and join them, but I've got this killer headache, and they're probably well into their game and I'd only be interrupting.

I look up at the sky, as though some answer will be imprinted there on the clouds. Instead, I see something that makes my stomach tighten.

Someone.

"Hey, down there!"

It's Tim, sitting in that dumb tree.

Man, my head hurts. "What?" I ask, irritation in my voice. Is he going to yell at me again for not sitting with him during lunch?

"Climb up and join me," Tim says, his voice high-pitched, hopeful.

Tim is the only thing standing between me and the sweet relief of iced coffee. I shield my eyes against the sun. "No thanks. I'm good." I guess Tim is over being mad at me for sitting with the guys instead of him and Dare in the cafeteria.

"Okay," Tim says, sounding hurt, which *really* annoys me. I can't help that I have a fear of heights. And even if I didn't, why would I want to climb into a stupid tree? What if someone saw me up there? What if Vasquez and the guys walked past after their game and saw me sitting in a tree? With Tim!

Norbert and Tim, sitting in a tree . . .

"You sure?" Tim asks. "Great view from up here."

For a moment, I wonder if he can see the basketball courts from up there and how cool that might be. I shake the thought from my head.

I look up at Tim and shout, "I'm sure!" And I head to Dunkin' Donuts, my head pounding like a jackhammer.

All Is Not Well

I jump out of Bob's branches and land so hard it hurts from my heels up through my knees. But I don't care. I run, my backpack thumping against my spine.

From a few yards behind him, I call, "Dunkin?"

He turns, and I try to read his face. Pain of some variety flashes across it. His face matches how I feel.

He keeps walking.

"Wait up." I run the rest of the way to catch up with him. And we walk together, fast, side by side, not saying anything. It's hard to match his stride because his legs are so long.

"So . . . ," I say, but the word hangs in the air between us.

I wish he'd say something. Anything.

It feels like he's trying to walk away from me. I wonder if I should just head back to Bob. But by then we're at Dunkin' Donuts, so I go inside with him.

I wait beside him, tapping the counter.

He looks at me, annoyed. Then, something shifts in his eyes. "You want something?" he asks, pulling out a five.

"Sure," I say. "Boston Kreme?"

He orders two Boston Kremes plus a large iced coffee.

Dunkin pays and drops the change into the tip jar. I consider this a good sign. He's a perfectly decent human, despite his aberration of sitting with the Neanderthals this week. He's new to school. I'm sure he just doesn't know better. Instead of being angry with him, I should help him figure everything out, show him that I would be a way better friend than any of the Neanderthals ever could be.

At our table for two, I watch Dunkin close his eyelids as he takes a loooooong swig of coffee through the orange straw. He blinks a few times, focuses on me and says, "Ah, the elixir. All is well."

When he picks up his doughnut, I grab mine and touch his in a kind of toast. "To the best kind of doughnut," I say.

Dunkin grins. "Yeah, this is my favorite, too."

I nod and take a sweet bite. "Glazed is my second favorite."

"Me too," Dunkin says, scarfing down the doughnut. "We have a lot in common."

"At least with important stuff, like doughnuts," I say.

Dunkin smiles, making me glad I hopped out of Bob, even though my heels and legs still ache from the long jump down. I want to tell Dunkin about what's going to happen to Bob in case he didn't notice the sign, but we talk about doughnuts and school stuff. I watch him relax the more we talk, and realize I'm feeling more relaxed, too. It's a good feeling starting to make a new friend. Dare's the best, but it would be great to have another friend, maybe one a little less . . . busy.

I'm feeling happier than I have this past week . . . until the door of Dunkin' Donuts swings opens and the worst possible things walk in. If I could have one superpower right now, I'd wish it were invisibility. I'd use that power because the entire army of Neanderthals—sweaty and loud—stand between me and freedom.

Unfortunately, I don't have superpowers. I don't even see an emergency fire alarm I could pull to distract them and run past, into the blazing sunshine. Into the arms of Bob. In fact, it feels like my butt is glued to the hard, plastic seat while I'm helpless to prevent the humiliation that's about to happen.

Why did I jump out of Bob and join Dunkin on his stupid coffee-and-doughnut quest? Why did I feel such a strong desire to give him another chance and follow him? Sure, it was great getting to know him a little better, but totally not worth dealing with what's about to go down.

Will I ever learn I'm better off when I stay away from other people?

Even if that means being hollowed out from loneliness.

THE NEANDERTHALS

I can't believe how much better I feel after sucking down that cup of iced coffee. It clears the fog from my head and takes away the jackhammer pain. I'd buy another one, but I'm out of money. I'm always out of money.

Tim and I talk about school and our love of doughnuts.

"Why did the doughnut go to the dentist?" Tim asks.

I shrug.

"He needed a chocolate filling."

"Ha." I shake my head, thinking Phin would appreciate Tim's stupid sense of humor. Then I realize I shouldn't be thinking about Phin. I'm here with Tim, and things are going well.

For the first time, I'm glad I ditched basketball.

When he asks, I show Tim the secret behind the disappearing saltshaker trick, and he's all kinds of impressed. He tries a bunch of times, but can't quite get it to work right.

"Takes practice," I say. "You'll get it."

Then, like a thunderstorm with dark clouds rolling in, the door to Dunkin' Donuts swings open, and Vasquez and the guys amble by—like an animal pack—their shirts drenched and their hair soaked with sweat.

Guilt stabs my heart. I should be among them, sweaty and spent. I feel like I played hooky. Then I realize I'm sitting across from Tim. There's no way to deny that fact.

Why didn't I go to basketball this morning and get the humiliation over with?

I make eye contact with Vasquez the same moment he notices me . . . and Tim. And I understand that what's about to happen is my punishment for ditching them after they've been nice to me all week.

I make a lame attempt at a wave. "Hey, guys." I hate how weak my voice sounds.

Vasquez comes over and stands right near me. Since I'm seated, he seems really tall. I try not to grimace from his vinegary stink.

"Seriously?" He's facing me with his back to Tim. "You ditched us for *her*?" He jerks his thumb toward Tim.

My muscles tense.

The cashier looks at Vasquez, and some of the other customers turn to see what's happening. Maybe they're wondering if a fight is going to break out. I hope not.

"Your loss," Vasquez says, and I get this ache because I know exactly what I'm losing. *Why did I let Tim come with me to Dunkin' Donuts? Why didn't he stay up in his stupid tree?*

"Yeah," one of the guys says. "We had a great bunch of games. You shoulda been there."

I'm not sure if he's threatening me or trying to be nice.

Someone pulls on Vasquez's sweaty jersey, and they conference near the drink cases. Vasquez nods, looks at me, then nods again.

I feel like bolting. I do not want to know what they're discussing—probably what they're going to do to me and Tim.

I glance briefly at Tim—long enough to see his blue eyes wide with fear.

Vasquez struts back over and brings the stink with him. He slaps his palms on our table and looks right into my eyes. It's uncomfortable, but I hold his gaze.

"The guys and I decided," Vasquez says, looking around at his posse, "if you come out for basketball tryouts in October, all will be forgiven."

A weight falls off me.

I nod.

Then Vasquez turns to Tim and bends lower so he's right in his face. "As for you . . . I can't even talk to you. I don't even know *what* you are."

The guys crack up.

Vasquez walks to the counter and all the guys follow in a pack. Then Vasquez looks back at me. "You comin' or not, Dorfman?"

He called me Dorfman. He wants me to join them. I hop up from the table so fast I bang my knee, but I don't care. My long limbs are always getting in the way.

Glancing back at Tim, I see his face is blotchy red, his

blue eyes swimming with hurt and disappointment. I turn from those piercing blue eyes and join Vasquez and the rest of the guys at the counter.

Bobby Birch bumps his shoulder into mine in a friendly way, so I know I'm back in. Forgiven for ditching their basketball practice this morning. Forgiven for the much bigger sin of sitting with Tim, even though I can't figure out why they hate Tim so much. He really doesn't seem like a bad guy at all.

I glance at Tim one last time.

He meets my gaze for a second, then rockets up toward the door and pushes it open. His doughnut wrapper is still on the table.

The guys' cruel laughter fills Tim's wake, and I know he can hear it.

I don't know if Tim can tell I'm laughing, too. But I am.

And I hate myself for it.

An Idea That Might Change Everything

That night at dinner, it's hard to eat because there's a rock in my stomach. Every time I think about what happened at Dunkin' Donuts—what happened with Dunkin and the Neanderthals—the rock grows a few centimeters. But the truth is, things could have gone much worse.

If only Dunkin had stayed with me instead of ditching me for the Neanderthals. We were having such a good time, or at least it seemed like we were. He even laughed at my stupid joke and he showed me the secret behind his cool magic trick. Why does Dunkin like those idiots? Why do I still even want to be friends with him?

Mom and Sarah are quietly eating. Meatball is curled on top of my feet, keeping them toasty. I'm forcing down a few pieces of corkscrew pasta when Dad says, "Tim, I think it would be a good idea if you got a haircut."

Mom makes a little gasp.

Sarah says nothing, but glares at Dad.

Meatball gives a whole-body shudder, then relaxes back onto the tops of my feet.

I look at Dad—at his determined eyes—and stab my fork into a piece of corkscrew pasta. "Okay," I say. "Tomorrow."

Mom and Sarah look shocked.

I stuff pasta into my mouth and chew without tasting, as though I'm chomping on bits of rubber. I think of Vasquez, calling me "her," which shouldn't make me angry, because that's how I define myself, too, but coming from his mouth, it sounded dirty, like something to be ashamed of. I think of Dunkin walking away and leaving me alone at that stupid table. Of the Neanderthals staring at me and talking about me while I was sitting right there, Dunkin among them. I heard their laughter. Mean laughter that followed me out of the store.

"Let's cut it all off," I say.

Mom chokes. "But, Lily, you said—"

"Don't call him that," Dad snaps, his cheeks reddening.

"She can call my sister whatever she wants," Sarah says, poking my thigh under the table.

Maybe Sarah wants me to stick up for myself against Dad, but I'm tired of fighting. "Buzz cut," I say.

Dad's got a goofy smile now. His cheeks have returned to normal color. "Oh, we don't have to go that far, Tim." Dad gives Mom a sideways glance. "Just a nice, short cut should do the trick."

As though a haircut will change who I am. But Dad keeps hoping. Keeps trying things, like only boy clothes and boy bedding in my room. And now a short haircut. Just like everything else he's tried, the haircut won't change who I am on the inside one bit. But it might change how people see me. It might even change how people treat me. And that's exactly what I need right now. Well, that and hormone blockers. Maybe if I give in on the haircut, Dad will give in on the hormone blockers. And that would be totally worth it.

Mom clucks her tongue and shakes her head. She looks like she wants to say something, but doesn't.

Sarah pushes back from the table and stomps upstairs.

I hate disappointing my sister, but I really think this might be a good idea.

I expect Meatball to follow her, but he doesn't budge from

his spot atop my feet. I guess he likes being close to the dinner table, in case someone drops something. But without Sarah here, his chances of being snuck a treat are slim.

I return to mechanically chewing my food, swallowing and not tasting. It doesn't matter. Mom and Sarah must think I've given up. Dad probably imagines he's won something, though I'm not sure what.

I'm the one who might win something. A short haircut is not such a big price to pay to finally fit in. I mean, it's not like I agreed to cut off my arm or my leg. Hair grows back.

Eventually.

The Cut

As the barber cuts off my hair, my head feels lighter, but I get an ache in the pit of my stomach, like I'm making a huge mistake that I can't take back.

I keep reaching for my hair, but it's not there anymore.

"Sit still," the barber grouses, like I'm a little kid.

So I put my hands in my lap, underneath the black cape, and sit very still. I peek at the floor around the barber's chair and feel like parts of me are scattered there. It's more painful than I imagined. I remind myself how much easier things will be at school. I'll be what they want me to be: Timothy James McGrother. Boy.

Whatever it takes to get through middle school.

And at home, things will be easier, too. At least with Dad.

I'm eager to see how everyone reacts to my new short haircut. It's blond and fine and reminds me of feathers. I want to pull it down and stretch it. It's really short. I'm so glad I didn't get it buzzed. That would have looked awful.

Mom says it looks good, but I can tell she's disappointed. And Sarah won't even look at me, which makes me feel terrible. But it will be worth it on Monday when I get back to school.

Monday morning, Dare says she hates it the minute she comes to the door. "You're not being true to yourself, *Tim*." She emphasizes my boy name and acts like I cut off my hair to irritate her. I don't bother explaining the truth—that it's temporary, so Vasquez and the Neanderthals will stop harassing me, especially in front of Dunkin. Then maybe Dunkin will feel like he can hang out with me, too.

As we get closer to school, I barely pay attention as Dare talks about her work with the horses Saturday and her uncle's visit Sunday. I'm thinking about what it will be like today. Maybe I'll start feeling more like a boy with the new haircut. It already feels weird not having hair on my neck.

I'm filled with hope as I approach my locker.

Why didn't I think of doing this sooner? Thanks, Dad.

I haven't even gotten my locker open when Vasquez

comes up and shoves me. Hard. My shoulder bashes into my combination lock. It hurts like heck, but what's more painful are the words Vasquez casually tosses off as he walks away: "Nice haircut, *fag*."

I can't win. No matter what I do . . . I can't win.

I trudge to each class and barely pay attention. At lunch, I'm rubbing my sore shoulder when Dare sits at our table. She nods toward the Neanderthal table. "Vasquez?"

I stop rubbing my shoulder. "I thought maybe . . . if I . . . it didn't matter."

Without an ounce of compassion, Dare says, "You're compromising. That's your problem." She leans forward. "Don't do what you think will make them happy. Do what will make *you* happy. It's not that complicated, McGrother."

She's right about me compromising. She's always right. "I thought it would be easier," I admit. "If I cut off my hair."

"Is it?" she asks, pointing her banana at me. "Any easier?"

I shake my head, and my hair doesn't whip around my face. It just sits there, out of my eyes.

It sits there, being exactly the wrong hairstyle for me.

A clementine bonks off my shoulder—my sore shoulder. And when I look toward the Neanderthals' table, they put their heads down and crack up.

Dunkin is sitting with them, of course. His head's not down, though. He's looking at me. And he's not laughing.

I want to hold his gaze, show him I can take whatever he and his stupid friends dish out. But the truth is, I can't. I look down, wishing I had my hair to hide behind, to make me feel a little more . . . like me.

What have I done?

The Letter

Sitting in Bob's branches after school, it doesn't matter that my hair is short.

Bob doesn't care. And his green leaves hide me.

I love this tree. I can't let it get cut down.

Something Grandpop Bob used to say pops into my mind: *The pen is mightier than the sword.*

When I was little, I didn't know what that meant. But now I know. Maybe I can save Bob. If I write a good enough letter, maybe I'll be like the Lorax and speak for the trees. At least for this one tree.

I pat Bob, gather my things and climb down.

There are new flamingos stuck in some lawns in our neighborhood. One of them is wearing a golf club cover on its head, which is hilarious since practically everyone around here is golf-crazy. Another flamingo is wearing a tiny Santa hat, even though it's not even Halloween yet. And a third has a miniature knitted necktie with bright colors. It feels like a good omen when the golf cart dudes don't come around and remove them.

Back home, Mom's in the kitchen making tea. I finally tell her about the sign and what's going to happen to Bob.

She gasps and puts her palm over her mouth, then shakes her head. "I can't believe it. Remember picnicking under that tree when you and Sarah were younger?" Her eyes get a far-off look. "You both put your dolls on the blanket to join the picnic. Sarah's was Miss Beasley and yours was, um, Minnie Mermaid?"

"Matilda Mermaid," I say.

Mom shoves my shoulder playfully. "You *loved* that mermaid doll."

I still do. "I have her on a shelf in my closet."

"You dragged that doll with you everywhere, even into the bathroom."

"I was totally obsessed."

"Matilda Mermaid used to drive your dad crazy."

I swallow hard, and we're both quiet. But I don't want to think about Dad right now. "Did you know Grandpop Bob used to read to me under that tree when you and Dad were both at work and he babysat?"

"Oh yes," Mom says. "Back when I was a lawyer and worked all the time." She lets out a big breath. "I'm glad that's in my rearview mirror."

"I remember envying Sarah because she got to stay at the shop with Dad and Grandmom Ruth and help make T-shirts, but I was too little."

"But you got to do cool things with Grandpop Bob. Right?"

"Definitely," I say. "And Sarah got stuck with Grandmom Ruth. Poor Sarah!"

We both laugh.

Mom puts her steaming mug of tea on the table and asks if I want one. I don't.

"I remember feeling so proud, walking into the little kid section of the library with him holding my hand. He'd let me pick out a bunch of books, and he'd choose some, too. Then we'd go out front and settle under our tree, all cozy and warm, for my own personal story time. It was pretty terrific."

Mom smiles, but her eyes look sad. "I miss your Grand-pop Bob."

"Me too." I take a sip of Mom's hot tea, just to melt the lump in my throat.

"And I can't believe the city plans to cut down that beautiful tree," Mom says.

"Not if I can help it. I'm going to write a letter to the city council to try and stop them."

Mom's whole face brightens. "What a great idea!"

"I'm going to tell them how important Bob is and that he shouldn't be cut down."

Mom cradles my cheek in her warm palm. "Of course you are, sweetheart."

I feel pretty good as I march to my room, ready to put pen to paper and battle for Bob. *The pen is mightier than the sword.* I pull out my favorite fuzzy purple pen from Dare and a sheet of the fancy stationery Mom gave me for my last birthday, and then I write the letter, which I had mentally composed during my walk home.

Dear City Council Members,

Please don't cut down the tree on the lot next to the Beckford Palms Library.

It provides shade for people walking their dogs. It provides a home for many species of birds and squirrels and insect life. People have picnics under it.

That tree has been there my whole life, and it's a very special place for my family and me.

I'm sure you'll agree that having the banyan tree on that property would be better for the community than a new park.

Thank you for your thoughtful consideration.

I think for a long time. I touch my too-short hair. Then I sign my name.

Lily Jo McGrother

The Proper Pronoun

Over the next few weeks, I check our mailbox for a letter from the city council about Bob. None arrives. I also check to see if the sign about his being cut down has been removed. It hasn't.

I don't know what else to do, so I worry. And I go to school.

Basketball tryouts are being held at the end of the day.

Vasquez and his Neanderthals have been so absorbed with that, they haven't bothered me as much as usual. It's been nice. I wish basketball season lasted all year.

Today in Mr. Creighton's class, he does a quick lesson on pronouns before we break into critique groups to work on our stories. He says some of us aren't using them correctly.

He. She. It. They. We. Them.

Mr. Creighton's right. Some people don't use pronouns correctly. For example, "she" is the correct pronoun for me. But people keep incorrectly referring to me as "he."

She.

I can't wait until the whole world calls me by the correct pronoun.

She.

Someday, they'll get it right.

She.

Someday . . .

READY OR NOT . . .

BASKETBALL TRYOUTS
IN THE GYM AT 4:15

As I change into my gym clothes in the locker room, I can't believe I managed to avoid playing pickup games with the guys this long. I made excuses, and they let me get away with them. It was almost as if they were okay with me not joining their pickup games as long as they knew I'd show for tryouts today and bring my A game.

Honestly, I don't know if I can bring my C game or D game or even my Z game.

But I'm not nearly as bad as I was. I've been working like crazy at improving and honing my skills.

Bubbie and I have worked together every night. She said I improved so much she might create a new line of videos—*Bubbie's Basketball Workout*—to add to her Bodies by Bubbie collection of products.

This made me feel really good.

Bubbie even got a few of her friends to challenge me to some pickup games at the rec center, which were hilarious, because her friends are each about five feet tall. But those ladies had game. They moved more quickly and more gracefully than I ever could with my long, awkward legs.

If I can barely keep up with a bunch of short, senior señoras, how will I ever manage with the guys on the court? Sure, I can sink baskets from the paint now and from the foul line sometimes, but actual running and dribbling? At the same time? With other guys chasing me? My legs will probably tangle and send me flying before I get a chance to shoot the ball.

Against my better judgment, I head toward the gym doors.

I hear the squeak of sneakers on the court and balls bouncing and know with complete clarity I'm not prepared. Not really. Not in the ways that matter. It's not as though I had a dad helping me with my basketball skills since I was little, like most of these guys I'm sure had. All I had was Bubbie and her friends helping me. That's not enough. That's never going to be enough.

My mind races through the myriad ways I might embarrass myself today. *Falling. Tripping. Missing the basket. Falling, tripping and missing the basket. Making a lame pass that doesn't reach its intended target. Catching a pass with my face instead of my hands.*

The possibilities are endless.

With a trembling hand, I pull open the door to the gym and step inside.

A Particular Kind of Pain

I peek through the small window in the door of the gym and see two things:

One: On the right-hand side, Coach Outlaw is yelling at the cheerleaders. Good. I'm not a fan of cheerleaders. I think a girl should play sports, like Dare does—she's a beast on the lacrosse field—not dress in skimpy skirts and cheer for the boys. "Rah. Rah. *Blah.*" Do you ever see boys cheer at girls' sports games, while wearing skimpy outfits?

Two: On the left-hand side, Coach Ochoa yells at the

boys. He's making them run different drills, while the assistant coach marks things on a clipboard.

I squint and see Dunkin. He's running a heat against Vasquez.

My stomach clenches as I watch Vasquez easily outrun him, even though Dunkin is taller. I expect Vasquez to make fun of Dunkin or something, but he pats him on the back and jogs to the next drill.

Pats him on the back. He'd never do that to me. More likely punch me in the back.

I'm dying to go into the gym and see how Dunkin does during tryouts, even though I know I shouldn't care about him. It's obvious he doesn't care about me or Dare. He won't eat lunch at our table and he barely talks to me, even less than he did before our Dunkin' Donuts situation, unless he has to during Mr. Creighton's class. Not exactly good friend behavior, but still, there's something about him that makes me want to keep reaching out.

I consider opening the doors and slipping inside the gym, except I don't want the cheerleaders staring at me, judging me. And Vasquez would surely notice me and say something cruel. In fact, I know the exact word he'll say.

Can't deal with that.

So I turn and walk down the hall, thinking I'll head to the outside sports fields and see what's going on there, or maybe I'll go to the Beckford Palms Library and lose myself among the shelves of books. I could even spend time with Bob, but the sign near him makes me so sad, it's hard to be there.

When I pass the utility closet near the water fountain, I remember what's inside, and I get an idea.

A crazy idea—my favorite kind.

Al E. Gator (aka Ali Gator)

The inside of the alligator head smells like ancient sweat.

It should. I don't want to think about how many students have worn this mascot costume before me. Have jumped around in it. Have gushed buckets of sweat inside of it while cheering for Gator Lake Middle.

Good old Al E. Gator—Gator Lake Middle's mascot for all football and basketball games. In my opinion, it should be named Ali Gator, but of course no one asked for my opinion.

I slip into the rest of the costume. It's like pulling on green carpeting. But there's something about being inside it that feels like Halloween and my birthday rolled into one. Something secret. Something magical.

I complete the transformation by putting on the alligator costume's oversized feet and hands, or paws and claws, as the case may be.

If there were a mirror in the utility closet, I could see how I look, but I can barely see out of the eyeholes. It's hot in the costume, like wearing a winter coat in summer, but it's also perfect because it covers every part of me.

I take a deep, sweat-smelling breath and open the door.

It's quiet in the hall. The only sounds are the distant squeaks of sneakers on the court, a whistle being blown and cheers being called.

I walk toward the gym, carefully placing each giant, green furry foot in front of the other. Then I grab the door handle with my Al E. Gator paw and pad inside the gym.

Through the small eyeholes, I see a couple of the basketball boys point and laugh, but when Coach Ochoa yells, "Focus or leave!" they go right back to the drills. Dunkin is concentrating so hard he doesn't even seem to notice I've walked in. Before I get yelled at by Coach Ochoa, I walk to the side of the gym and stand behind the cheerleaders. I make a few dumb moves, so people will think I'm one of the dopey jocks in the costume—probably assume I'm someone from the football team.

I have fun dancing and making the cheerleaders giggle. Even Coach Outlaw laughs, but she waves me away. "We're working here."

If that's what you want to call it. I back up—sweat dripping into my eyes—shuffle my feet, twirl my hands around and keep an eye on the opposite side of the gym—the basketball side.

What I see surprises me.

SUPERCHARGED

I'm surprised when my shots go in the basket.

I'm surprised when I keep up with the guy who's guarding me and the guy I'm guarding. I'm surprised when my legs don't twist together like a pretzel and I don't fall on my face during dribbling drills. I'm utterly shocked when I beat a few guys during timed runs.

Thank you, Bubbie and the sassy señoras!

I'm so focused on not humiliating myself, I barely notice when someone comes into the gym wearing an alligator costume. *School mascot?* I guess he has to practice his routines, too, but it doesn't look like he's practicing—just goofing around behind the cheerleaders. The alligator is kind of hilarious, which helps me relax, so I end up playing even better.

Several days later, Coach posts a list of the kids who made first cut. And right there on the list is "Norbert Dorfman." It's the only time I've been happy to see my name.

The guys who made the cut try not to cheer too much because the guys who didn't make it are hanging their heads and slinking away. Each of us knows that in a few days, when the final list of names is posted, any one of us might not be on it. Well, Vasquez and a couple of the other guys will be on it. That's a given.

The threat of not making the final cut seems to make each of us try harder at practice. I know I'm giving it everything I've got. It's almost like something has given me superpowers on the court. And I know exactly what that something is. Not Bubbie. Not the sassy señoras. Not the goofy mascot. Something else.

When the final team list is posted, I'm shocked and thrilled to discover my name on it.

I knew cutting back a little on my meds was a good idea. It's given me zip and energy to keep up with the other guys. I sleep less, too, which means more time to practice. At first I just forgot to take a couple doses. I didn't mean to skip any medicine because I knew Mom was trusting me to take my pills every day. But doing well on the court is super important, so it seems like a good plan to "forget" to take my pills a bit more often now.

As we're all crowded around the list and the guys see their names (or don't), Vasquez pulls me into a huddle with the other guys who made the team. They chant, "We are Gators! We are Gators! WE ARE GATORS!!!"

I join in.

Our voices blend together, and the vibrations ripple through me like an electric current. I feel supercharged.

"WE ARE GATORS. WE ARE GATORS. *WE ARE GATORS!!!*"

This is the most exciting thing that's ever happened to me. And the most terrifying. From now on, these guys are counting on me to help them have the best season ever.

And I'll do whatever it takes to make that happen.

I can't wait to tell Bubbie and Mom the great news.

I wish I could tell Dad.

IT'S TIME TO GO

After school, I drop my backpack near the stairs.

"Don't get too comfortable," Mom says. "We're going out."

"Where?" I ask, but before she answers, I've motored to the kitchen and grabbed a sawdust and raisin muffin. I'm so hungry I could eat twenty of them, even though it's like chewing on ground tree bark. My mouth stuffed with the first bite, I shout, "I made the team!" Sawdust crumbs spray everywhere.

Mom leans against the kitchen counter and narrows her eyes at me. "Is that why you're so excited?"

Why can't Mom be happy for me? This is the biggest news of my life. And I didn't think I was acting *that* excited. Just happy. Really, really happy. "The stuff Bubbie did helped a lot." I shove another bite of muffin into my mouth and walk in tight circles—two steps forward, turn, two steps forward, turn, two steps, turn. I count the things Bubbie did on my fingers and talk with my mouth full. "The drills. The dribbling. The running. The throwing. The drills."

"You already said that one." Mom's looking at me strangely, like I messed up, so I start again. "The drills. The dribbling. The—"

149

"Norbert?"

"Don't call me that!" I shriek.

Mom reels back, like I pushed her. "Okay," she says. "What should I call you, then?" Her arms are crossed. Her eyes look tired with dark circles underneath. I hope she hasn't been crying again. I didn't get why she was crying so much before. I mean, it's not like—

"Norb?"

I bob from foot to foot. "Yeah?" I should probably do some basketball drills right now to use up some of this energy. I could probably sink a hundred three-pointers in a row the way I feel.

"Let's go," Mom says.

I'm not sure why, but her words grate on me, like they're rubbing my nerve endings.

"And bring your meds," she adds.

I stop moving, which isn't the easiest thing for me to do right now. "Where are we going?" I ask, breathing hard through my nose.

"Calm down," Mom says.

"I AM CALM!"

"Just grab your meds and let's go. We'll stop at Dunkin' Donuts afterward."

That softens me. A little. But I'm not happy about this. "Where did you say we're going?"

"I didn't." Mom looks at me like she's trying to figure something out. Like I'm hiding something. "We're going to a new psychiatrist. There's only one in the whole area who specializes in bipolar disorder, and it took me forever to get this appointment, so let's get moving. I don't want to be late." Then Mom mutters, "Sorry he couldn't get you in sooner. We never should have waited this long."

"But we saw my psychiatrist right before we left Jersey," I remind her.

"So?"

"So, do we have to go now?" I ask. "I feel great. See?" I do a bunch of jumping jacks and some pushups, like Bubbie would if there were a few unoccupied moments. "I feel absolutely fantastic."

"I'll bet you do," Mom says, but not in a nice way. "Please grab your meds. We're going." She snatches her purse from the counter and waits by the front door.

Upstairs in the guest room, I look at my pill bottles. Way too full. I must have been skipping more doses than I realized. I shake some out from each bottle and wrap them in a tissue. Then I shove the tissue under some papers in my trash can. I feel bad about that because of how expensive my antipsychotic medicine is and how hard I imagine it is for Mom to pay for things since Dad . . . Anyway, I really didn't need all those pills. I do much better . . . feel much better when I skip a few doses. And Mom wouldn't understand that.

Pill bottles in hand, I jog downstairs, grab another sawdust and raisin muffin and hustle to the car. While I wait for Mom, I tap a complicated melody on the car window with my fingers. "What took you so long?"

"I was right behind you," Mom says. "I only stopped to lock the door." She looks at me like I'm crazy.

I can't be crazy. I've never felt better. *Right, Phin? I wish he were here. Why isn't he here?*

In the car, my leg bobs up and down so much it feels like I might drill a hole in the floorboard with my sneaker. "Let's go!"

Mom shakes her head, starts the car and pulls out of the driveway. "Yes, let's."

HAVE YOU TAKEN YOUR MEDICINE?

By the time we get to the office building, every cell in my body is irritated. It was torture being trapped inside the confined space of the car. I slam the door and follow Mom inside the building. Another closed-in space.

"Norbert Dorfman?" a lady asks, and walks Mom and me back to an office.

The lady annoys me by the way she says my name. Mom annoys me for coming back with me. I'm not a little kid.

"Hi, Norbert," a man behind a desk says.

"I don't like that name," I say, even though I know I'm being rude and I have no idea who this guy is. Except another doctor.

Mom looks shocked. Not by the fact that I don't like my name, I'm sure. She already knows that. "Ahem."

"Sorry," I say, even though I'm not. I'm pissed and I don't want to be here. I cross my arms over my chest.

"That's okay, Norbert," the man says in an overly jovial tone, making sure to use my name again.

I wonder what would happen if I punched him in the face.

Knock it off!

I turn my head quickly to the left to see who said that.

"Norbert," the man says, using my name for the third time. "I'm Dr. Daniels. It's nice to meet you." He waits, but I don't say anything because it's not nice to meet him, and I don't feel like lying. "How are you feeling today?" Dr. Daniels taps a pen on his desk.

"Okay. Good, I guess." I lean forward in my chair. "Great, actually. I found out I made the basketball team." I give Mom a glare because she didn't make a big deal about it, and it was really hard work to make the team.

"Besides making the team—congratulations, by the way—how are you feeling? Anxious? Up? Down? You seem very up to me right now, and maybe a little agitated, too."

"I'm okay," I say, sinking back in my chair. But I feel like a jack-in-the-box whose spring might pop me out of the chair at any moment.

"Norbert?" The doctor folds his hands and rests them on his desk.

I wish he'd stop using my name. And I wish he wouldn't fold his hands like that. It's like he's pretending to be calm so I'll stay calm.

"Are you taking your medication regularly?" Dr. Daniels asks.

I nod, surprised at how easy it is to lie.

"Never missed a single dose?" he asks, like he knows I'm lying.

"I might miss a dose here or there, but not often." I think of the pills wrapped in a tissue in the trash can at home.

"Did you bring your medication with you today?" He looks at Mom instead of me when he asks this.

Mom nods at me, so I reach into my pocket and hand the doctor the pill bottles.

He examines the labels and looks inside each bottle.

"We'll have to get labs to determine his blood levels," he says to Mom. Then Dr. Daniels presses his palms flat on his desk and looks at me. "Did you take your dose this morning, Norbert?"

"No," I say. "I forgot."

"Here." Dr. Daniels reaches behind him, grabs a bottle of water from a small fridge and hands it to me along with my meds. "Would you take your medicine now, please?"

"Now?"

Dr. Daniels nods and waits, hands folded on his desk, like he has all the time in the world. Like we're not paying for that time. Like he's not a dumb jerk-face doctor who's trying to make me do something I don't want to do. I know those pills will slow me down, make it harder for me to be awesome on the basketball court.

I hear Mom tapping the arm of her chair. I picture her chewed fingernails and wish she'd stop tapping.

I'm so uncomfortable, trapped in this office with Mom and the doctor staring at me. My leg bobs a million miles a minute, but I can't stop it. I wish Dad were here. He'd sweet-talk the doctor out of making me take my medicine. He could charm anyone. Mom called it manipulation, but Dad said it was his secret superpower—the charm factor. I look from the doctor to Mom and back to the doctor and consider bolting. I have enough energy to run all the way home, if I wanted to. Maybe all the way to New Jersey!

"Norbert?" the doctor says, using my stupid name *again*. *What would Phineas do?*

"Sweetheart?" Mom says. Her voice sounds worried. I don't like that sound in her voice. It makes me think of the not-good times with Dad. It makes me think of—

"Sure," I say, and gulp down the pills in front of the doctor and my mom. I feel like an animal in the zoo. "Happy now?" I direct the question to Mom.

She inhales sharply but doesn't answer.

The doctor wastes more of my time by asking a bunch of stupid questions—I could be practicing basketball. And when he asks how I feel about what happened to my dad, I lie, then change the subject. Finally, he gives Mom an order for a blood test and prescriptions for refills of my two medicines.

The last words Dr. Daniels leaves me with are: "We don't want you to end up in the hospital again, Norbert. Keep taking your medication."

Fantastic!

Back home, I don't even tell Bubbie about the basketball team. I just give her a quick kiss on the cheek and go to my room, which isn't even really my room; it's just some dumb girlie guest room. Why did the doctor have to say that about ending up in the hospital? It reminds me of that awful time over a year ago in New Jersey when my good mood spiraled way out of control and I had to stay in the hospital for a couple weeks of consistent meds and therapy until I was stable again. And it makes me think about Dad, which makes me feel rotten. And I had been feeling so great. I wish I hadn't taken my meds in the doctor's office, even though the doctor and Mom were watching. The medicine makes me sluggish. Lazy. Foggy. Tired. Soooo tired . . .

All I want is to lie down and go to sleep. I plump my pillow, lay my cheek on it and stretch out on the bed so far that my feet dangle over the end of it. I'm totally wiped out.

Night night.

I pop my head up, my heart pounding. "Who said that?"

Where Are We Going?

We hear the chant from down the hall while we're taking a math quiz. "We are Gators. We are Gators!"

Kids in my class laugh softly. I strain to hear if Dunkin's voice is part of the chorus, but can't tell.

"WE ARE *GATORS*!"

More laughter. "Basketball team must have been announced," Dwayne McCabe whispers.

"You're taking a quiz," our teacher snaps.

I go back to the math problems in front of me, but now I'm distracted by the chanting. Still, I think I get them all correct.

After school, I open the mailbox in front of our house and pull out a community newspaper, a bill from the electric company and an envelope from the city of Beckford Palms. There's a palm tree on their logo and a small crab on a beach, off to the corner. There's also a flamingo, which makes me think of the flamingo mystery we're having here in Beckford Palms Estates. I wonder if various neighbors are putting them out on their own lawns—a secret society kind of thing. If so, maybe I should put one out on our lawn. I could put one of Dad's reject T-shirts on it. That would be funny.

I drop my backpack on the end of my bed and think about changing into a dress. It's been too long since I've done it, and I know it would make me feel more relaxed. I really want to change, but something tells me not to. Something always tells me not to.

I can't wait another minute to open the letter from the city. Carefully, I lift the flap and am already planning to visit Bob and read the letter aloud to him. I might even yank that stupid sign out of the ground—if it's still there—and lay it on the sidewalk so the trash collectors can haul it away.

I just know it's going to be good news. Why else would they bother to write back to me?

Grandpop Bob was right. The pen *is* mightier than the sword.

I flip onto my stomach, unfold the letter, smooth out the creases and read.

Dear Lily Jo McGrother,

Thank you for your letter and for your concern about our community.

We've had several public meetings about the lot of land near the Beckford Palms Library. It was unanimously decided to use that lot for a park that the whole community will enjoy. Planners were not able to incorporate the banyan tree into the park's design because of its size, so it's scheduled for removal to make room for the building of a new community park. Some new shade trees will be planted in the area following construction of the park.

Thank you again for your concern.

Sincerely,

Mayor Teresa Higginbotham

I drop my head onto the ugly brown comforter. It smells like feet.

The pen is not mightier than the sword.

I failed Bob.

Mom barges into my room without knocking. "Let's go."

"Huh? Where?"

"We have an appointment," she says, and walks out.

I roll off the bed, put the letter in my desk drawer and rush downstairs.

Mom *and* Dad are in the foyer, looking at me.

"Dad?"

His hands are on his hips, his foot tapping, like he's planning to wear a hole in the floor. Meatball whines nearby, like he wants to go, too.

"You're not going, Meatball," Mom says.

"Lucky you," Dad mutters.

"Lovely," she says to Dad. She waves a hand at me and opens the door. "Come on."

I walk out first and they follow. *Did I do something wrong?*

After we pile into the car, Mom zips out of the driveway like she's in the Indy 500.

Dad looks out the passenger-side window and taps a rhythm on the glass with thick fingers. "I don't see why I have to come to this. I don't see why—"

"Stop!" Mom must hit the brake for a second, then the gas, because we jerk forward, then back. No one says anything as we pass the entrance to our neighborhood and turn left, toward the library. We are driving way above the speed limit.

I hear Dad breathing—fast and shallow, like an animal caught in a trap.

I'm dying to know what's going on and where we're going, but I understand when to keep my mouth shut.

When we pass by Bob—he's so beautiful—and the stupid sign in front of him, I swallow a lump in my throat. I want to tell Mom about the lousy letter I just got from the city, but I know now's not the time.

Mom swerves the car into a parking spot in front of a three-story office building. "We're here," she says flatly.

"Whoopee," Dad replies.

Mom gets out and slams her car door.

Dad gets out and slams his.

I get out, too, and gently close mine.

What's going on?

The Doctor Is In

After the psychologist introduces herself as Dr. Klemme, she asks Mom and Dad if she can talk to me by myself.

As my parents leave the office to go back into the waiting room, I hear Dad hiss, "See, I don't know why I needed to be here."

Mom doesn't reply, or at least I don't hear her answer before she closes the door to the doctor's office.

"So," Dr. Klemme says, folding her hands in front of her

and placing them on her desk. "What would you like me to call you?"

The question surprises me. In a good way.

"Some of my patients prefer to go by a different name than is listed on their birth certificates."

My whole body tingles. *Who is this woman?*

"For example, a patient might like to go by the name Janet instead of James."

I take in a slow breath. *Lily.* I think of Dad in the waiting room. Now I know why he's so angry. Mom took us to a therapist especially for me. The vein in Dad's temple is probably pulsing like crazy right now.

"My name is Timothy. Some people call me Tim."

I instantly feel awful. I feel wrong.

"Okay," Dr. Klemme says. "I'll call you Tim, then. But if you ever want me to call you by another name, simply let me—"

"Lily." I sit up taller.

"Hmm?"

I speak louder, but not loud enough for Dad to hear, in case he's anywhere near the door to the office. "I'd like you to call me Lily, please. Lily Jo McGrother is my name." With those words, a weight is lifted off my chest.

There's a hint of a smile on Dr. Klemme's mouth, and she makes a note on the chart in front of her. "Lily," she says. "Such a pretty name."

And for the first time in a long time, my shoulders are

pulled back and my chin held high. *Screw you, Vasquez and your evil band of Neanderthals. Here, in this office, I can be Lily Jo McGrother.*

And feel safe.

The Other Side of the Door

I end up telling Dr. Klemme all about Bob and the letter I got.

"I'm so sorry," she says.

And I can tell she really means it.

"Lily, do you mind if we talk about your hormone blockers?"

I get a tingle in my stomach. I think of how I had to pluck a few new mustache hairs this morning and how much it hurt. I think about how my voice cracked the other day when I was talking to Sarah—a reminder that it's going to get deeper soon. I think about how horrible I'll feel when things grow more down there. "Okay."

"Your mother told me that your father would rather you didn't get them. How will you feel when you grow hair on your face and around your penis, when your voice deepens and your shoulders broaden?"

I can't believe she says the word *penis* just like that. *I'm NOT okay with hair growing around my penis, because I'm not okay with my penis.* "Not okay," I say quietly. Then I think about how I can't stand the thought of those things happening and that if I don't do something to stop it, all of it will definitely happen. And soon. "Not okay at all," I say loud enough for Dad to hear. "I'm not okay with any of that happening to me." Tears well up, and I look down at my lap.

"Lily?"

I don't look up, even though I know it's rude not to. Even though she's using the name I asked her to use.

"Lily, why do you think your father doesn't want you to get the hormone blockers?"

A hot tear leaks out, but I swipe it away with the back of my hand and bite the inside of my cheek to keep more from escaping. "He doesn't like . . . he doesn't like . . . who I am." I look up at the doctor, another tear streaking down my cheek. "I mean, who I really am."

Dr. Klemme hands me a tissue, then stands, which surprises me. "Lily, I think it would be a good idea now if you waited in the other room with your mother and I spoke to your father. I think he's the one I need to talk to right now."

She comes around her desk and puts her hand on my back as she leads me to the door. "I believe there may be some things about what's going on with you that your father may not fully understand or appreciate yet."

In the waiting room, Mom looks at me, her eyes prying, like she's trying to read my mind and find out what the doctor said to me, but Dr. Klemme told me that unless I plan to harm myself or someone else, whatever we say in her office is completely confidential. She promised she wouldn't tell my parents anything I said in there, unless I wanted her to.

Dad looks surprised when the doctor asks him to come in. As soon as Mom rises to join him, Dr. Klemme says, "Just Mr. McGrother right now. Thanks."

When Mom returns to her seat, I sit next to her.

She reaches over and holds my hand. She doesn't say anything, just gives my hand a gentle squeeze. I give her hand a squeeze, too, so she'll know I appreciate her taking me to this doctor.

Then the door closes with Dad on the other side of it.

A Welcome Surprise

When Dad finally comes out of the doctor's office, his eyes look glassy.

Mom gets up and grabs his hand. I hear her whisper in his ear, "You okay?"

He nods—barely—but he doesn't look okay. He looks like his body's here, but his mind is far away. *What happened to him in there?*

Dad glances over at me and tilts his head, like he's trying to figure out who I am. Like he's never seen me before.

The doctor follows Dad into the waiting room. "How about if you come back in two weeks, and we'll see how everything's going?" she asks. "I'll need to see only Lily for that appointment, unless, of course, there's something you feel you need to tell me."

I check Dad's face to see if he's angry that the doctor called me Lily, but his face doesn't change. He still looks like he's somewhere else. Dazed. I'm not sure he even heard her call me Lily.

The doctor hands Dad an envelope and says, "You'll need this where you're going."

I'm dying to know what's in that envelope. I hope it's something better than what was in the envelope I received earlier today from the mayor.

Mom shakes Dr. Klemme's hand, and I do, too. I hope she knows the handshake means "thank you." I'm grateful to have someone who understands me, someone I'll be able to talk to who isn't Mom or Sarah or Dare. Another person on my side.

My whole world feels bigger.

As soon as the three of us are in the car, Dad says, "Go to the endocrinologist's office," and hands Mom the envelope. He looks straight ahead when he speaks. "The address is on the front. We need to give them the letter inside."

Mom doesn't start the engine.

"Let's go," Dad says. He waves his hand forward. "Before I change my mind."

I know what this means because I read all about hormone blockers on the Internet. If my parents say it's okay and a psychologist or therapist writes a letter saying it's okay, I might be able to get the blockers. *Go, Mom. Go! Before Dad changes his mind.*

"I think we need an appointment to go there," Mom says. "Don't we?"

In the backseat, I bite my fingernail. I'm listening hard and hoping harder.

"Well, we're already out, so let's go and see if they can take us," Dad says.

Mom starts the car and drives. "Well, okay, then."

At the endocrinologist's office, they manage to squeeze us into their schedule.

The endocrinologist asks me a million questions about how my body's been changing and how I feel about those changes and even about some of the things I did when I was a little kid, like wore Sarah's dresses and played with dolls. My heart thrums as I answer each question. All the while, I'm thinking *please, please, please let this happen.* It would almost make up for the bad news about Bob. *Almost.*

I don't even mind the pinch from the needle for the blood test, because I know if everything goes right, I'll finally be able to start getting hormone blockers.

I can't believe Dad actually agreed to this. Mom and I watch him sign the form that gives permission for me to get them.

What did Dr. Klemme say to him?

THE DECISION

When I blink awake, I see Bubbie walking into my room, carrying a tray.

I think I'm still dreaming, but when she says, "Breakfast in bed for my new basketball star," I know I'm awake. And I feel terrific again. Mom must have told Bubbie the good news about my making the team.

I sit up, lean back against the headboard and rub my eyes.

"I told you," Bubbie says, setting the tray over my legs on the bed. "You're going to be the next Jordan Jordache! Look what treats I made for you. I was so excited when your mom told me the great news last night." She points at the things on the tray. "Here's a delicious egg-white omelet with spinach and mushrooms. You'll need the egg whites for protein now that you're a big basketball star." Bubbie squeezes the bicep of my right arm. "Hmm. Lots of protein. And maybe some weight lifting, too, Norbert."

It feels nice that Bubbie is making a fuss, like I wish Mom had done yesterday. I still have energy, but it's muted. Probably from taking the meds yesterday. That's what they do—dull my energy, creativity and drive. I know they do some good things, too, but I'm not sure it's worth it.

"Okay," Bubbie says, still pointing at things on the tray. "There's half a grapefruit. The vitamin C helps your body absorb protein from the omelet. And a green drink full of nutrients and minerals. Don't you feel healthier already?"

I sniff the green drink. It smells like cucumbers. I hate cucumbers.

Once when I was little, I threw up after eating a bunch of cucumber slices and that was the end of that. Turned out I had the flu, but I always blamed the cucumbers. Dad knew never to give me cucumbers again because when I threw up, most of it landed on his sneakers.

"Where are the doughnuts and coffee?" I ask Bubbie. "Breakfast of champions!"

She makes a fist. "Breakfast of *chump*-ions! You're in training now, mister."

I take a few bites of the strangely white egg thing to make Bubbie happy. Healthy food and I go together like cucumber vomit and Dad's sneakers.

"I'm proud of you, Norb," Bubbie says, leaning forward and kissing my cheek.

After Bubbie leaves, I eat most of the breakfast and pour the green drink down the bathroom sink. Then I sit at the white desk in the guest room. My pill bottles are in front of me, like two tiny soldiers. I feel like knocking each of them over, just to show them who's in charge. Instead, I stand and pace, then sit again.

I have a decision to make before I go to school. Mom's still trusting me to take the meds on my own. I don't want to disappoint her, but . . .

If I take the meds, I'll be foggy, slower and potentially unable to do what I need to for the team. I don't want Vasquez to think I'm letting him or the other guys down.

If I don't take the meds, I'll have tons of energy and will feel more like myself. But . . . well . . . sometimes there's too much energy. Too much everything and my brain sort of short-circuits. And there's a chance I could end up in a hospital again. But I could monitor myself really carefully and keep that from happening. *Can't I?*

Mom told me she set up the blood test for two weeks from today. It will show whether I've been taking the meds or not. It measures the level of one of the medicines in my bloodstream. The other pill I take can't be detected by a blood test—just through my behavior. And if the mood stabilizer level is too low in my bloodstream . . . the doctor will know I'm not taking it. And then if he doesn't like how I'm acting or how Mom tells him I'm acting, he might put me in the hospital, where they'll *make* me take them. And that would suck. I wouldn't be able to help the team at all then.

I need my levels and behavior to be good for the blood test, which means taking my meds for the next two weeks. Consistently. No missed doses.

I swallow my pills and wash them down with water from the bathroom sink. It tastes gross, and I feel like the pills are already making me duller, which is ridiculous because I just swallowed them.

"Happy now?" I say to no one, except my reflection in the bathroom mirror.

My reflection doesn't reply.

I consider this a good sign.

ANYTHING AND EVERYTHING IS POSSIBLE

In the crowded hallway at school, Tim and Dare stand at Tim's open locker. They look happy, leaning against the row of lockers, talking. I wish I were standing with them. I remember how comfortable I felt talking with Tim at Dunkin' Donuts that day before Vasquez and the guys came in. I remember how it felt like we had so much in common, like we could become good friends. He had been so nice to me right from the very first time meeting him. Vasquez and the guys are great to hang out with and all, but it's not like I could tell them anything—not anything that matters. They don't really listen or care about anything that's serious. If I tried to tell them how I felt about something important, they'd just make fun of me. We only talk about basketball and girls and, to be honest, make fun of other people. I haven't had a truly good friend since Phineas. But he's not here now . . . so I head toward Tim and Dare.

Just to say hi. To see what happens.

Vasquez and a few of his friends suddenly rush through the crowd of kids. Vasquez slams Tim's locker closed and screams, "Score!"

While Vasquez and the guys rush off, it feels like a stone is sinking to the bottom of my stomach. *Why does he do things like that?* Tim and Dare weren't doing anything to them. They were just talking. And now they look miserable instead of happy. What if Tim's fingers were in that locker when Vasquez slammed it? Or his head?

Dare calls after him, "Neanderthal," which I think is a good comeback.

Tim, I notice, looks down and says nothing.

I can't go over and say hi now because they'll lump me in with the basketball guys, even though I'd never do anything mean like slam his locker.

So I steer a wide arc around them, looking at the floor the whole time.

At lunch, Vasquez and some of the guys throw fat red grapes at Tim. The guy whose lunch they're taking them from, I notice, gets to eat only a couple of his own grapes, so I bet he's not too happy that Vasquez and the guys decided to use them as ammunition. And I know Tim can't be happy getting pelted with these abnormally large grapes. They must hurt, especially with how hard Vasquez is throwing them. Why isn't there ever an adult around when this stuff is going on?

Dare is glaring hard at our table. Her eyes are like laser beams. If she could, I'll bet she'd make our whole table burst into flames. And I wouldn't blame her. She's just sticking up for her friend. She's not a stupid coward, like I am.

This must stink for Tim. I could get up right now and sit at their table. That would show Vasquez what I think of how he treats Tim. But I can't. No way can I throw away something as amazing as making the team. Nothing like this has ever happened to me. Maybe when the season's over, I'll find a way to sit at Tim and Dare's table. Maybe when the season's over, I'll be able to walk away from this table.

"You ready for the first practice?"

"Huh?"

"Dorf," Vasquez says, "I asked if you're ready for our first official team practice."

"Oh yeah," I say. "Totally."

But am I? I feel so worn-out and sluggish.

Vasquez throws another grape, and it hits Tim in the ear. "Booyah!"

Tim reaches up to touch his ear, but he doesn't turn around.

Even when most of the guys at our table are cracking up loud enough for him and lots of other people in the lunchroom to hear, I'm silent. But being silent doesn't feel like enough.

After school in the locker room, the guys change fast, like they can't wait to get into the gym and start practicing.

I change fast, too, not because I can't wait to get to practice, but because I hate locker rooms. I feel so uncomfortable with my abnormally tall and hairy body, but it doesn't feel quite so bad here with the basketball team. At least a lot of the guys here are tall, too—not quite as tall as I am, but I don't feel like a complete freak among them.

Vasquez whips his T-shirt at the back of my legs.

I jump forward and bang my knee on the bench.

"How great is this?" he asks, ignoring the fact that I looked like a klutz and banged my knee.

"Great," I say, but actually I'm nervous. What if my decent playing during tryouts was a fluke? What if I get on the court today and embarrass myself? I should have practiced yesterday. Plus with the meds, I'll probably be a little slower than normal. "Great," I say again.

"You bet it is," Vasquez says, tying his sneakers tight. "This is going to be the most awesome season yet." He smacks me in the chest with the back of his hand. "We're eighth graders, with a couple good years under our belts, and now we've got you—our secret weapon. You're probably going to be a famous basketball star one day."

"Dorf. Dorf. Dorf!" the guys chant, and I can't believe how good it feels. Like the opposite of the laughter at Tim in the lunchroom.

"Best. Year. Ever," Vasquez says, as though this is college ball or the pros, instead of an eighth-grade basketball team.

But really, it does feel like a big deal, especially when we all run out onto the court together and Coach claps. "Here come the future state basketball champions!" he shouts, and we hoot and holler and dribble and shoot.

Like anything and everything is possible.

Like everything is right in the world.

You Know I Love You . . .

I get up extra early so I can eat breakfast with Sarah before she leaves for school. I haven't seen her much lately.

"Hey, sis," Sarah says, her mouth full of granola.

I nod, loving every time she calls me sis, even though I'm wearing boy clothes and my hair is still pretty short. Reaching up to touch it, I can't wait for it to grow long. This time, I'm not going to cut it, no matter what Dad says. But I have a feeling Dad won't mind my long hair anymore.

It feels like everything's changed with him since yesterday, in the best possible way. If my blood test comes back okay, I'll start on the hormone blockers soon, and that's all thanks to Dad's change of heart. I'm still dying to know what Dr. Klemme said to him, but it's up to him if he wants to tell me.

Dad's drinking coffee and has his newspaper shield in front of his face. But he lowers it and looks at me.

I smile.

He puts the paper up again.

What's with him? Sarah mouths, and points her thumb at Dad.

I shrug. With Dad, sometimes, it feels like one step forward and two steps backward. Today feels like it might be a two-steps-backward sort of day, but that's okay because yesterday was about a thousand steps forward.

"How's school going?" Sarah asks, slurping the last of her almond milk from the bowl.

"It's okay." I don't tell her about Vasquez and the Neanderthals, which is definitely not okay. "I like Language Arts class a lot."

"Of course you do," Sarah says. "You're such a word nerd."

She's right. I am a word nerd; I love books and writing and probably always will. "How's school going for you?" I ask, pouring some granola into a bowl.

"It's school," she says. "I wish I were in college already."

"Me too," I say, which is kind of hilarious because I practically just started eighth grade.

"Did you feed the dog yet?" Dad mumbles from behind the newspaper.

Sarah looks annoyed. *I've got to go,* she mouths.

"I'll do it," I say, and watch my sister sling a bag over her shoulder, rinse her mouth at the kitchen sink and head out.

I fill Meatball's dish with half a cup of dry kibble. He can barely keep his wiggly butt still on the floor until I give him the signal that it's okay for him to eat. "You're some dog," I tell him, referencing one of my favorite parts of *Charlotte's Web*. I scratch behind his ears. "Some dog."

Dad lowers his newspaper and looks at me while I pick at the dry granola in my bowl.

"You know I love you," Dad says. "Right?"

I stop chewing. "Right."

"Just wanted to make sure you knew. That's all." Newspaper shield goes back up.

I resume chewing. "I know."

"Good," he says from behind the paper. Then he lowers it again and looks at me. Really looks. "You happy about the hormone blockers?"

I swallow. "Of course."

"You're absolutely sure that's what you want?"

"Absolutely!" A part of me is afraid he's going to take it all back, say I can't get them after all.

"Good," Dad says, running a hand through his hair. "Because they're expensive."

A wave of guilt washes over me. "I know. I'm sorry."

Dad puts the newspaper down and looks right at me. "You're worth it. And don't forget that."

I go over and give him a big squeeze.

He acts startled.

Then he hugs me right back.

I'm in a terrific mood by the time Dare arrives to walk to school together.

When I tell her about the hormone blockers, she squeezes me tighter than an anaconda. I can't breathe, and I don't care, because I really do feel terrific.

"Knock, knock," Dare says as we head out of Beckford Palms Estates.

"Who's there?" I ask.

"Interrupting cow," Dare says.

I stop walking, face her and shield my eyes from the sun. "Interrupting cow wh—"

"Moooooooo!" Dare cracks up and bumps my hip. "Get it? Interrupting cow says—"

"Yeah, I get it." I shake my head and keep walking. "I get—"

"Moooooooo!"

"Oh my gosh, please st—"

"Moooooooo!"

As I walk to school, I feel like the luckiest person on the planet.

Moooooooo!

At school, while Dare and I stand at my open locker and she keeps moooooing every time I say something, Dunkin lumbers toward us. My breath catches. It would be so nice if he started talking to me in school. I'd love to know if he made the team. I'm sure we could be friends if only it weren't for . . .

Vasquez and a few of the Neanderthals burst from a crowd of kids, and Vasquez slams my locker closed. "Score!" he yells, and runs off.

"Neanderthals!" Dare screams after them.

I silently watch not Vasquez, but Dunkin, who instead of coming over, makes a wide arc around us, head down.

Was he going to come over if Vasquez and the Neanderthals hadn't done that? Why does Dunkin keep sitting with them? Doesn't he realize Vasquez is an ASSasaurus and the rest of the Neanderthals are baby ASSasauruses? And if he keeps hanging around with them, he's probably going to turn into an ASSasaurus, too!

"Can you believe this?" Dare asks.

"Of course I can. Vasquez is always doing obnoxious things. I'm glad my hand wasn't in my locker. Or my head!"

"Not that," Dare says, waving her hand dismissively in the direction Vasquez went. "This!" she says, flicking a flyer stuck to the wall near the lockers.

"The eighth-grade holiday dance," I say. "So what?"

"It's only October, and they're putting up a flyer about a dance in December. It's not even Halloween yet! There should be a law against advertising holiday stuff this early."

I read the small print on the flyer. "*Semiformal. Eighth-grade students only.* It's the big annual dance," I say. "Who cares when they put it up?"

"*Who cares?*" Dare puts a hand to her hip. "It's like people putting up Christmas decorations in July. It's like someone planning a Thanksgiving meal at . . . at . . . Groundhog Day. It's way too early, McGrother. Heck, I don't even know what I want to be for Halloween yet. And that's really soon!"

Someone from the lacrosse team walks past and shouts, "Hey, girl!" to Dare.

"I don't know what I want to be for Halloween, either," I say, even though I definitely do have an idea. "Are you going?"

"Trick-or-treating?" Dare asks. "Does a dog sniff another dog's butt to say hello? Of course I'm going. I already found an extra-long pillowcase to collect all the candy."

"I didn't mean Halloween," I say. "I know there's no force on earth that could stand between Dare Drummond and a fun-size Snickers bar."

Dare makes an exaggerated bow. "You know me so well."

It's true. I know everything about Dare Donilynn Drummond and she knows everything about me. *Everything.* "I meant are you going to the dance?"

Dare's eyes shift to the left, like she's thinking about something. "I don't know," she says, gripping my shoulders. "Like I said, it's way too early." She kind of shoves me toward class. "See you at lunch."

I whip around. "Hey, Dare?"

"Ye—"

"Mooooooo!"

She shakes her head at me.

"I got you," I say under my breath, still feeling pretty terrific. Even the Neanderthals can't make me feel bad today.

THIS IS SERIOUS

Coach Ochoa has us gather around him in a semicircle on the gym floor. He gets down on one knee and grimaces.

"Guys," he says, "I'm not getting any younger and I won't be coaching at Gator Lake forever."

Some of the guys whisper to each other.

It feels like I'm an extra in some sappy Hallmark movie.

"I really love coaching basketball." He looks each of us in the eyes. "But do you know what I love more?"

"Winning!" the guys yell.

"That's right," Coach says, standing with a wince. "And this year, I want us to win."

"Oh yeah!" Vasquez shouts.

"Not just some games."

"No!" everyone yells.

The assistant coach stands off to the side, holding a clipboard and nodding at whatever Coach says.

I still haven't added my voice to the chorus because I don't want to shout the wrong thing and sound like an idiot.

"Not just District," Coach says, putting both hands in the air. Now it feels like I'm at a revival. I half expect someone to shout, *Hallelujah!*

"No!" the guys yell.

"This year," Coach says, pumping his fists skyward, "I want to go all the way."

I hold back a giggle; I'm so mature.

"I want to win State."

"State!" the guys scream. "State! State! State!" They begin to clap, so I do, too.

Coach signals us to settle down. "And you're the ones who are going to make that happen. Being on this basketball team is an honor, boys. Representing Gator Lake Middle School is an honor. Each of you was chosen for this team for a reason. Except you, Diaz." He points to a short guy in the front. "Your dad asked me to make you the team's statistician, so you're the statistician. And water boy."

Diaz nods and laughs nervously.

I'm so glad I'm not Diaz right now.

I'm lucky to be part of this team. To be on the inside, not the outside, like the kids who were cut. I get to be here with these guys, preparing to be the very best at something. I wish Mom could see me. And Bubbie, since her help got me here. I know Dad would be so proud.

Don't think about Dad. Not now. Not when I'm feeling so happy.

"So I need to ask you beasts one more question." Coach looks at each of us again, then says, "Are . . . you . . . all . . . in?"

"Yeah!" everyone shouts. Even Diaz. Even though he's just the statistician and water boy, and cheerleaders probably never go for the statistician and water boy.

The vibrations from each person's voice give me energy. I want to scream, *All for one and one for all!*

I'm about to do it, too, when Coach blows his whistle.

Everyone scrambles up, and we're directed to split into two groups. Half go with Coach Ochoa to one side of the gym; the other half go with the assistant coach to begin drills.

I'm with the assistant coach to practice layups, using both our right and left hands. It feels awkward when I shoot with my left.

The rest of the team is at the other end, running back and forth about a million times.

"Suicides," Diaz whispers to me. "I'm glad I'm only the statistician."

My stomach clenches. *Suicides?*

"Wonder how long before someone upchucks," Diaz whispers. "Someone always upchucks during suicides."

"Dorfman!" the assistant coach yells, and I realize it's my turn to shoot a left-handed layup. I miss the shot by a mile and run to the back of the line. After several shots, I'm sweating like a maniac and am so thirsty. I remember how important it is for me to have water with my meds so I don't dehydrate, but I don't want to be the only one going out to the hall to get a drink.

One of the guys running suicides staggers off to the side near the bleachers and throws up.

"There it is," Diaz says.

"Diaz!" Coach shouts. "Find maintenance. Tell them we need a cleanup in the gym."

"Sure thing," Diaz calls, and jogs out.

He's lucky to leave the gym because he doesn't have to smell the odor, which is wafting to where we're practicing layups. I feel sorry for the guys who are running back and forth at top speed. Back and forth. Back and forth. With a pile of upchuck a few feet away.

I can't believe Coach Ochoa doesn't stop practice until the gym floor is cleaned, but he doesn't.

And the kid who threw up doesn't go to the nurse or home. He doesn't even sit. He goes to the hall—probably to rinse his mouth and get some water—and comes right back to running.

I wish I could go out and get a drink.

Man, this basketball stuff is serious.

Hope I can keep up.

THE REAL REASON

When the sides switch and it's time for me to run suicides, I'm grateful the puke has been cleaned.

I don't want to be embarrassed by the guys I'm running against, so I give it all I've got. Pump my arms. Move my legs. Pump my arms. My legs tangle with each other, and I go sprawling.

Coach offers two words of encouragement: *"Get up!"*

The kids on the team are silent as I rise to my feet. Without even brushing myself off, I get back to the business at hand—running—even though both knees and my right wrist hurt and I feel a little like crying.

After suicides, I lean against the wall, sure I'll never be able to catch my breath. My legs hold me up almost as well as cooked noodles would. I've never been so ready to go home and climb into my bed in my life. But, apparently, Coach hasn't finished with us.

"Three-point shooting contest, boys. I'll try to end practice every day with something fun."

This is fun?

A few boys cheer at Coach's announcement.

I try to shoot by pushing off with my leg muscles, like Bubbie taught me, but there's nothing left in them, so I miss a bunch of shots and look like a loser in front of the guys. I feel like throwing the ball across the gym in frustration. I'm positive I'd have more energy and stamina if I weren't taking my meds.

When practice is finally over, the guys funnel into the locker room, red-faced and slumped forward, but Coach taps my shoulder. "Dorfman, stay."

My feet grow roots into the gym floor. *Is he going to make me run extra suicides by myself? Shoot layups or three-pointers?* Then a voice in my head says, *Maybe he's going to tell you that you did a great job.* A half smile forms on my face, but when Coach backs me up against a wall with thick padding, my smile disappears and my mind switches, racing to the thousand possible things I did wrong during practice.

Coach Ochoa squints, and a fan of wrinkles spread beside his eyes.

He's so close that I smell aftershave and something sour on his breath. His morning coffee, maybe.

My legs tremble, more like twigs than tree trunks.

"Listen, Dorfman." Coach pokes my chest with his right index finger. *Is he even allowed to do that?* "Why do you think I picked you for this team?"

I wish Vasquez were here instead of in the locker room. He'd know the right answer. He'd shout it out with great enthusiasm.

Apparently it was a rhetorical question because Coach answers it himself. "You're on this team for one reason and one reason only."

This time I venture a guess, my voice shaking like a leaf in a gale: "Vasquez?"

"What?" Coach steps a millimeter closer. "No! Why would you say that?"

I'm literally looking down at Coach, but it feels like he's so much taller than I am.

"You're on this team because of your height, Dorfman." Then, as though I'm too stupid to know what "height" means, he says, "Because you're tall."

I wish Coach would back up and give me room to breathe. I wonder if my sweat is dripping on him.

"I can teach you a lot of things. I can teach you to run and shoot. I can teach you to dribble well with your right *and* left hands. I can teach you a good number of plays. But there's one thing I can't teach you, even if I had all the time in the world. Do you know what that is?"

I do know because Bubbie already explained this to me, but there's no way I'm saying it. So I stand there, awkward and embarrassed.

"Height." Coach sprays spittle on me, but I don't wipe my neck. "I can't teach height. Dorfman, you will spend so much time on the bench this season your butt will get splinters. But when I put you on the floor, you'll throw the other team into a panic. They'll think you're a scoring machine. It's all about intimidating them with your height. Got it?"

I nod, but I don't want to get splinters in my butt. I don't handle pain well.

"And I will teach you how to catch passes from your teammates under the basket and put them up all day long." He gets even closer. "Dorfman, are you in 110 percent?"

I nod furiously, even though 110 percent is a statistical impossibility.

"I can't hear you," Coach says in an ominously low tone.

"Yes, sir!" I shout. "I'm in 110 percent."

"Good man," Coach says as he claps me on the upper arm and shoves me toward the locker room. "Go get changed. I'll see you tomorrow. And don't shrink overnight." Coach laughs at his own lame joke.

I laugh, too, even though it wasn't funny.

In the locker room, Vasquez asks, "What'd Coach want?"

I can't tell him Coach only picked me because I was tall, not because of all the hard work I did with Bubbie. "Nothing." I shrug. "He just said I did a good job today."

Vasquez pounds me on the back. "That's awesome. Coach doesn't usually take the time to throw someone a compliment. See, I told you you're going to be a superstar. See you tomorrow, man."

I nod and open my locker. "Tomorrow."

Time for a Change

At lunch, Dare hands me an iced blueberry Pop-Tart from her double pack before I even sit. I take it as a good omen that she'll be receptive to what I need to tell her. With Pop-Tart in hand, I lean across the table and whisper in her ear, "I've decided to make small steps. I know I've said this before, but this time I mean it. I think it's important now that I'll be getting the hormone blockers. Small steps toward being me."

What I don't tell Dare is my reason—my endgame—for doing these small steps. My big idea. But she'll find out.

Dare raises an eyebrow as I sit, and she passes me her other Pop-Tart.

It's her way of saying she forgives my past failed attempts and approves of my new resolve.

If she only knew how much resolve I'll need for my final goal.

I take a huge bite and let the sweet taste linger on my tongue.

That night, I paint my fingernails bold blue with shimmery sparkles. I think they go nicely with my eyes. It's not the first time my nails were painted.

When we were younger, I'd beg Sarah to paint my nails, and of course she did. We'd play spa, and she'd do my nails and give me a facial, which consisted of putting a warm washcloth over my face, then smearing on Mom's Noxzema until it tingled so much I made her wash it off. Eventually, Dad put his foot down about spa days. And at sleepovers, Dare and I would paint each other's nails outrageous colors. But I always used polish remover before coming home.

This morning, I feel so good when I look at the blue, sparkly polish on my fingernails. Mom's already at the yoga studio, and Sarah's left for school. Meatball couldn't care less what my fingernails look like as long as I feed him breakfast before I leave. Dad, of course, has the newspaper shield in front of his face, so all my worrying about how he might react is for nothing.

Dare notices immediately, of course. She bumps her hip into mine and nods. "You weren't kidding, McGrother, about those small steps."

I waggle my fingernails at her. "No I wasn't. You like?"

"I do." She looks at the chipped green polish on her own fingernails. "It's awesome, Lily."

Lily.

Who knew a little bit of Sarah's nail polish with sparkly bits could make me feel so good?

Unfortunately, Dare isn't the only one who notices my first small step.

At my locker, as soon as Dare leaves, Vasquez swaggers over. He nods at my nail polish, then actually spits on me. *Spits!* "Nail-polish-wearing fag!"

I make sure no teachers are looking, but really, there never seems to be a teacher around when Vasquez and the Neanderthals bother me. That's why I've got to start sticking up for myself. So I give Vasquez the finger—my blue polished fingernail held high—as he walks away. That's my second small step—standing up to the Neanderthals, at least a little.

On my way to homeroom, as I wipe off the place Vasquez spit on me, I wonder what the rest of the day will hold. I admire my polish one more time. I don't care what Vasquez says or thinks about it; I think it looks great.

I can tell that some of my teachers notice my polish throughout the day, even though they pretend they don't. I also hear a couple kids whisper about it in some of my classes, but nobody else really bothers me.

I'm sure when a biological girl paints her nails, she doesn't think much of it. But to me, this is huge and it felt right. I took a step today—a small step toward being me and feeling more comfortable in my own skin—and I survived, only a little worse for the wear, thanks to Vasquez.

My next small step will take more bravery.

The next day, I put on Mom's lipstick. It's a really subtle shade. But still. To me, I'm putting lipstick on myself because wearing it makes me feel happy. To the outside world, I know I look like a boy wearing lipstick.

Sometimes, our hearts see things our eyes can't.

"Nice, McGrother," Dare says when she sees me. She gives me a fist bump. "You're getting there." Then she's quiet for a moment, which is really rare. Dare looks into my eyes. "I'm proud of you."

I smile.

"Also, you have lipstick on your teeth."

I wipe my front teeth with the side of my finger and ask her if it's gone.

"All clear, girlfriend."

I hold myself tall as we walk to school. Dare called me "girlfriend."

Bring it!

Vasquez slams my head into my locker. For a second, I can't hear anything except the ringing in my ears and the word "Fag!"

Only one thing is louder—the voice in my head: *I am not a fag.*

I AM A GIRL!

Such a Monday

Monday, I wake hopeful, even though it means another day of middle school and dealing with Vasquez and the Neanderthals. It's also Halloween, which will be so much fun with Dare.

For today's small step, I carefully draw Sarah's black liner under my eyes, which makes the blue in them stand out. I didn't know my eyes could look so pretty. Bare lips today. It's all about focusing on my eyes.

"Dad?" I watch as he lowers the newspaper. Holding up the backs of my hands, I wiggle my polished nails. "I'm leaving for school now."

He looks at my nails and at my eyes, then ruffles the newspaper. That's it. Ruffles the newspaper like he's annoyed, then puts it back up like a shield.

Small steps for me. And small steps for him.

At least he didn't scream. He didn't tell me to wash my face and take off the nail polish. And really, he could have been a beast about either thing.

I want to squeeze Dad into a big hug, but feel like it might be too much right now. So I simply say "Thank you" with my eyes to the back of Dad's newspaper, hoping my mental message gets through to him.

Thank you, Dad, for giving me the space to be me.
Thank you for allowing me to take small steps.

Before school, Vasquez doesn't pay a visit to my locker, and I'm so relieved. Maybe it won't be so bad for a Monday. Maybe Vasquez will be absent today. Maybe he contracted some bizarre illness that will keep him out of school the rest of the year.

Imagining that scenario makes me smile for much of the day . . . until PE.

In the locker room, I change as fast as I can. I hate being undressed in there, so I never am. I wear gym shorts under my pants on PE days. I'm uncomfortable enough about my body without having other guys looking at it, judging me.

"McGrother," Vasquez says, blocking me from leaving the locker room.

"What's under those?" He eyes my gym shorts.

I try to march past him—head down, plow ahead—like Dare would have done.

But there's no marching past Vasquez. He's a mountain, plus two of the Neanderthals have shown up as reinforcements, blocking my way.

"Yeah," Bobby Birch says, and laugh-snorts like I imagine a hyena would. "What's under those?" He points to my gym shorts again, as though that's any of his business.

Vasquez tilts his head. "Well, McGrother. Whatcha hidin' under there? Hmm? Whatcha got inside?"

I channel my inner Dare and growl, "The same thing that's inside yours." *Unfortunately!* Then I shove Vasquez so hard with both hands, he stumbles backward.

It's all I need to get out of there, into the relative safety of the gym.

I hate the boys' locker room.

I hate PE.

I hate Vasquez, Bobby Birch and the entire band of Neanderthals.

In the gym, Coach divvies us up into four sections for two games of volleyball. "Set. Spike. Block." Coach claps his hands to each word. "Set. Spike. Block."

Then he blows his whistle, which means we're supposed to start playing.

Most of the girls drag their way to the courts and get into position. Dare's in the group on the other court. Some of the boys are excited; maybe because they like to hit things. I don't know. I wish PE weren't required. I'd much rather do something civilized, like read in the school library. Too bad they closed that when I was in sixth grade. Then they fired the nice librarian, Ms. Tarr. Budget cuts, someone said. If they didn't have enough money, why didn't they cut a few sports programs instead? Now there's a big, book-filled room on the second floor we're not allowed to go into because "there's no supervision." Mom even volunteered to sit in the library a few hours a week so the kids could at least go in and use it, but the principal said no thank you.

I hate this stupid school.

When Coach leaves the gym to talk to another teacher, Vasquez manages to spike the volleyball right into my face. It's like a planet hurtling a million miles an hour toward me and then colliding. I bring my fingers up to my nose, expecting a waterfall of blood. But none comes.

"Nice nail polish!" someone yells from the other side of the net.

Laughter.

"Yeah, blue's your color, Tim," some guy says in a fake high-pitched voice. "Matches your eyes."

More laughter.

"He's such a fag!" Bobby Birch says.

"Yeah, *she* is," Vasquez adds.

More laughter.

"Stop it!" Dare's voice.

Then silence.

"What's going on over there?" Coach bellows. "Mc-Grother, come on. Get up. Let's see you spike that ball!"

I lower my hands from my nose. I rise from the floor and toss the ball back to the person on our team who's supposed to serve next. Then I bend forward, rest my hands on my knees and glare at Vasquez. "Let's go," I say, my voice choked.

My teammate serves the ball . . . right into my back.

"Sorry!"

I. Hate. Volleyball.

HALLOWEEN, PART I

Vasquez decides we'll have a group costume for Halloween.

He doesn't strike me as the group costume kind of guy, and I'm worried what it might be. He'll probably make us all dress up as Freddy Krueger or something dumb like that, which I guess would be okay, although not very original. One year, my dad came up with a great group costume. He dressed as a firefighter, Mom was a Dalmatian and Mom and a friend of hers made me a fire hydrant costume. I'm not kidding. Back then I thought it was hilarious.

Mom and Dad walked me all over the neighborhood. I remember getting a ton of good candy that year. I remember Mom and Dad laughing a lot, too, and chatting with neighbors. I remember some lady telling me, "Sorry, I ran out of candy," and dropping two quarters in my bag. Two quarters!

That was the last good Halloween with Dad.

I was eight.

There are a buttload of pink flamingos wearing tiny Halloween costumes stuck into random lawns in our neighborhood. They're funny, but I wonder for a second if they're really there. I look around to see if anyone else sees the flamingos. Maybe my medicine is making me see things. I'm taking all my doses like the doctor wanted, but maybe seeing pink flamingos in Halloween costumes is a rare side effect.

When some kids, dressed like hockey players, kick one of the flamingos out of the grass, then crack up, I realize I'm being a complete idiot. Of course the flamingos are really there. My mind is fine. *Isn't it?*

It takes f-o-r-e-v-e-r to walk to Vasquez's house. Of course I'm sweating the whole way, because even though it's Halloween, it's still a million humid degrees outside. In New Jersey, I used to worry about having to wear a coat over my costume because it would be so cold. Here, I worry about applying enough deodorant to combat excessive armpit sweat.

Way #10 to die in South Florida: drowning in my own armpit sweat.

By the time I knock and go inside Vasquez's trailer home, the other guys are already squashed around a small table, playing poker. Vasquez's older sister, who is introduced as Francesca, is finishing up sewing five basketball T-shirts together at the sleeves.

"We're going as Siamese quintuplet basketball players," Vasquez says, as though he invented a cure for acne or something. "Awesome. Right?"

"Awesome," I say, faking enthusiasm and squeezing in at the small table. The thought of being stuck that close to these guys, especially when I've been sweating like Niagara Falls, seems like a mild form of torture.

Turns out I'm going to be the guy in the middle because I'm the tallest. "Awesome," I say again.

Everyone abandons the poker game, stands in a straight line and lets Francesca put the T-shirt built for five over our heads. When she gets close to me, I notice she smells like strawberries, and I decide I'm a big fan of strawberries. Maybe I'll try a strawberry-filled doughnut next time I'm at Dunkin' Donuts.

We have to put our arms around each other's waists because the T-shirt built for five forces us to stand so close together. There are two guys on either side of me. I know this is supposed to be fun—a crazy Halloween with the guys—but I have the makings of an ugly headache and don't feel like doing this. I wonder what Tim and Dare are doing tonight. Probably something really fun.

One of us smells sour, like he hasn't taken a shower in a while. I worry it might be me, but since we're all attached by the dumb T-shirt, I can't even secretly sniff my pits.

I wonder why I agreed to do this, but realize it wouldn't work without me. We need five people, like on a basketball team. And I'm that fifth guy. Just like on the court, the guys need me.

Part of me feels like I'm too old to go out for Halloween. Last year when I went out with Phineas, I was sure that was the last time I'd go out. But here I am, stuffed into a T-shirt built for five.

Francesca takes a photo of us, then stands on her toes and kisses her brother on the cheek.

He wipes it off, and all the guys make oohing and aahing noises.

"Shut up," he says, and punches the guy next to him with his free arm.

I'm glad I'm not standing next to Vasquez.

We all shut up and wait for him to tell us what to do next.

I know what I want to do—go home and climb into the guest bed. My bed. The meds have been making me so tired lately, and this walk over here in the heat wore me out.

When I ask Vasquez if I can have a drink, Francesca holds a glass of water for me and pours it into my mouth. Of course, I choke and spill water down my neck, and all the guys laugh.

Terrific!

"Let's go to Beckford Palms Estates," Vasquez says. "They'll give out bigger candy bars. Not like the cheapskates in this neighborhood. They'd give out a single Skittle if they could. In Beckford Palms, sometimes you get a whole handful of candy at each house. Those people have some serious money."

My cheeks heat up, and I feel like I'm guilty of something, even though I don't really live in Beckford Palms Estates. Technically, it's Bubbie's house. Still, I wish I could shrink away, but unfortunately I'm too tall for that.

"You guys ready?" Vasquez asks.

He sounds pumped.

"Ready!" the guys say.

I say it, too, even though the only thing I'm ready for is sleep. Or a giant cup of coffee.

"Bring me back some good candy," Francesca says before disappearing into one of the rooms down the hall of the trailer.

Outside, getting down the few steps from the door, we realize how hard it is for five people to move in sync.

I'm *not* looking forward to this.

It turns out to be kind of fun trick-or-treating with the guys.

We end up doing stupid walks together.

"Right. Left. Right. Left," Vasquez says to keep us walking in sync, but someone always messes up, and we burst out laughing.

There are about a thousand kids trick-or-treating in Beckford Palms Estates. I never saw so many people here before. An army of pint-sized princesses, aliens, monsters, cheerleaders, football players and characters from movies have descended on the neighborhood.

"Kids come from other neighborhoods for the good candy," Vasquez explains. "Let's go get our share before they hog it all up."

That's when we try to run . . . and end up in a five-person heap on the ground.

We manage to get up, coordinate our walking and knock on the first door.

People crack up when they see us. Some make sure to give us five pieces of candy, even though there are only two pillowcases—one at each end.

"That's the most original costume I've ever seen," some lady says as she drops candy into our pillowcases.

A man pushing a little ladybug in a stroller says, "That's what I call teamwork."

I'm grateful the neighborhood is large enough that we travel many blocks and never end up on the street with Bubbie's house. I don't know how I'd deal with that one. Besides, Bubbie is probably giving out healthy muffins or something that the guys would use as ammunition to launch at other kids.

When Vasquez starts complaining that his bag is getting too heavy and someone else says his feet hurt, we decide to head back to Vasquez's place. I try to figure out if there's any way I can duck out and go home, but I can't see how I could manage that without them knowing I live in this rich neighborhood, so I stay in formation and head toward the entrance.

I'm so exhausted, though.

Three people around our age approach from the opposite direction. They're laughing and look like they're having so much fun. I know one of them. Wait. Two of them.

Just as they're about to walk right into us, my heart thuds. *Do something!* I purposely put my leg in front of Bobby Birch, the guy next to me. He trips and we all go down in a heap, just like I'd hoped.

I bash my right knee on the sidewalk, but it's totally worth it.

"Damn!" Vasquez yells. "Who did that?"

Bobby starts to say something, but doesn't.

As the five of us try to right ourselves, I glance behind us and watch Tim and Dare and another person walk past.

Safely.

I smile, feeling good that I finally did one small thing. And Vasquez doesn't even know about it.

When we manage to get up, I slip out of the costume. "Sorry, guys," I say, "but I've gotta go." And I jog out of the neighborhood by myself like I'm heading to some other neighborhood, but I plan to make a wide loop and come right back.

I hope Vasquez and the guys don't catch me doing it.

When I finally get to Bubbie's house, I'm thirsty and tired, but I think that Halloween was pretty good after all and nothing bad happened (thanks to me!).

Turns out Bubbie gave out packaged granola bars to the trick-or-treaters.

Mom is eating one when I walk into the house. "How was trick-or-treating?" she asks, wiping crumbs from the corner of her mouth.

"Pretty great," I say, and this time I'm not even lying.

An Unexpected Guest

I'm all dressed up and almost ready for Halloween way before Dare is supposed to arrive.

In the lunchroom today, we agreed to stick with tradition and trick-or-treat in my neighborhood, since everyone knows they give out the best candy. We realize we're getting too old, and this will be our last year trick-or-treating, so we want to go out with a bang and collect the most candy ever.

I'm scratching under Meatball's chin when Sarah comes into my bedroom, wearing her Wonder Woman T-shirt and holding out her makeup case like it's Wonder Woman's magic lasso of truth or something.

"I'm ready!" she says.

"You know you're only putting makeup on me, not saving the planet from evil. Right?"

"Whatever," Sarah says, putting her case on my desk. "My magic makeup case will save you from being a merely mediocre mermaid."

"Nice alliteration," I say, taking a deep breath, sitting and facing the giant *W* on Sarah's chest. Not for the first time, I wish my boobs looked like hers. Developed. Unmistakably feminine. *Someday,* I tell myself, I'll be able to move on to female hormones. Then I'll finally, *finally* get the body that matches who I am—more curves, fewer angles. I decide to talk to Dr. Klemme about this at our next session together. I know she'll understand.

Sarah uses bright blue eye shadow that matches my sparkly costume.

"Stop squinting," she admonishes.

"I'm not," I say while squinting. "I'm afraid you'll poke my eye out."

"Well, stop squinting," she says, brushing on the color. "Or I will!"

"That's reassuring." I try not to move.

The blue eye shadow, black eyeliner and mascara look gorgeous, but my favorite part—my absolutely favorite part of this year's costume—is the wig. A bright blue, long-haired wig that Sarah bought me from Walgreens with her babysitting money.

"I've got the best sister on the planet," I tell her.

"What a coincidence." She pokes me in the nose with the tip of her finger. "I do, too."

I admire myself in the mirror and make a fish face. It feels so good to have long hair again, even if it's only a cheap drugstore wig.

"Company coming up," Mom calls.

Sarah stands to the side, hands on her hips. She totally looks like Wonder Woman with that stance.

I sail onto the bed and pose like a mermaid on a rock at sea. Dare is going to love my costume.

When she enters my bedroom and another girl comes in behind her, I sit up fast. Dare hadn't mentioned bringing someone else. She and I always trick-or-treat together—just the two of us. It's tradition. And it's our last year.

Who's this new girl? What will she think of me . . . dressed like this?

The Pirate in Pink

Dare's dressed as a pirate, with an eye patch and a plastic sword tucked into her belt. She's wearing these great swashbuckling boots, which I realize are her riding boots.

"Nice costume," I say, hoping she'll say the same thing to me.

The other girl is dressed as a pirate, too. Pink bandanna. Pink eye patch. And a pink plastic parrot on her shoulder.

I wish I looked like her—lovely eyes (one of which is covered by an eye patch), smooth skin, medium-sized boobs under a puffy pirate blouse and fluorescent pink nail polish on her toes that are poking through these cool Grecian-style sandals.

"Lily," Dare says, exploding with happiness. "This is Amy. Amy, this is Lily."

I nod toward Amy, and she gives me a big smile. "Nice to meet you, Lily."

She scores points for using my real name, but I don't like that she's showed up unannounced and uninvited.

"Well, I've gotta go help Mom give out candy," Sarah says, and slips out.

I don't want Sarah to go. When Meatball trots out after her, his tags jingling, I feel especially vulnerable.

Dare punches me in the arm. "Great costume, Lil. You look good in blue."

Amy laughs, but I can't tell if she's laughing with me or at me.

"Thanks," I say shyly. "Sarah bought me the wig and did my makeup."

"She seems like a cool sister," Amy says. "My sister is a boy." She looks at me, and her face grows a deeper shade of pink than her eye patch. "I mean," Amy stammers. "I . . . I . . . was trying to be funny. I mean I have a brother, not a sister. That's all." She looks down and shakes her head. "Sorry. I'm an idiot."

"It's okay," Dare says, putting her arm around Amy's shoulders and squeezing tight. "Right?" Dare glares at me.

"Of course," I say. "It's fine. What you said was totally funny." I make a lame noise that might pass as a laugh.

I look at my best friend—my only friend—with her arm around this girl's shoulders.

What's happening here?

Almost Perfect

As soon as Mom sees me, she claps her hands over her mouth. "Let me grab my camera." She runs off, leaving us—two pirates and a mermaid—at the bottom of the staircase.

I thought Sarah and Meatball might be in the kitchen, but I don't see them.

Dad strides over, and when he sees me, his eyes go wide. For a microsecond, I hope it's because he thinks my costume is terrific.

"Timothy," Dad says in a low, ominous voice, and I die a million deaths in front of Dare and Amy. I had thought we were making such progress.

Dad signals me with his eyes to follow him.

"Be right back," I say, trying to keep my voice from cracking.

I follow Dad through the kitchen and into the laundry room.

He slams the door and grabs my upper arm with thick fingers.

I don't try to wiggle out of his grasp.

Dad bends low so he's right in my face, and I smell chocolate and peanut butter on his breath. "I've been understanding. Haven't I?" he asks in a quiet, barely controlled voice.

I nod, because if I do anything more than a subtle nod, tears will slip from my eyes and mess up the makeup Sarah put on.

Why is Dad ruining Halloween?

He releases my arm, but continues to talk in a soft, scary voice. "I've let you walk out of the house wearing nail polish."

I hide my fingers behind my back.

"And that . . ." He swings his arm in the air. "That stuff you wore on your eyes the other day." He looks into my eyes now. "I let that slide. Right?"

I nod again, sure Niagara Falls is about to erupt from my tear ducts.

"But this . . ." The vein in Dad's temple throbs, and I worry it will burst. "This is too much," he says. "Too far. Don't you understand?"

I think of Vasquez and our daily ritual at my locker. *I understand plenty.* I wish Dad understood how much this costume means to me, especially the wig. Plus I've loved mermaids since childhood, when I became obsessed with *The Little Mermaid.* He should remember that.

While Dad's breathing his chocolate and peanut butter breath on me, and the vein throbs blue beneath the skin of his temple, I wonder what Dare and the new girl are doing. They're probably talking about me. And Mom's probably standing there with her camera, wondering what's going on. It will be so embarrassing to go back out there after this.

It would be easier if I lived here only with Mom, Sarah and Meatball. Dad could live in that little apartment over his T-shirt shop with Grandmom Ruth. They could complain about me over their morning cups of coffee. But the thought of Dad leaving makes me feel sad and empty. I don't want him to go anywhere. I just wish he'd stop doing things like this. He seemed to be doing so great.

Dad grabs my shoulders. "Don't you realize?" he says,

his voice breaking. "The minute you go out of the house dressed like *that,* you're not safe. There are rotten people out there who would hurt you, Tim. There are . . ."

He lets go of my shoulders and drops down on one knee. "Timmy, don't you see? All I've ever wanted is to keep you safe, keep you from getting hurt."

The way Dad's looking at me, he seems so vulnerable, like Niagara Falls is about to explode from *his* tear ducts. Or from his heart.

"But, Dad, you don't need to—"

He grabs me into the most bone-crunching hug he's ever given me. "I love you so much, son."

His words are almost perfect.

Halloween, Part II

Our pillowcases are heavy, bulging as we head back toward my house.

"What does a Jewish pirate say?" Amy asks.

Dare and I look at each other, then shake our heads.

I'm glad the awkwardness of joining them near the staircase after Dad's talk is behind us. And no matter how worried Dad is, there's no way I'm changing out of this mermaid costume. I worked too hard to get to this point. I'm not turning back again.

Mom snapped a few photos—I'm sure I did not look my best mermaid self—and we headed out. I can't believe that was more than two and a half hours ago.

"Ahoy vey!" Amy says.

I laugh a little.

"Boo!" Dare bellows in Amy's face. "Boo!!!!"

"That's not nice," Amy says, shoving her.

"It's Halloween." Dare shrugs. "'Boo' is a perfectly appropriate thing to say."

Amy holds her pink parrot in Dare's face. "Aaargh!"

They knock shoulders and keep walking.

I get a little pang of sadness, because Dare is supposed to knock shoulders with me. To feel more included, I share the one pirate joke I know: "How much is a pirate willing to pay to get his ears pierced?"

They stop walking, and Amy taps her chin. "A peg leg?" she asks.

"How is that even funny?" Dare asks.

"I have no idea," Amy says. "It sounded like it might make sense."

"It makes absolutely no sense," Dare says.

"You make no sense," Amy replies.

"That makes no sense," Dare says.

No one is paying attention to me, but I say the punch line anyway: "A buck an ear."

I wait for a response, but none arrives because they're bantering back and forth. "A buck an ear," I say louder. "Get it? A buccaneer."

"Oh." Amy nods. "I get it."

"Not funny, McGrother." Dare pokes me in the side with her fake sword.

"Ouch," I say, even though it didn't hurt.

"Who knows any mermaid jokes?" Amy asks, finally making me feel included.

"I know one," Dare says. "But it's stupid."

"Stupid's good," Amy says. "Tell it."

"Okay. Where does a mermaid go to the movies?"

"The dive-in!" Amy shouts, and jumps like she's on *The Price Is Right* and guessed the price to win a brand-new car.

"Yup," Dare says, smiling. "You got it."

"I got one! Woohoo!" Amy does an uncoordinated pink pirate dance.

"I'm impressed," Dare says. "Not with your dancing ability, mind you. That's just embarrassing." Dare points her swashbuckling fake sword at Amy. "But shiver me timbers, matey, your joke-figuring-out talents are totally awesome sauce."

Naturally, Amy's got to do a few more awkward dance steps. This makes me like her.

I was worried about getting harassed after Dad's talk, but it hasn't happened. Maybe when people see me, they don't see a boy in a mermaid costume. Maybe they see three girls walking down the street. At least, I hope that's what they see because that's exactly what it is.

"One last pirate joke," Amy says. "Knock, knock."

"Who's there?" Dare asks, brandishing her fake sword.

"Interrupting pirate."

"Interrupting pirate wh—"

"Arrrrrrgggghhhh!" Amy says, and cracks up.

Dare and I exchange glances. She mouths the word *Mooooo,* and it makes me feel great, like she and I share a private joke.

I'm about to chuckle a little to make Amy feel good about her lame pirate joke when I see them.

Everything shifts.

Nothing is funny anymore.

Dad *was* right. I'm completely exposed and vulnerable out here. I shouldn't be outside dressed in a mermaid costume, no matter how good and right it feels. Dad understood something I wasn't ready to know. One minute we're telling stupid pirate jokes and the next I'm in serious trouble.

Straight ahead are five Neanderthals, their heads poking out of some weird basketball shirt built for five, with Dunkin—the tallest—in the middle. Vasquez is on one end, his arm free to do all kinds of damage. All he'd have to do is drop the pillowcase. His head is turned the other way, though, looking back at something.

I wish that seeing Dunkin brought me a sense of comfort—like he'd stick up for me or something—but I know that's a fantasy, and I have experience in what Vasquez and his crew are capable of.

The Neanderthals are only a couple yards away, heading right toward us, and Dare and Amy, apparently, are too oblivious to realize what's about to happen.

My stomach clenches as I understand how ugly this is

going to get. The moment Vasquez sees me wearing a mermaid costume, I'm done.

Dare tugs on my arm, and when I turn and see her, eyes open wide, I know she's noticed what's coming.

There's no way to avoid them, because they're taking up the whole sidewalk. And they'd see if we suddenly darted across the street.

As Dare leans over to whisper to Amy, the Neanderthals drop in a heap, as though someone pulled an invisible rug out from under them.

Dare yanks me, but she doesn't have to. I'm moving as fast as my constricting mermaid costume allows. We scoot around them—past the squirming heap—but I can't resist glancing back.

They're a tangle of heads, two arms and scrabbling legs. Vasquez is yelling. The only one from the heap looking at me is Dunkin.

And he smiles.

That's when I know.

Somehow, Dunkin engineered the collapse so Vasquez and the Neanderthals wouldn't see me. Dunkin's grin tells me he did this for me, to protect me.

I try to say "thank you" with my backward glance before I allow Dare and Amy to pull me away.

I'm going to find a way to pay him back. I knew Dunkin was good deep down inside. I knew he wasn't like the other Neanderthals. And now I owe him big.

Before long, we're at my house and Amy says, "What's Captain Hook's favorite place to shop?" She waits a few seconds. "A secondhand store."

"Good one," I say, relieved to be past the danger.

Dare groans.

"You guys look exhausted," Mom says when we walk in. She puts her arm around my shoulders and kisses me on the cheek. "And happy."

"Relieved" might be a more accurate word. Maybe Mom feels a little relieved, too, now that I'm home safely.

Dad's in the living room. He definitely looks relieved to see us—to see me, home and unharmed—but he leaves as soon as we dump our stashes on the floor to begin trading. I know sometimes it's just too much for him, but at least he's trying.

The three of us have collected tons of amazing candy. And three granola bars.

When we begin trading, Amy starts up with the jokes again. I realize I made a new friend tonight, and I'm glad Dare brought her.

Sarah comes over, says hello and picks all the peanut butter cups from my pile. I let her because she's Sarah . . . and I'm not a huge fan of peanut butter cups anyway. I prefer Twizzlers and anything with caramel.

As I sit in the living room, trading candy with my new and old friends, shooing away Meatball and watching Sarah bite into a peanut butter cup, I'm so glad Dad's dire prediction didn't come true, or it would be a very different end of the night.

And I have Dunkin to thank for that.

Score: The Blue Mermaid and friends—1, Vasquez and the Neanderthals—0.

November Daze, Er, Days

I decided I've taken enough small steps for a while, although going out in a mermaid costume with a wig, full makeup and nail polish felt more like a gigantic leap. So as I head to school these cool November days, all I have on my fingernails is some chipped polish. I leave the makeup home and wear jeans and T-shirts, especially my favorite of Dad's rejects: *The Bu Strippers*. Dad definitely did that one on purpose.

Even though I'm trying to fly under his radar, Vasquez still calls me "Fag!" at every opportunity. But he's stopped slamming my head into my locker, so that's an improvement. And I'm incredibly creative when it comes to avoiding him in the PE locker room. One day I leave class early, so I'm changed and in the gym before anyone else arrives. Another day, I end up in the nurse's office with a "stomachache." And another time, I manage to help a teacher the entire period and get out of PE altogether.

Dare talks about Amy a lot now. She moved here from Portland, Maine. She can't get used to our humid weather.

And she misses her friends from her old school, since she was pulled out just after the start of her eighth-grade year, because her mom got a job down here at South Florida Waste Management.

I think Amy's great, so I don't mind that she's started to join us for stuff. She's a little heavy on the dumb jokes, but there are worse things. And she's taken to giving me Pop-Tarts at lunch, since she's joined us at our table, so I'm totally good with that.

And even though it's still a month away, kids are already talking about the eighth-grade holiday dance. Whenever someone mentions it, my stomach does somersaults because of the idea I came up with the day I first saw the flyer.

Part of me can't wait for the night of the dance.

Another part is terrified.

All I know is that the night of the eighth-grade dance is going to be an important one.

The First One

Mom drives me to the endocrinologist's office because Dad couldn't get away from the T-shirt shop, and I can't believe this is going to actually happen.

"One of the side effects you may experience," the doctor tells me as I sit on a table in a small exam room, "is tiredness."

I nod, eager for him to hurry up and give me the shot, but he takes his time explaining a few more things.

My whole body tingles as I pull my shorts up to expose my thigh. *No more facial hair. No deep voice. No Adam's apple. No new hair growing down there. No anything else growing down there!*

"That's it?" I ask after the doctor plunges the needle into my thigh.

"That's it," the doctor says. "See you next month. Call if you have any problems."

I had expected the shot to really hurt, but it didn't.

The only one who looks like she's in pain from the whole thing is Mom when she goes up to the counter to pay for my shot. Hormone blockers are expensive. Mom's face loses its color as she signs the credit card receipt.

But then she wraps her arm around my shoulders as we walk out of the office. "Let's go get ice cream sundaes."

"Why?" I ask.

Mom bends onto one knee and looks into my face. "To celebrate, Lily. We need to celebrate this milestone."

"Yes," I whisper, feeling the full impact of how important today is. How important that injection was. "We do need to celebrate."

And we do!

ON THE BENCH

I wish there was something I could take or do to make me feel less nervous about our first game. We've been practicing like crazy, and I even put in some extra hours with Bubbie. But I'm sure the team we're playing has been practicing like crazy, too.

Since I passed my blood test with flying colors a little while ago, I've decided to cut back on my meds. Just a little. To give me that extra edge on the court, but I don't know if it will be enough.

My stomach is in one big knot. If only I could talk to Dad about this, everything would feel better. I should visit him. We should visit him.

In the locker room, the guys are pumped. Especially Vasquez. They're jumping around and pounding each other on the backs. "We've gotta win the first game," Vasquez says.

"We'll win," Birch says, slopping his arm around my shoulders. "We've got Dorfman."

"Dorf. Dorf. Dorf," the guys chant.

I wish the game were already over.

All this pressure isn't good for me. I won't do anything but screw up with all this attention. I don't know why I even agreed to join the team. I should have just hung out with Tim and Dare. I might have gotten made fun of, but at least I wouldn't be in this position now—with everyone looking at me, expecting so much from me. I mean, I do okay during practices—I've actually improved a lot—but I know I'm going to make a fool of myself during a real game.

Coach pokes his head into the locker room. "Let's go, boys. It's time."

Vasquez grunts like a caveman, and we run out of the locker room after him.

I'm surprised when there's an announcer whose voice fills the gym. "Please welcome for the first home game of the season, our own *Gator Lake Gators*!"

We jog through a tunnel the cheerleaders have formed. The stands are filled with people clapping and cheering and stamping their feet. I know Mom and Bubbie are among them.

I feel the vibrations in my chest. The energy in the gym is amazing. It sets my brain into mega-overdrive.

No wonder Vasquez was so excited to get out here.

After the other team is announced—the Lions from Lakeside Middle—we put our hands over our hearts and listen to a girl from school belt out the national anthem. "Ohhhh, say can you seeeee . . ."

The starting lineup jogs onto center court.

I'm not in the starting lineup.

I'm on the bench, where Coach said I would be. Except the bench is not actually a bench. It's a row of black plastic chairs. So the splinters Coach had warned me about were metaphorical. Metaphorical splinters don't hurt.

The other team gets the ball, but Vasquez runs beside the player, steals the ball, dribbles it back to our side, passes to Birch, and we score the first two points of the game on an easy layup.

Even though I'm no superstar, I could have made that shot.

Everyone on the bleachers goes wild, even though it's only two points.

Two points becomes four, then six, then nine, until . . . we're way ahead in the second half and everyone on our team has had a chance to play. Except me.

I'm sure Coach plans to put me in, so I'm totally prepared to hear my name, launch onto the court and immediately score a couple three-pointers. I'm not nervous anymore. I'm excited. I'm ready.

When the final buzzer sounds and we win by thirty-six points, the place erupts. Feet stamping. Cheerleaders leaping. People clapping and screaming. The noise in the gym is overwhelming.

But I feel like an idiot because I was the only person on our whole team who didn't play. Not even for thirty seconds. It wasn't even worth changing into my basketball uniform. And everyone saw me sitting there the entire time.

I know I'm supposed to cheer for my team while I'm on the bench, which I did, but it would be nice to play a little, too. To know what it feels like to be out there during a real game, with people cheering. Especially the first game of the season with Mom and Bubbie in the stands.

Maybe Coach forgot I was there. Maybe I should talk to him.

On the way into the locker room, Coach pounds me on the back. "Like I told you, Dorfman. Lots of bench time. Then when we really need you, we're going to call you out, and you'll be our secret weapon."

I guess it's not a bad thing to be a secret weapon.

"This was only the first game," Coach says. "You'll definitely get to show your stuff soon."

What Coach probably means is, *You'd better up your game, Dorfman, or I'll never play you. I have eyes,* he's probably thinking. *I see how lousy you are during practice compared to the other guys.*

"Thanks," I say, feeling like a fraud.

The guys in the locker room are high-fiving. I high-five a couple of them, but mostly I feel like a loser because Coach didn't put me in, and all the guys must know it's because I'm not good enough.

Mom and Bubbie are waiting outside the locker room, along with the other parents.

With my head down, I say, "Let's go," and keep walking.

They follow me outside.

"Great game, honey," Mom says.

I swivel around. "Were you watching? I didn't play."

"You'll show 'em next time, bubela," Bubbie says, patting me on the rear end, which annoys me.

"If he ever plays me."

"He'll play you," Bubbie says. "If he's got a head in that brain of his."

"You mean a brain in that head of his," Mom says.

Bubbie waves a hand. "That's what I said."

When we're in the car, Mom turns to me before she starts driving. "Norbert, your team did great. It was really fun to watch. I'm sure you'll play next time."

Bubbie unwraps a protein bar and hands it to me. "Replenish your energy."

I look out the window and don't take the bar.

"I've got nothing to replenish, Bubbie. Thanks anyway."

She withdraws the protein bar and says nothing the rest of the way home.

I think that maybe I need to take even less of my medication. Maybe that will make a difference in my energy level and playing ability, but right now I sink into the backseat, feeling like the world's biggest loser. And the ride back seems endless.

A New Sign

Dare, Amy and I go to the first basketball game of the season.

We end up at the top of the bleachers in the back, which is annoying because there's a group of obnoxious boys near us, who scream and stamp their feet constantly, even during moments of the game when extreme enthusiasm is not warranted, like when a referee slips on some jock's sweat and lands on his keister.

We stay for the whole game, and the Gators win, of course.

I feel kind of sorry for the other team. They never had a chance.

I feel sorry for Dunkin, too. It looked like every other player got floor time except him. It would have been nice to watch him play.

Of course, we can't leave without Amy sharing a basketball joke. "Why was Cinderella thrown off the basketball team?"

Dare and I wait for the answer.

"She ran away from the ball."

"That's actually not bad," I say.

Dare knocks into Amy's shoulder, and Amy smiles.

It's good to get away from the crush of people in the gymnasium, and the cool air outside feels great. I love when we get a reprieve from the humidity. The temperature cooled off on November fifteenth, just like I told Dunkin. I wonder if he noticed.

During the walk to Beckford Palms Estates, I'm behind Dare and Amy because the sidewalk is too narrow to fit three people.

I miss hearing some of the jokes, but I hear their laughter. It feels like they might be laughing at me. But I know that's not the case when they each give me a big hug as soon as we arrive at my house.

I watch them walk off together.

Inside, Sarah is knitting something while petting Meatball with her bare foot. She agrees to help me with a plan I came up with.

We walk out to Bob. It's weird being here at night. Everything looks different in the dark.

Sarah helps me tape a sign I made over the sign that's already there.

PLEASE SAVE THIS TREE.
IT'S SCHEDULED TO BE CUT DOWN.
CALL BECKFORD PALMS CITY HALL AND TELL
THEM TO SAVE THIS BEAUTIFUL TREE.
THANK YOU!

In school the next day, I wonder how many calls come in for Bob. I wish I'd thought of this sooner. If lots of people call to protest, they'll have to leave Bob alone.

After school, I see Dunkin running down the hall.

"Hi," I say.

He seems really happy to see me, but looks a little confused. "I have to get to practice."

I point in the opposite direction he's going. "Isn't it that way?"

"Oh yeah," he says, and changes direction.

"You okay?" I call.

"Never better!" he yells, breathless.

It feels great to talk to Dunkin, even for a few moments. I haven't forgotten what he did for me on Halloween.

I hurry to Bob, expecting a crowd gathered around the sign. Maybe even news people, reporting on the story. I'll bet dozens of people called the city to complain. If all that happens, Bob will definitely be saved.

When I get to the tree, there are no people.

And no sign.

Not our sign anyway. That one's been torn away, and the only sign remaining is the one announcing the clearing of the land.

Score: Bob—0, City Hall—1.

Maybe you really can't fight City Hall.

Maybe the pen isn't mightier than the sword.

Maybe there's nothing I can do to save Bob.

I sink onto the ground and lean back against his solid trunk and whisper, "Sorry, Bob. I tried."

He answers with a sad-sounding rustling of leaves, and a fire ant crawls onto my leg and bites my thigh, right near where I got my second hormone blocker injection.

VASQUEZ'S DAD

The second game, early the following week, is much different.

224

Our opponents—the Woodrow Wilson Warriors—are amazing. Stealing balls and outscoring us practically from the tip-off.

Vasquez curses every time he comes to the sidelines for a timeout.

Coach tells him to watch his mouth before our team gets slapped with a technical.

The crowd in the bleachers is subdued for this game, except for one man who yells things like, "Come on, Johnny, you shoulda had that!" or "Johnny, that was yours!" He must be Vasquez's dad. And he's pissed.

The more Vasquez's dad yells from the bleachers, the quieter Vasquez gets when he comes over to the sidelines. In the locker room at halftime, Vasquez is silent, brooding, like water about to explode into a boil.

No one goes near him. No one says anything to him. I consider patting him on the shoulder, but refrain.

We're well into the fourth quarter when Coach taps me on the back and says, "You're in, Dorfman."

I'm so startled I trip when I get up, but quickly right myself and check in at the table where Diaz sits with someone who runs the scoreboard. When I jog onto the court, I feel everyone looking at me, and even though I should know, I don't remember where I'm supposed to position myself.

Vasquez shouts my name and passes me the ball. Hard. But my hands manage to hang on to it. I hope Bubbie's watching. Two guys run toward me at the same time, so I pass the ball back to Vasquez, and the guys move toward him like magnets. Except the ball doesn't go into Vasquez's hands, like I'd intended. One of the guys from the Warriors snatches it and dribbles toward his own basket and scores.

I grab my head and watch in horror.

It surprises me when Coach doesn't replace me for messing up.

I get in position under our basket, like I was taught. Vasquez passes the ball to Landsberg, who feeds it to me, like we practiced a million times. I reach up to drop it in, but it rolls off the other side.

I do the same boneheaded thing one more time.

Then Coach pulls me.

A couple people boo from the stands. They are booing me because I hurt my team. They are booing me because I don't belong on the court. They are booing me because I'm tall enough to be a basketball superstar, but I'm a basketball superdud, even with all my practicing. I'm too slow. I *could* be a basketball superstar, if only . . .

I sit the rest of the game, and by the time the final buzzer blasts and we lose 98–59, I've made up my mind. I know exactly what I need to do.

The guys gather to trudge into the locker room, heads down. But Vasquez is still on the floor, looking into the eyes of his dad, who is screaming and red-faced.

Vasquez doesn't say a word, simply maintains eye contact.

He's still getting reamed out by his dad while the rest of us file in to get reamed out by Coach.

"Vasquez!" Coach yells. "Get over here."

Neither Vasquez nor his dad respond.

I think Coach is going to go over and tell Vasquez's dad that Vasquez is supposed to be in the locker room with the team, but he doesn't. And we all go in without him.

I always thought of Vasquez as this tough guy, but right now I'm worried for him because his dad is big. Mean. I wish Coach went over and made Vasquez join us in the locker room. I wish someone—a parent, a teacher, a coach from the Warriors—someone!—did something because Vasquez's dad looks way too angry.

My dad may have a lot of issues—*a lot*—and he might have accidentally embarrassed me sometimes, but he'd never do something like that to me in front of all those people.

ALMOST UNSTOPPABLE

The moment I wake, I think about how badly I played at last night's game. How muddled and foggy I felt both on and off the court. How I let my team down in such a big way.

Then I take my two pills for today, wrap them in a tissue and stuff them in my pocket. On the way to school, I drop them into a trash can and am surprised by how easy it is.

I immediately feel better, even though I know that's impossible.

During lunch, we talk about basketball. And girls. And food. No one talks about Vasquez's dad. And Vasquez himself is oddly quiet today, except when he grabs the tangerine from someone's lunch and hurls it at Tim.

"Bull's-eye!" he shouts when it smacks Tim hard on the side of his head.

Tim doesn't even turn and face us.

Dare stands and glares.

And Vasquez? He finally looks happy. Like Tim's head was a substitute for someone else's—someone he could never throw a tangerine at . . . and live to tell about it.

I dump what's left of my lunch and spend the rest of the period in the bathroom. I keep thinking about that tangerine smacking Tim in the head. He didn't do a single thing to deserve it. It's not Tim's fault Vasquez's dad is a jerk.

Between the image in my mind of Tim getting beaned by the tangerine and the gross smell in the bathroom, I feel like I'm going to hurl, but I force myself to wait in there until the bell rings.

I wish I didn't feel so alone. I know I shouldn't, but I wish Phin were here.

During practice, I'm still slower than the other guys and sort of uncoordinated when it comes to shooting. I even accidentally hit the assistant coach in the back with one of my passes. He gives me the stink eye, but doesn't say anything.

It's okay, I remind myself. *I have to hang in there until all the meds are out of my system and I start performing better. Just a little more time with no medication and the other teams won't be able to stop me.*

No one will.

Thankful, Part I

Mom puts a veggie lasagna in the middle of the Thanksgiving table, and we all hold hands.

I'm holding Sarah's hand and Grandmom Ruth's. Her skin is tight and dry.

Mom tells us to say something we are thankful for.

Sarah starts, "I'm thankful for the Knit Wits and the chance to make the world suck less."

Dad clears his throat and nods toward Grandmom Ruth.

"Sorry," Sarah says quietly. "And I'm thankful for my family." She squeezes my hand.

"I'm thankful for my family and friends," I say, giving Dad a special nod because he made sure I got my hormone blockers. "And for all this good food Mom made for us."

"Me too," Dad says. He leans over and kisses Mom's cheek. "And I'm glad Grandmom Ruth could be here with us. Sorry you can't be here, too, Pop." Dad looks up at the ceiling.

Grandmom makes a tight-lipped smile, but when I look at her, the smile disappears. I desperately want to let go of her prune-like hand, but don't.

"That was nice," Mom says. "I'm grateful for my husband, my mother-in-law and my two beautiful daughters."

Grandmom Ruth gasps and drops my hand like a hot potato.

"Let's eat," Mom says.

THANKFUL, PART II

Bubbie, Mom and I sit outside for Thanksgiving dinner, which feels weird because in New Jersey it's way too cold to sit outside, but here it's a really nice day—warm, but not too warm, and the sun's shining.

My health-crazed bubbie actually cooked food that looks and smells delicious.

"It's okay to splurge once in a while," she says, putting a container of European butter on the table.

I pile my plate with turkey, candied yams, string bean casserole and three rolls, slathered with butter. "Mom?"

"Hmm," she says, focusing on cutting her turkey.

So I say it a bit louder: *"MOM!"*

I must say it too loudly because both Mom and Bubbie look at me, startled, like a siren went off or something. But it's a good thing I got their attention because what I have to say is super important, especially at Thanksgiving, when we should be all about family. "I was thinking, maybe we could go visit Dad."

Mom looks like I punched her in the face.

Bubbie tilts her head. "Visit?" Bubbie asks. "Your *dad?*"

"He must be lonely there," I say, taking a big bite of roll.

Mom gasps. Maybe she choked on a piece of turkey. She should put some gravy on it so it's not so dry.

"Isn't that a great idea? When can we go? How about right now?" I leap up, but Mom presses a hand to my wrist and I sit again.

Then Mom says something that really throws me for a loop. I expect her to tell me of course it's a great idea, of course we should visit Dad, especially on Thanksgiving. But what she actually says is this: "Phineas, have you been taking your medicine?"

It's my turn to look like her words punched me in the face. *Phineas?* I turn to see if he's behind me.

"Earth to Norbert," Mom says.

Bubbie reaches over and taps my hand. "Norb?" she says quietly. Her eyes look worried. "Did you hear your mother?"

Did I?

"She asked if you've been taking your medicine, bubela."

Have I? I almost turn to ask the only person who might know.

Mom says something to Bubbie about getting me to the psychiatrist right after the holiday, but her voice sounds far away.

I sit there, staring like a deer in the headlights—my heart going a million miles a minute.

"Sweetheart?"

What's happening?

THE DOCTOR AND THE DECISION

Mom gets me an emergency appointment with the psychiatrist.

He asks if I've been taking my meds, and I show him the nearly empty pill bottles and nod.

"Norbert," he says.

I hate the sound of my name in his mouth, but I know to shut up about it.

"I'm concerned about your behavior. Some of the things you've been saying."

I nod but say nothing, even though I want to talk a million miles a minute and it feels like holding back a roaring ocean.

"I'd like to talk about your father. Is that okay?"

I nod again, even though it most definitely is not okay.

"You understand that he's gone. Right?"

I know exactly where he is. "Yes," I say. "I know he's gone."

"And that he's not coming back."

I nod, hoping a fake tear will squeeze out, but it doesn't. This doctor might have a whole bunch of framed degrees on the wall, but he doesn't know everything. For example, he doesn't know that my dad is somewhere getting better. He's thinking the same stupid thing everyone else is. But they're wrong. They're all wrong.

"Have you had any unusual stress?" he asks. "Maybe at school or with friends?"

I think of Vasquez and the team. I think of Tim and Dare. "Nope," I say, hoping my voice sounds cool, calm. "No unusual stress."

"Okay," he says. "You actually seem pretty good to me. Reasonable. Calm. We'll order another blood test," the doctor says to Mom. "And we'll go from there."

Mom clutches the form to get the blood test like her life depends on it.

And I'm so happy to escape from that office.

It looks like I'll have to take my mood stabilizer for a while. That's the one the blood test will measure. But no one will know if I don't take the other medicine—the antipsychotic. That's the one that slows me down the most anyway. That's the one that keeps me from doing my very best on the court.

BOING! BOING! BOING! BOING! BOING! BOING! BOING!

The following Monday, after school, I sit with Mom at the table and fill her in on what's been going on while she stuffs padded mailers with Bubbie's DVDs. "I got a B on a test and an A on my Language Arts project and finished all my math homework in school and volunteered to help the counselor put up a bulletin board about bullying and I'm hungry and—"

"Norbert," Mom says way too slowly. "You feeling okay? You seem a little amped up. You were terrific at the doctor's office, but—"

"I'm great," I say, which is the truth. I couldn't be better. My head's exploding with ideas, like a million light-bulbs going off with bright flashes. And I've been able to accomplish so much without wasting time on stupid stuff, like sleep. "I made five free throws in a row during practice and a bunch of layups and the guys were patting me on the back and I can't wait for the next game and I'm going to be totally awesome."

"I'll bet you are," Mom says, stirring her coffee in annoying lazy circles. "Sweetheart, you understand how important it is to take both of your medicines every single day. Right?"

Mom looks at me like her eyes are lie detectors or something, but I won't be the fly in her web. I won't fall into her trap. My team needs me. I have to be like this—alive! "Of course I understand," I say, forcing myself to slow my speech, even though it's like holding back a freight train. "Super important," I say in a measured tone. "I totally get it." *But it's not as important as being a great b-ball player for my team so we can win the state championship.* "Don't worry,

Mom." I feel like my eyes are open too wide, my heart beating too fast, my mind whirring like race cars barely able to stay on the track. "No need to worry. I've got it all under control." And I pat the back of her hand to make her feel better.

"Me?" Mom says. "Do I look worried?"

I look at the crease on her forehead. "Yes, you do."

She laughs and comes over to pull me into a tight hug, but it feels like she's trapping me. Suffocating me. I can't wait to break free and get outside to practice, practice, practice, practice, practice, practice, practice.

I feel Mom's eyes follow me as I walk outside. I'll have to be careful because she's really paying attention now. I'll keep taking my mood stabilizer, but I won't go back on those antipsychotics. The doctor and Mom think they're good for me, but they're not. I do much better without them. I'll just have to keep myself in check.

Once out back near the pool, I throw the ball against the wall over a thousand times. Maybe two thousand. I can't actually keep count because a lot of other thoughts are zipping around in my brain, like maybe I'll get a basketball scholarship and end up in the NBA with all kinds of product endorsements and how proud Dad would be. I love the thoughts that are zooming around and wish I could hang on to them longer, but Bubbie comes out. "You have to give it a rest, bubela. It's great that you're practicing so much, but that's it for tonight."

I love the rhythm of the ball hitting the wall, then hitting my hands, faster and faster. I know with each throw, I'm getting better and that will show on the court. *When did it get so dark?*

"Norbert, did you hear me?" Bubbie asks. "You have to stop now. Our neighbor called to complain about the noise."

I want to listen to Bubbie, but it feels so good to keep going.

Boing. Boing. Boing. Boing. Boing. Boing. Boing.

Besides, how much noise can one lousy basketball make? I hate this fancy neighborhood. Where I used to live, a neighbor wouldn't complain about something dumb like that. They'd be glad kids were practicing basketball instead of breaking into cars.

Boing. Boing. Boing. Boi—

Bubbie snatches the basketball from my hands. "Stop!"

I storm inside and take a long shower, hoping it'll relax me. But the spray feels like needles pricking my skin and does nothing to slow my racing thoughts.

In bed, I'm wild awake, thinking and planning and wishing I were still out back throwing the basketball. At least it's a way to use up some of this endless energy. Inside the house, I feel boxed in. Maybe I can do pushups or deep knee bends, like Bubbie does. Or I can practice jumps. Or . . .

Suddenly, I don't have the energy to do any of those things. I lie still, my brain barely containing the thoughts ricocheting around inside my skull.

Finally, I summon the strength to roll onto my stomach and I'm painfully aware of only one thing: the muscles in my arms are screaming in agony.

Maybe I overdid it.

To Whom?

At lunch, Amy has a drama club meeting, so it's just me and Dare at the table.

She taps me on the hand with the edge of her apple Pop-Tart and tilts her head toward the Neanderthals' table.

"Yeah?" I ask, not wanting to look for fear of flying fruit hitting me in the face.

Dare nods and whispers. "Look at Dunkin."

I turn and look. "He's talking," I say. "So what?"

Dare leans forward and says with impeccable grammar, "To whom?"

I look again, paying more attention to what I'm seeing, and realize Dunkin is talking to someone over his left shoulder.

Only there's no one standing over his left shoulder.

"Weird," Dare says. "Right?"

I look again. "Who do you think he's talking to?"

Dare shrugs and takes a huge bite of Pop-Tart.

The guy next to Dunkin shoves him and says something, and then Dunkin faces forward and stops talking to the no one over his left shoulder.

Strange.

Jerk!

Dare, Amy and I have nothing to do after school, so we get dinner from the vending machine and hang around to watch the basketball game.

I kind of want to make sure Dunkin is okay, since he was acting weird at lunch.

He's not.

Right after halftime, he commits an unpardonable sin. He makes a basket for the other team. He must have gotten confused and shot at the same basket he used before the break.

His teammates scream at him. Some throw their hands onto their heads, like they can't believe what they're seeing.

People in the stands yell mean things, like "Loser!" Some laugh. Some boo. Even the adults. Especially the adults.

One man near us screams, "Get him off the court!" The guy looks exactly like an older version of Vasquez, which makes me shudder. Must be his dad. "Coach!" he screams. "Get him off the court! He'll cost us the game."

Coach pulls Dunkin and reams him out on the sidelines. It's painful to watch Dunkin bob from foot to foot as Coach screams at him. And if that's not bad enough, people are still calling out from the stands, ganging up on him. I know how rotten that feels when everyone is against you. *Why can't people leave him alone? It was an accident, a mistake.*

238

"It's no big deal!" I scream, surprising myself. "Leave him alone!"

People in the stands turn and look at me.

Dare and Amy look at me.

Even Coach looks up.

I slink down low, wishing for the ten billionth time that my hair were long enough to hide my face.

At least Coach stops yelling at Dunkin. And when Dunkin glances up, I give him a quick thumbs-up, so he knows at least one person is on his side.

He smiles for the briefest second, and I feel like maybe I've paid Dunkin back for the time he saved me from the Neanderthals at Halloween.

Dare, Amy and I decide to leave before the game is over. I can't wait to get across the gym floor and out of there. Just before I get to the doors, I see Dunkin. He's seated on the sidelines, muttering to himself. That can't be good. I wish there was something I could do to help him, to tell him it will be okay, that it's only a game and not worth the stress.

With my hand on the door, I look back at the bleachers. The cheerleaders are standing by, waiting for an opportunity to shake their pom-poms. The guy who must be Vasquez's dad is laser focused on the game.

I shake my head, open the door and breathe in the air of the empty hallway.

As the three of us walk toward the exit, I think of Dunkin. I'll bet he wishes he could walk out with us, away from the pressures of the game, away from the obnoxious people in the stands.

"Next game's Friday," Dare says as we walk down the hall. "An away game."

"Oh well," Amy says, because we don't go to away games.

"I hope that guy—Vasquez's dad, I guess—doesn't go to the game," I say. "He's a loudmouth jerk."

"Jerk," Dare agrees, shaking her head.

"Jerk," Amy says.

"Jerk," I mumble, but I can't stop thinking about Dunkin, about how strange it is that he's been, well, sort of talking to himself lately. *What's going on with him?*

And we walk out of school into the cool night air.

AN IMPORTANT NIGHT

During the day of our away game, I feel like tonight something important is going to happen. I keep thinking about Dad and feel like it's going to be a hugely meaningful evening. I'm just not sure why.

In school, I can barely sit still. It feels like forever before the game will get here. When the last bell finally rings, I explode from the classroom and meet the guys outside the bus.

"This is going to be amazing!" Vasquez says.

I'm hopping from foot to foot. "Amazing," I say, because it is. *"Amazing!"*

"What are you doing?" Vasquez asks me. "Do you have to take a piss or something?"

240

I stop hopping from foot to foot, but inside my head, I'm hopping, leaping, sprinting!

"You'd better not do anything to screw this game up," Vasquez says, and hits me in the chest with the back of his hand.

"No way," I say. "No way." He has no idea how amazing I'm going to be tonight, but I'll show him.

Some of the other guys give me the stink eye because I scored a basket for the other team in the last game, but I don't care because this is a whole new game. And I'm a whole new me. I feel like Superman, Batman and Spider-Man combined into one incredible person.

"Are we ready for this?" Vasquez asks the guys.

"Ready!" I scream way too loudly.

The guys look at me like I'm crazy, but I know I'm not. I'm terrific!

"Chill out, Dorfman," Vasquez says.

"Sorry. Just excited."

He pats me on the back. "Save it for the game."

The game. I can't wait to get to the game.

I'm Not Moving

I'm scared to death, but I know it's my last chance to save Bob. Nothing else has worked. My words have failed. It's time for action.

A date for Bob's removal was added to the sign—today's date!

So I climb high up into his branches with supplies—a backpack containing four water bottles and an empty one (just in case), two peanut butter and jelly sandwiches, a package of iced blueberry Pop-Tarts, a jacket if it gets chilly, a flashlight and a copy of *The Lorax* to give me strength and remind me why I'm doing this.

My stomach is so nervous. It feels exactly like it did that summer day I put on Mom's red lily of the valley dress and went out front when Dad was unloading groceries from the car.

Like that day, I know what I'm doing now is hard, but important.

That's why I'm sitting in Bob's sturdy branches—terrified, determined—and skipping school, something I've never done.

I don't know what's going to happen, and I wish I weren't here all alone, but I know one thing: like Julia Butterfly Hill, who stayed in a redwood tree for two years to save it, I'm not moving.

I probably should have brought more food. And water.

For some reason, knowing I can't go to the bathroom makes me have to go, but I'll have to hold it. I open *The Lorax* and start reading, but it's hard to concentrate. I wonder when they're going to come with the equipment to cut Bob down and what's going to happen when they see me sitting here. *Will they even see me?*

I'm in the tree for hours. My butt, back and legs are stiff

and sore. The sturdy branches are really hard and uncomfortable, and every ten minutes or so, I have to flick off a fire ant that crawls too close.

I watch people enter and leave the library. I look at the clouds and occasionally see a bird fly past. I wonder what Dare is doing now. Probably hanging out with Amy. They've become inseparable lately, always trying to outdo each other by telling the worst jokes.

Yesterday when the three of us were at the vending machine, Dare said, "Knock, knock."

Amy smiled. "Who's there?"

"Two."

"Two who?"

"To whom!" Dare said, and cracked up.

Amy laughed once.

"Classic grammar nerd joke," I said.

They both looked at me, and I felt like I was intruding on their private moment or something, which is totally dumb. It was just a knock-knock joke.

While I shift my weight, trying to get more comfortable, I wonder what Dunkin's doing. I hope he's stopped talking to himself. If he keeps that up, everyone's going to make fun of him, especially the Neanderthals, even if he is on the team.

I shift again. It's impossible to get comfortable up here, but I'm not coming down until the city promises to leave Bob alone.

I wonder how Julia Butterfly Hill felt when she lived in her redwood. She was probably scared. Not only did she have to worry about loggers, she had to deal with all kinds of weather and wind because she was really high up. She stayed up there through two years' worth of nighttimes. How terrifying. She must have really loved that tree.

I pat Bob and read *The Lorax* to him. If someone saw me, they'd probably think I was talking to myself. And they'd also think I'm crazy, because I am sitting in a tree when I'm supposed to be in school. "Don't worry," I tell Bob, putting the book in my backpack and grabbing a Pop-Tart. "I'm right where I'm supposed to be. I won't let them hurt you."

I've just taken my first delicious bite of the blueberry Pop-Tart when a big orange truck pulls up.

I shove the Pop-Tart into my backpack and inhale deeply. "This is it," I tell Bob. "Hang on. Okay?"

He doesn't answer, not even a slight rustling of his leaves. The only sound I hear is the wild thrumming of my heartbeat. But I know somewhere deep in his roots, Bob senses what's going on and is probably panicked.

Three guys, all wearing orange hard hats, get out of the truck.

One of the guys is on the phone. The other two are getting things from the back of the truck. I shouldn't be surprised they don't notice me. Apparently, people even forget to look up into the tree they're planning to cut down.

I wonder if I should say something to let them know I'm here.

The guy on the phone finally looks up.

"Oh shit," he says into the phone. "I'll call you back."

He puts the phone away and squints up at me. "You gotta get outta that tree, kid. We're cutting it down."

"No, you're not," I say in a small but determined voice.

"What?" He cups a hand around his ear.

"You are not cutting this tree down." I almost say *Bob* but catch myself, because I don't want the guy to think I'm a weirdo.

He removes his hard hat and runs his hand through his hair, which reminds me so much of Dad. *Dad.* He'll probably kill me for doing this.

"Oh, come on!" the guy says. "Are you serious? Shouldn't you be in school? Is it a day off or something?"

The other two guys stand beside him. All three look up at me.

I'm really glad I climbed higher than I usually do. I wouldn't want them reaching up and grabbing for my foot or something. "I'm not moving!" I yell down, glad my voice isn't trembling, even though I am.

"Terrific," the first guy says, and the three of them go over to the truck to talk. Even though I strain, I can't hear what they're saying.

One of the guys comes back. "You'd better come down now. We don't want you to get hurt."

"I won't get hurt." I wonder if I should stop talking to them. *Did Julia Butterfly Hill stop talking to the people who wanted her out of the tree?*

"You have to come down," the guy says in a serious voice.

He seems like a nice guy. I'm sorry to do this to him, to ruin his workday, but saving Bob is more important than that. "I can't come down."

"Why not?" he asks. "Do you need help to get down?"

"I can't," I say, gritting my teeth, "because I'm not letting you cut down my tree!"

The guy reels back. "What's that supposed to mean? You don't own this tree. The city does." He waves his hand dismissively and stalks away.

That's when I decide to stop talking to them.

The guy who was on the phone at first comes over again. "Well, you have about five minutes to climb down before the police get here."

I hunker down, even though my back and legs are so sore. *Not moving.*

Hang On

By the time a police car pulls up, my body is as tense and rigid as Bob's branches.

At least it's only one police car. I had imagined a bunch of cars squealing up, lights flashing, sirens blaring. Still, I'm scared. I don't want to get taken to jail. Or shot at! I probably should have asked Mom or Sarah for help, but I wanted to do this on my own. *Don't cry,* I tell myself. *And don't climb down, no matter what they say!*

A female officer gets out of the car and talks to me through a bullhorn, which is totally dumb because I'm not that far away. I almost say so, but remember I'm not going to talk to anyone.

"Come out of the tree, little boy," the officer says through her way-too-loud bullhorn.

I feel my cheeks flame. *I'm not little. And I'm definitely not a boy, even though today I happen to be dressed like one—much easier for tree climbing!*

"What's your name?" the officer asks through the unnecessary bullhorn.

Which one?

It doesn't matter because I say nothing.

"Tell me your parents' phone number so I can call them," the officer says. "You won't get in trouble, but I need to let them know where you are."

I definitely don't answer.

"Little boy," the officer says through the bullhorn. "Come down now or we will have to call the fire department and have you removed. These men have a work order from the city to clear this land. We do not want you to get hurt."

I squeeze my backpack so hard my fingers bleed white, but I say nothing. Bob's a part of nature. How can the city own him? How can anyone own nature? If people stood up for trees, we wouldn't have such a big problem with pollution and melting polar ice caps and vanishing species of animals. Trees are the planet's lungs, taking in dirty air and releasing clean air. Everyone who's fond of breathing should protect them.

"If I have to call the fire department," the officer says, "your parents will be charged for them to remove you."

I swallow hard and wonder how much it costs to call the fire department. I thought it was free. Don't taxes pay for the fire department . . . and schools . . . and the library? I almost yell down, *Liar!* because I realize the officer is trying to trick me.

"It's going to cost your parents hundreds of dollars if the firemen have to remove you from the tree," she says through the bullhorn. "Maybe more. So come down now."

I think about how hard it must be for them to pay for my hormone blockers every month and don't want them to have any extra expenses because of me. But I'm not coming down.

A few people stop and look up. Maybe if people looked up more often, they would have realized how majestic Bob is and that he shouldn't be cut down to build some stupid playground. I wish the onlookers would leave, though. It's embarrassing enough to be up here without everyone staring at me.

But then I realize lots of people are exactly what I want. If enough people gather around and see what's going on, maybe they'll stop Bob from being cut down. Perhaps they'll be the difference that keeps Bob standing. Now I'm glad people are pointing at me and talking to each other.

I wave at them. Maybe someone will call the news station. Maybe—

"Move along," the officer says through the bullhorn as she shuffles people away. "Nothing to see here. Keep moving."

And they do. *Chickens!*

While the officer is shooing people away, one of the hard-hat guys comes back beneath the tree and looks up at me.

We lock eyes.

"Just come down," he says. No bullhorn. No bull. "Please. Come down."

I shake my head no, and he looks sad, like I disappointed him. And I feel like I have disappointed him, by doing what feels right.

This morning, I thought trying to save Bob would feel heroic, like I'm doing something important and good for the world like Sarah's Knit Wits Club, but instead, it feels like I'm being a pain in the butt to all these people.

For the first time, I wonder if I should climb down. It would be so much easier. I could go to the bathroom. I could shake out the pins and needles from my legs and butt. I could get something good to eat.

A warm wind whips through the branches, and I hang on tight. Bob's leaves make a rustling sound, like he's talking to me. *Hang on,* the leaves say. *Hang on to me.*

I remember all the times Bob provided me a safe haven. I think of how happy and relaxed I've always felt in his branches. How I named him to honor Grandpop Bob. I think of other kids who might need a place to go when they're having a hard time, or need a little shade or something beautiful to look at. I think of how defenseless trees are. And how good they are.

Someone needs to be brave for them.

I won't climb down.

Even when the fire truck pulls up.

SIT STILL

I'm one hundred percent alert and focused while sitting on the sidelines of the game. I'm ready to go in and make big plays. I'm prepared to sink shot after shot under the basket. No mistakes. No excuses. Pure awesomeness!

Even though the game's going on, I pop out of my seat, pace a few times in front of the other guys on the bench, then return to my seat. Pop up, pace, return. The third time I do this, Coach grabs my arm and forces me into a chair. "Knock it off, Dorfman! I'm trying to coach a game here!"

It's impossible to stay in my seat, though. How do the other players do it? Aren't they keyed up, too? My knee bounces like a jackhammer. I remember Dad's leg used to do that sometimes. His leg used to do that when he was . . . *PUT ME IN ALREADY, COACH!*

He doesn't. Not once the entire game.

By the time we're back on the bus heading home, I don't think I'll be able to sit still a second longer. I get up, walk the aisle, then return to my seat. "I'm okay," I say. "I'm okay." I do this repeatedly, thinking I'll explode if this bus doesn't stop soon and let me off.

"Dorfman!" Coach screams. "What the hell's with you tonight?"

"Yeah!" Vasquez yells. "You're getting on my nerves. Sit down already!"

"And *shut up*," Bobby Birch says.

Everyone laughs.

I sit, the echoes of their laughter rolling over me in waves. I stare out the window into the endless night. And I try desperately to keep myself from exploding.

And the Score Is . . .

I wish I could hear what the firefighter and the officer are saying to each other.

The guys from the tree-cutting company have made themselves comfortable on the lawn, under the shade of Bob. *See?* I want to tell them. *Doesn't Bob make this the best spot in Beckford Palms?*

I'm about to pull out the Pop-Tart I had started earlier—I'm hungry!—when the firefighter walks over. He looks up. He scratches his head. "You coming down?"

I shake my head no.

"Your parents know you're up here?"

I nod my head yes, even though it's a lie. This morning, I pretended I was leaving for school, but came here instead. The only one who knows is Dare . . . and probably, by now, Amy. I didn't even tell Sarah.

The firefighter goes back to the police officer and says loudly, "I'm not pulling a kid out of a tree. If something were to happen, then—"

"What?" the police officer shrieks.

I knew she didn't need that bullhorn.

The firefighter moves closer and says something too quietly for me to hear.

"You've got to be kidding me." The police officer steps back and crosses her arms. "Well, what am I supposed to do? Shoot him?"

My eyes go wide.

The firefighter throws up his arms, like there's nothing he can do.

The police officer shakes her head, like she's pissed.

And the firefighter gets in his truck and leaves. *Guess my parents won't be charged for that after all!*

I'm so excited I can hardly sit still in Bob's branches, because I realize I won the first battle of this war.

Score: Lily (representing Bob)—1, Beckford Palms's Finest—0.

"I thought I'd find you here," Sarah says, looking up at me. "You okay?"

I nod, but tears prick at the corners of my eyes because I feel decidedly less okay than I did after the firefighter drove away. That was a couple hours ago. Now I desperately need to pee, but don't want to do it in a bottle in front of the police officer and the tree cutters and the people who have stopped to stare. I'm super hungry and all I have left are Pop-Tarts. I never thought it could happen, but I'm officially sick of Pop-Tarts. I'm also sick of sitting here. My legs keep getting pins and needles, no matter how much I shake them out, and the rest of me feels like one giant ache. And I'm especially sick of these people who are standing here but doing nothing to help.

The sun is starting to go down, and it's getting chilly.

"Can you get me something to eat?" I ask, my voice scratchy from not using it.

The police officer walks closer to Sarah, like she's a shark who smells blood. I can tell she'd stop Sarah from passing anything up to me. I should pee in the empty bottle and drop it on her head.

Sarah looks at the officer, then at me, then at the officer. She bites her thumbnail. "I'm calling Mom."

Panic rises in my throat, but I realize I could use reinforcements. "Go ahead," I say.

When Mom's car pulls up, a wave of relief that I hadn't expected washes over me. Now it won't be me against the police officer and tree cutters. Mom will tell them what's what. She'll send up food and anything else I need. She'll take care of everything.

Mom gets out of her car and marches over.

I can't wait to see her give it to the police officer.

"Lily McGrother!" she screams up at me. "Get out of that tree."

Mom's words are a punch in the gut.

"I mean it," Mom says, hands on her hips.

Where did my yoga-breathing, peaceful-poses mom go?

Sorry, Sarah mouths, but I know it's not her fault. Mom would have figured out where I was eventually.

"And when we get home, you're grounded for skipping school today."

A couple of the tree guys laugh, and I want to disappear like the saltshaker from Dunkin's magic trick. Even the police officer smiles. I'll bet she's loving this. She probably thinks I'm going to slide right down out of the tree and make her job easy.

Well, I'm not.

"Mom," I say as quietly as I can, feeling my cheeks flame fifteen shades of red. "They're going to cut the tree down."

It's like a spell is broken. Mom finally stops looking at me with her laser-beam eyeballs and glances around at the workers, the police officer, Sarah, the onlookers.

Then she focuses on me again. "And this involves you how?"

"They're going to cut this tree down today. Right now." I want to say: *The tree we had our picnics under,* but instead I say, "Remember? I told you about it. I wrote a letter, but it didn't work. I put up a sign, but it didn't work. So now I'm sitting here." I wish she understood how important this was. "The only thing standing between this tree and their chain saws"—I point to the three hard-hatted guys—"is me."

"Well, that's very noble of you, Lily."

I'm glad she uses my real name.

Mom looks at the police officer. "But I think it's time for you to come down now."

I let out a breath and say, "If I come down, the tree comes down, too."

Mom holds up a finger, then walks over to talk to the workers and the officer.

While she's talking with them, I try to get my wild heartbeat to slow. I thought Mom would be with me, not against me. How am I supposed to fight the whole world by myself?

Sarah cups her hands around her mouth. "Hey, you okay up there?"

I don't answer because I'm really choked up. Mom shouldn't have yelled at me like that, especially in front of everyone.

"I think what you're doing is awesome!" Sarah screams.

"Me too!" a guy standing nearby says.

"Yeah," a young woman says, waving her fist. "Stick it to the man."

I have no idea what that means, but it makes me smile. Maybe I'm not entirely alone, even if Mom isn't on my side. I have all kinds of renewed respect for Julia Butterfly Hill for doing this for two years. I'm finding it difficult to do this for one day. I know I'll have to come down sometime. Even though today's only Friday, eventually Monday will arrive, and I can't miss another day of school. I can't stay up here forever.

"Honey," Mom says, her voice softer. "I appreciate what you're trying to do here. I really do. But it's too late. They have orders from the city."

"I'm not coming down!"

"Then I'm coming up."

The police officer and the workers look as shocked as I feel when Mom climbs up Bob's trunk. Sarah has a stunned look on her face, too. Apparently, Mom's years of yoga have made her ridiculously strong. And agile.

"Oh, terrific," the officer says. "Now I've got two loonies up there."

"I can't stand her," I whisper to Mom when she settles near me.

"Yeah," Mom answers. "I can see why."

We're quiet as Mom gets her bearings.

"It's nice up here," she finally says.

"Right?"

Mom wobbles.

I reach for her.

She steadies herself and nods. "You know you can't stay up here forever."

"I know," I say, surveying the crowd.

"And you really shouldn't have skipped school. They called me, and I didn't know where you were and—"

"I'm sorry," I say. "I should have told you. I didn't mean to make you worry."

"I know." Mom reaches out and touches the back of my hand. "I think you're the bravest person I know."

"Thanks."

"Seriously, Lily. You're an amazing, strong and wonderful human. The world is lucky to have you."

While Mom's saying these astonishing things to me, the three tree cutters leave.

"Mom, look."

She grabs onto a branch and peers down. "Wow. That's a good sign."

"Don't get too excited," the officer calls up. "They'll be back first thing in the morning. They have to clock out at a certain time today."

My stomach drops. *They're coming back tomorrow. I can't stay here all night!* "Mom." A few tears leak out. "What am I supposed to do?"

Mom looks up at the late afternoon light filtering through Bob's leafy branches, then into my eyes. "Lily, what do you want to do?"

I take a shaky breath and pat my tree. "I want to save Bob. But they're coming back tomorrow." I lean back, defeated. "Guess there's no winning this war."

Mom tilts her head. "Are you giving up, then?"

Am I?

Thanks, Dad

"By the way," the officer calls up to Mom and me through her bullhorn, "I've been in touch with the mayor's office. This tree is coming down first thing tomorrow. No matter what." She takes a few steps toward her car, then turns back. "And I hope for your sakes you're not still here when that happens."

When the officer drives off, Mom looks at me. "Lily," she says. "I'm going to let you stay up here. All night if you want, because it looks like it will be your last time in Bob. But I'm going to be here at the base of this tree the entire time. You'd better be incredibly careful." She takes a deep breath. "And you've got to climb down in the morning before the guys start cutting."

I don't tell Mom I have no intention of climbing down in the morning. But I'm glad she's okay with me being up here tonight. And that I won't be alone.

Carefully, slowly, I lean forward and manage to give her an awkward hug.

Mom hugs me and pats my back. It feels so good.

"Anything you need help with before I climb down?" I whisper to Mom.

And since it's getting dark and the last of the onlookers left when the police officer did, Mom helps me pee in the bottle. It's disgusting, but I realize that for once in my life, I'm glad I have male anatomy.

Mom takes the bottle down with her to "dispose" of it.

I use water from one of my drinking bottles to wash my hands.

I sure hope Bob appreciates all I'm doing for him.

Mom gets me a sandwich from Publix and some fresh fruit and brings it up to me.

Afterward, she and Sarah set up lawn chairs and sit at the base of Bob, eating the food Mom bought for them.

It's like we're having a picnic together, except they're down there and I'm up in a tree. And it's dark, except for the glow from the streetlight.

Normal people don't have picnics in the dark.

But who wants to be normal?

Dad arrives, and Mom hands him a sandwich and a banana.

"Tim!" he calls up in a voice that makes my breath catch.

"Hey, Dad." I expect he'll tell me to come down, and I have a feeling that if he does, my resolve will melt like an ice cube on a sweltering sidewalk.

My butt and back are incredibly sore. Gnats fly near my eyes. I have fire ant bites on my arms and legs. I'm exhausted and achy. If Dad insists, I have a feeling I'll be down in a heartbeat, with the rest of my family.

And I will hate myself for it.

"I don't like this," Dad calls up. "I wish there were another way." He clears his throat. "But I'm proud of you for standing up for something that doesn't have a voice to stand up for itself."

Dad's words surprise me. They warm me. They remind me of the dad I know and love. Remind me of what I'm sure Grandpop Bob would have said. "Thanks" is all I can manage.

My eyes have adjusted to the dark, and the nearby streetlight allows me to see Dad nod, then join Mom and Sarah for dinner. He paces while he eats.

"Bob," I whisper in my quietest voice. "I have the best family."

He rustles his leaves to tell me he knows. And maybe to say thank you.

I look at my family, eating and laughing below me. Then I pull my jacket from my backpack and settle in for what will probably be a very long night.

At least I don't have to pee anymore.

RUN, NORBERT. RUN!

When the bus pulls into the lot at school, it feels like my teammates are moving in slow motion to make their way off—purposely—to annoy me. I want to push past them, but force myself to wait.

Finally, FINALLY, I'm free in the breezy December air. Tim was right about it getting cooler after November fifteenth. I thought I'd never survive the heat and then, like a switch was flipped, it cooled off. Not New Jersey cold, but enough to keep me from sweating to death.

Mom waves from where she's leaning on our car, and I jog over. It feels good to be moving. To be in forward motion.

"How'd you do?" Mom asks. "Sorry I couldn't make it to the game."

"Didn't play," I say, shifting from foot to foot. "Not even one minute. Warmed the bench the whole game."

"Again?" Mom asks, glaring toward Coach, who is standing near the bus.

"It's okay," I say, even though it isn't. "Team won."

"That's good, I guess," Mom says. "Hey, let's get home. Bubbie's baked some blueberry flaxseed muffins for us."

"As awesome as that sounds, I need to move."

"Huh? I drove over here to pick you up." Mom's looking at me in *that way* again. Really staring into my eyes. "Don't be mad at me, but I went in your room today and checked your medicine bottles."

I am mad. Incredibly mad. My-head's-going-to-shoot-off-my-neck mad. "I'm not mad," I say, trying to stand still. It's impossible. I jog in place a little.

"It appears you're taking your pills," Mom says. "The bottles are nearly empty." She reaches up and puts her fingertips on my shoulders so I can't keep jogging. "But are you?" she asks.

People mill around us in the parking lot.

I wrap my antipsychotic pill in a tissue every single day and dump it in a trash can. "Absolutely," I say, pulling back from her and jogging in place again.

"Because it seems like you're not taking them, Norbert. It seems like you're not doing so great. Do I have to start watching you take them again, like we did in New Jersey?"

"No! I'm fine!"

"Honey—"

"Mom, I'm absolutely, one hundred percent, terrific, fine, great and wonderful. I need to move. That's all. I was cramped on the bus and now I need to move." In truth, I want to burst out running like an Olympic athlete after the starting pistol, but I force myself to jog in place a few seconds longer. *Act normal. Hold it together, Norbert.*

Run, Norbert. Run!

I look over my left shoulder.

"Norbert," Mom says, "you're not acting—"

Run, Norbert. Run!

"See you at home, Mom." I throw my sports bag and backpack on the trunk of the car and take off.

As I'm running, I expect Mom to pull alongside me and make me get into the car, but she must have gone back home. I'm alone and it feels so good to move fast—to make my body match the energy inside my mind.

I feel like I could run all the way back to New Jersey—twelve hundred miles—and I bet I could, too, but Dunkin' Donuts seems like a more practical destination.

So that's where I head.

UP A TREE

I'm slurping down my large iced coffee and carrying a bag with four Boston Kreme doughnuts. I wish Dad were here to help me eat them. *Dad.*

I'm near the tree Tim calls Bob and trying unsuccessfully not to think about Dad when I see something so strange that I blink several times to make sure I'm not hallucinating.

Three people are sitting in lawn chairs under Bob, like they're having a picnic or something, except it's nighttime. The man has a flashlight on, so I can see his face. I've seen him before. But where?

I clutch my bag of doughnuts more tightly and figure I'll motor past the weird picnickers and head back to Bubbie's house.

"Hey, Tim!" the man yells into the tree.

I realize he's calling to someone who's sitting in the tree. *Tim?*

"I'm heading home to take care of Meatball. You need anything?"

"I'm good, Dad. Thanks."

That's when I see him—Tim!—sitting way up in the branches of Bob. At night. *Maybe Mom was right. Maybe I should be taking my meds after all.*

Even though I'm still a ball of energy, I stop moving. My breath comes in short gasps. "Tim?" I call. I don't know why I do it. I should have kept going.

Four people look at me—three from the ground and one from the tree.

"Dunkin?" Tim asks. "What are you doing here?"

It's like Earth stops spinning. *This* must be the important thing I was meant to do tonight. I can feel it in every molecule in my body. I walk closer to the tree and to the people who I guess are Tim's family. "Hi, I'm Nor—" Then I stop myself. "Dunkin," I say. "Tim's friend from school." And I know that's right. I am Tim's friend, even though I should have been a whole lot nicer to him. Sat with him in the lunchroom. Given him a Pop-Tart once in a while. Something.

Everything is becoming clear now.

"Hi, Dunkin," they say, and his dad shakes my hand.

"Well, I've gotta go," Tim's dad says. "Be careful up there. Don't fall out."

"I won't," Tim says.

Why is he sitting in the tree?

"Climb up and join me," Tim calls to me.

"Can't," I say, not even thinking about it. I feel like running again. Every cell in my body is pushing me to move, move, move.

"Oh." Tim sounds disappointed.

Outside of helping him at Halloween, I haven't been much of a friend. But I could be one now. As a way of thanking him for sticking up for me during the game, when everyone else was yelling at me for scoring a basket for the wrong team and for all the mean things Vasquez and the guys have done, all the fruit lobbed at his head. All the insults.

This was the important thing. Be a friend to Tim.

"Okay," I say, despite my fear of heights. "Here I come."

I throw my empty coffee cup into a nearby trash can, grip my bag of doughnuts, reach up for a branch and . . . falter.

"Go around the other side," Tim says. "There are more things to grab on to."

Tim's right. The twisty trunk on the other side is loaded with places to hold on to, so I climb.

The moment my feet leave the ground, I tremble. *I can't do this.* Even though I'm only a few inches off the ground—I'm paralyzed—and my body feels like it's made from lead.

"You can do it, Dunkin," Tim says.

Can I?

Of course you can.

I look over my left shoulder to see who said that. My heart thumps wildly.

No one's there. But it feels like someone is. Someone very familiar. The same someone who had whispered a few things to me in the lunchroom the other day, then disappeared.

"You don't have to," Tim says. "If you're too nervous."

I look up. It's not that far. And Tim's up there, waiting.

So I climb.

ONE QUESTION

It's not until I'm on the branch across from Tim that the fear settles in. It courses through my veins like ice water. My legs go weak and my heart jackhammers so hard my ears ring.

"Dunkin?" Tim whispers.

I can't answer.

"You okay? Do you want me to call down for my mom or something?"

"No."

I want to ask Tim what's going on, why we're up in a tree at night. I have a million questions spinning around my brain, but fear keeps my mouth sealed.

"I can't believe you climbed up here with me." He reaches out and touches the back of my hand. "You're crazy, but thanks."

I want to shrug to show him it's no big deal, but I can't move.

We're quiet. Then I finally look at Tim and ask, "So, why are we here?"

Tim lets out a huge breath. "Today's the day the city had scheduled to cut down Bob."

"Oh no." I realize this really is a big thing, and now I'm part of it.

"But they didn't," Tim says. "They didn't because I was sitting up here."

"That might be the coolest thing ever," I say. "Does this means we're protesting?"

"I guess we are."

"Cool."

"Yeah, it is pretty cool." Tim nods, then slaps at something on his arm. "Bite number nine or ten. I've lost count."

I don't want to know what kind of bite and I don't want to think about what might be crawling around on this tree with us, so I pull out my phone and let Mom know where I am. Except I don't tell her I'm in a tree. That would totally freak her out, especially with how worried she's been about me lately. I just say that I'm with a friend. Mom says to be quiet when I come in because she's going to bed. She has a migraine.

Perfect.

Tim gives me a Pop-Tart from his backpack, and I give him a Boston Kreme doughnut from my bag. As we're munching on our treats and Tim's sister is singing softly below, I realize that besides first getting on the basketball team, this is the most fun I've had since moving to Beckford Palms. A picnic in a tree. At night! Phineas would love this. I wish my brain were calmer, though, because it's racing at such wild speeds, I feel like the rest of me is going to jerk, and I'll fall out of the tree.

If that happens, all the king's horses and all the king's men wouldn't be able to put Dunkin together again.

"Lily," Tim's mom says. "I'm running home to get me and Sarah sleeping bags. Need anything?"

Tim looks at me and tilts his head.

"I'm good," I say.

"We're good!" Tim yells down.

"Okay. Be right back, then."

Tim's mom drives away, but his sister stays. Below us, she's curled in a chair, reading a book with a flashlight. I don't know her at all, but there's something about her I like already.

"Hey," I say to Tim. "Maybe you should get a job working in a tree."

"Huh? I don't think there is such a thing."

"Then you could be a branch manager," I say. "Get it? Branch manager."

Tim shakes his head. "Oh, I get it. Unfortunately."

But I can tell he's smiling. Jokes are not my best thing. I wish I could do a magic trick for Tim, but it's too dark. "Wouldn't it be cool," I say, "if we could live up here?"

"We might have to if we want to save Bob," he says.

"My butt's already sore," I say. "How long have you been up here?"

"My butt's so sore it's numb," Tim says. "I've been up here the whole day."

"No way!" I say too loudly.

Tim nods.

Then I whisper, "You cut school?"

"Had to."

"That's awesome," I say. But what I really want to do is ask Tim a question that I haven't been able to get out of my head. Instead I ask another question. "Didn't you need to . . . pee or anything?"

"Nah," he says. "I've got a bladder of steel."

I nod, but don't believe him. If I go the whole school day without peeing—which I sometimes do because the school bathrooms are disgusting—by the time I get home, my bladder's about to burst. But that's not what I really want to know. There's a niggling question that's been knocking on the inside of my skull, demanding to be let out and answered.

So I ask.

"Why did your mom call you Lily?"

I Am a Girl

I think I'll die of embarrassment when Dunkin asks me about needing to pee. I can't believe when the lie rolls so easily off my tongue, but I don't think he believes me. I mean, who has a bladder of steel? Maybe Superman, but not a mere mortal. I should have told him the truth—I peed in a bottle. Big deal.

But Dunkin's asking about peeing is nothing—*NOTHING!*—compared to the heat I feel in my cheeks when he asks *the* question. I'm glad Mom respects me enough to call me Lily, but why did she have to do it at that moment in front of Dunkin?

I look at Dunkin, who climbed up this tree to be here with me. He shared his doughnuts with me, too. I could lie and keep lying. Sometimes I feel like that's all I do.

"Dunkin?"

"Yeah? I'd lean closer, but I'm scared of falling."

"You don't have to lean closer," I say.

"It was just a mistake when your mom called you Lily. Right? A weird mistake."

Ouch. Am I a weird mistake?

I wish I could stay in this tree forever, but I know someday I'll have to climb down. Someday I'll have to go back to school. And someday, I'll have to face Vasquez and the Neanderthals. It will be infinitely harder to do that if Dunkin repeats a single thing I'm about to tell him.

I take so long to answer that Dunkin says, "Don't worry. You don't have to tell me. I'm sure it's a thing between you two. None of my business."

The way he says this is so sweet that something inside

me cracks. "Dunkin," I say, loud enough for only him to hear. "You climbed up here with me. You trusted me, even though I could tell you were scared. Of course I'm going to tell you." *You're my friend.* "Remember the first day I saw you?"

"Yes."

Stars twinkle above, through Bob's big, leafy branches, and a cool breeze rustles. The air smells clean, with a slight hint of salt from the ocean. And Dunkin and I are sitting in this magnificent tree to save its life.

"Remember I was wearing a dress?"

"Yes," he says. "You said your sister dared you."

I look down at Sarah, slumped in the folding chair. She's so amazing. I can't believe she's here, supporting me. Just looking at her gives me the courage to continue. "That's my sister, Sarah," I tell Dunkin. "She didn't dare me." I wait for a response to my admission, but Dunkin's quiet. If he had said one word, I might not have gone on, but his silence is allowing me the space to keep going. "I wore the dress because I wanted to."

In my head, the words come out like cymbals crashing at the grand finale of an orchestra. But in reality, my words are whispered, barely able to be carried on the cool wind.

"But why . . ." Dunkin doesn't finish his sentence. I'm sure his face is a picture of confusion, but it's hard to see it clearly in the dark. I'm glad for the dark, though. Without it, I wouldn't have the guts to keep talking.

"I look like a boy. I have boy parts." I can't believe I said that. "But I feel like a girl. I always have." I let out a breath. "Does this make any sense?" I wonder how it could make sense to someone who was born into the body that matches who they are.

Part of me knows Sarah and Dare would be proud of me for speaking the truth, but another part is terrified of what the truth might set into motion for me. That part wishes I could take every word I just said and stuff it back into my mouth, especially since Dunkin is silent.

"Are you okay?" I ask, which is a stupid thing to say.

"I, um . . ." He runs a hand through his curly hair. "It's just that . . ."

"It's okay," I say, feeling like it's anything but okay. I'm sure he'll laugh about this with Vasquez and Birch and the other Neanderthals in school on Monday. I don't know why I thought I could trust Dunkin. Even my dad is having a hard time with me being me. How did I expect this new boy would understand? *Stupid!*

Dunkin's words come like gifts from the darkness. "It's just that I never met anyone before who was transgender," he says. "Or at least I don't think I have."

I can't believe Dunkin named it. "Well, that's what I am," I say. "Transgender." I'll have a lot to talk to Dr. Klemme about on my next visit.

Dunkin's foot is tap, tap, tapping a million miles a minute, while the rest of him is still as a petrified tree.

I thought this would take longer to explain, be more complicated. But there's really not much more to it than what I said. "Do you, um, have any questions?"

"Nope," Dunkin says. "Well, I do have one question."

Uh-oh! My throat goes dry, and I can barely scratch out the word: "Yes?"

"Do you have any more Pop-Tarts?"

"Pop-Tarts?"

"Yeah," he says. "I'm totally starving."

Ready

When I wake, it's light out, and I can't believe I fell asleep in a tree. Every part of me is stiff and sore and numb. I have to pee worse than yesterday. Across from me, Dunkin is awake, his eyelids open wide.

"Hi," I say, running my tongue along my teeth, which feel thick like fur and taste disgusting. *Why didn't I think of tossing a tube of toothpaste in my backpack?*

Dunkin raises his eyebrows. "Hey."

I melt. Why didn't I realize how cute he is before? Maybe he didn't look so cute standing near Vasquez and the Neanderthals. But here, in Bob, he's adorable.

"I can't believe I stayed up here all night."

I blink a few times. "Me too!"

"We did it," Dunkin says.

"Yeah," I say, patting Bob's bark. "I guess we did." I peek

down below. Mom and Sarah are still asleep in their chairs. Dad's not there. I'm sure he came during the night to check on us, but probably had to get to the shop early to make some mistakes on a few T-shirt orders.

Yesterday comes back to me in unpleasant waves. The nasty police officer. The firefighter who refused to pull me down. The workers who were here to cut down the tree. Mom. Dad. Sarah. And the miracle of Dunkin climbing up here with me, even though he looked terrified to do so— that's something only a friend would do. I recall the things I shared with Dunkin last night in the dark. Things so few people know about me.

"Dunkin?" I whisper.

"Yeah?"

"You can never, ever tell anyone what I told you last night. I'm not ready."

He tilts his head.

"About me being a girl."

"Oh," he says. "Are you sure?"

I reel back. "Am I sure you shouldn't tell anyone or am I sure I'm a girl?"

Dunkin shakes his head. "Never mind. Stupid question. I didn't sleep much." He glances over his shoulder. "Or the night before that, or . . . My brain's going haywire. But, don't worry. I won't tell anyone. It's just that . . ."

"What?" I ask, a little annoyed. Plus I have to pee so much it hurts.

"What do you want me to call you?"

"Wow."

"'Wow'? That's a dumb name."

We both crack up.

"Dunkin, that might be the nicest thing anyone has ever asked me."

He shrugs, like it's no big deal, but it totally *is* a big deal. That one little question is so respectful and thoughtful, Dunkin has no idea how much this means to me. I had a feeling Dunkin would make a great friend. "You can call me Tim," I say. "For now. I'll let you know when that changes."

"Okay."

"And Dunkin?"

"Yeah?"

"Thanks again for asking. That was really cool."

He shrugs again.

"Hey, won't your mom and dad be worried about where you are?"

"Oh crap." The color drains from Dunkin's face. "My mom will flip if she gets up and I'm not there. But she had a migraine last night, which usually means she sleeps late." Dunkin looks at me. "And I, um, don't have a dad right now."

Do I say I'm sorry? Do I ask a question? I bite my thumbnail.

"I mean he's somewhere else. He's—"

"Rise and shine!" It's the police officer, talking through her stupid bullhorn.

Mom and Sarah startle awake and scramble out of their sleeping bags.

"Oh jeez, there's two of them up there again now," the officer says, not through the megaphone, but I hear her loud and clear.

Mom stands beside the officer, cups her hands around her mouth and asks, "You two okay up there?"

Dunkin nods, so I answer, "We're great."

"Still here?" the officer says to my mom.

"Yup," Mom answers, folding her sleeping bag. "Still here."

"Not for long," the officer says. "The mayor's coming."

"Well, whoop-di-do," Mom says.

Sarah laughs.

Go, Mom!

I make sure everything's in my backpack and whisper to Dunkin, "I hate to say this, but we'll probably have to climb down soon."

"Lily," he whispers, like he's trying it on for size. "This was the most fun I've had in a really long time."

I can't help but smile. "I guess it was kind of fun. But you don't have to call me Lily. Yet."

"Sorry," Dunkin says.

"Totally okay."

Dad pulls up in his car, gets out and walks to the base of the tree. "How are you?"

"Fine, Dad. We're fine," I say. "Did you hear? The mayor's coming."

Dad runs a hand through his wiry, red hair. "Of course she is."

The tree-cutting guys return. It's the same three from yesterday.

"Holy mackerel," one guy says. "There's two kids up there now."

I see one of the workers smile, but he covers his mouth with his hand.

When Mayor Higginbotham arrives, she plants her hands on her hips and takes in the situation. Then she approaches Bob. "Did one of you write me a letter?"

"Yes," I say, my voice catching because my throat is so dry. "I did."

"Well, you must really love this tree to go to all this trouble." She doesn't say it in a mean way.

"Bob's worth loving that much," I call down.

"Who?" The mayor looks around.

"The tree," Dunkin says. "This tree is worth the trouble."

"Oh." The mayor shields her eyes and says, "Well, I came here personally to tell you how much I admire your persistence and dedication."

I bite my lip because I know what she's going to say next.

"But there's nothing that can be done at this point." She pauses. "I'm sorry."

I don't believe there's nothing that can be done. They could build the playground somewhere else or build it around Bob. Or not build it at all. But I don't say those things because I know their minds are set. Also, I have to pee so badly it feels like my bladder will rupture, and there's no way I'm peeing in front of anyone, especially Dunkin. Besides, every part of my body hurts. And I'm starving.

I want to eat a big breakfast, brush the fur off my teeth, take a hot shower and climb into my soft bed under the ugly brown comforter and sleep for, oh, the entire rest of the weekend.

There's a long pause, where everyone is looking up at us.

"Are you ready to come down now?" the mayor asks gently.

I look at Mom. At Sarah. At Dad. There's so much love in their faces. Then I look at Dunkin, this wonderful new friend, who called me Lily, and he nods.

"Yes," I say, grabbing my backpack. "We're ready to come down now."

Sorry

After we climb down from Bob's branches, Mom and Sarah give me bone-crushing hugs. Mom even hugs Dunkin. He seems so awkward and tall in her embrace. It's kind of funny. Dad claps a hand on my shoulder and squeezes.

"Dunkin, do you think your parents would mind if you joined us for breakfast?" Mom asks.

"I'll check," he says, pulling out his phone. "But I'm sure my mom will say yes."

I wonder what Dunkin was going to tell me about his dad before the rude police officer interrupted. I almost wish he'd told me some deep, dark secret up in Bob's branches so we could be even. And I can't wait to tell Dare that the officer is more annoying than Interrupting Cow!

Mom takes my hand. "Let's get out of here, sweetheart."

"Just a minute," I say.

And even though I need to pee desperately and I'm sore and hungry, I stand there, feeling the ache of every limb in my body as the chain saws whir and slice through Bob's branches.

Thunk. Thunk. Thunk.

Branch after branch falls to the ground.

Thunk. Thunk. Thunk.

With each piece, a severed memory of my time in the tree lands, time with Grandpop Bob.

Thunk. Thunk. Thunk.

Dunkin and I stand beside each other as one guy climbs up a rope to reach the upper branches and fells them one by one—chain saw whirring and sawdust flying.

Sarah is on my other side, and Mom and Dad stand behind us, their hands on my shoulders.

It's like they're all holding me up, in a way I couldn't hold up Bob any longer.

And I stay—we stay—until the last branch is down and

Bob is left an ugly, gnarled stump. A proud stump. I think of how many people won't know the beauty he was.

"We'll pull that out Monday," one of the guys from the crew says.

The mayor thanks the workers and the police officer and even shakes my hand and my family's and Dunkin's hands before leaving.

I give her credit for staying and watching the massacre.

It takes Mom and Sarah, each pulling a hand, to uproot me from my spot and get me into the car.

If I weren't in the backseat next to Dunkin, I'd dissolve into a puddle of tears.

We both look through the back window at Stump Bob as Mom drives us away.

I'm sorry, Bob. I'm so sorry.

Breakfast

Mom orders me an omelet, hash browns and fruit cup, but I can't eat.

All I can do is picture Bob being taken down branch by branch and not being able to do anything about it. I decide I don't need to see the stump pulled from the ground Monday. In fact, I don't need to walk anywhere near the area for a long time, which means I won't be able to go to the library—my other sanctuary.

Our ordeal doesn't seem to inhibit Dunkin's appetite. He

eats a huge pile of pancakes, scrambled eggs and home-fried potatoes. I'm shocked to watch Dunkin down not one or two, but *five* cups of coffee.

"You must be really tired," I say.

Dunkin turns over his other shoulder and says, "Not right now."

"Dunkin?"

He looks at me, startled.

"Is everything . . . okay?" I'm still so grateful he joined me up in the branches of Bob for the last time.

"Sure. Of course. Great. Terrific!"

Dunkin's talking fast, but five cups of coffee will have that effect on a person. I know I don't have to, but when Mom and Sarah go to the bathroom, I whisper, "Are you sure my secret's safe with you?"

He reels back. "Of course. I can be trusted one hundred percent. Why would you even ask?"

I nibble one small chunk of honeydew. "Just checking."

"No worries."

"Hey, how was your mom when you asked about joining us for breakfast?"

Dunkin grins. "I lucked out. She didn't answer—probably still sleeping—so I left a message that I went out to breakfast with a friend and would be home soon."

I nod and poke at my fruit. I decide I'll bring the rest of my breakfast back for Dad, since he had to go to the shop, and I feel like I'll never be able to eat again anyway. I can't get the images out of my mind of my tree being dismembered, perfectly healthy pieces of a majestic tree in great heaps on the ground. I try to think of something else.

"Dunkin?"

"Yeah?"

"You know that dance? The big eighth-grade dance before the holidays?"

He nods.

"Well, I was wondering. Are you going?"

"Are you?" he asks.

"Yes," I say, taking a deep breath. "I'm definitely going."

"Cool," he says, grabbing a piece of cantaloupe from my bowl and popping it into his mouth. "Then I'll go, too."

I think about what it might be like. "Perfect."

THINKING

I like Tim's family, especially his mom and sister. His dad scares me a little, but I'm not sure why, and I really don't want to think about it. I'm so hungry and the ache in my head tells me I need coffee stat. Lots and lots of coffee loaded with lots and lots of sugar.

While I'm eating and drinking, I think about what Tim told me last night. I don't mean to, but I keep staring at his face, at those electric blue eyes. He kind of looks like a girl, except for the hair—not short, but much shorter than when I first met him. I wonder if this is why Vasquez calls Tim "fag" all the time. Does Vasquez know about Tim being transgender? But if he does, "fag" isn't the right word anyway. One thing has nothing to do with the other. Besides, I hate the word "fag." Kids at my old school used to call me "fag" sometimes or use the word "fag" to mean "weird."

The more I think about it, the more I don't like Vasquez . . . or the guys on the team. Too bad because I'm going to be playing with them all the way to the state championship, so I'd better get along with them, at least until then.

I know Tim's the real deal because he trusted me enough to share that secret. And he shouted when Coach was reaming me out, and gave me a thumbs-up when everyone else was booing. That's what a real friend does—sticks by you when no one else will.

I'll bet I could trust him with my secret. Secrets.

I look over and watch Tim *not* eating breakfast. I want to do the disappearing saltshaker trick for him—to cheer him up—but I don't have any magic in me today. And Tim probably wouldn't be in the mood anyway. I'm sure seeing his favorite tree get cut down hit him hard. It's tough to lose something you love and know there's nothing you can do about it. It's unbearable to realize you couldn't have stopped it, no matter what—

Stop thinking!

But—

Just stop!

Did He Tell?

Monday, I'm in the locker room and Vasquez comes over. "Where's your nail polish, fag?"

I don't answer, but a panicked part of me wonders: *Did Dunkin tell him?*

"I don't see any," Vasquez says. "Want me to borrow my sister's to give to you?"

I say nothing, but I tremble involuntarily and hate myself for it. Vasquez hasn't really bothered me too much lately. *Why is he doing this now?*

"You people make me sick," Vasquez says, and shoves me into the locker.

The back of my head smacks the metal of a lock. There's an explosion of pain, so I reach back, expecting to feel the warmth of blood, but my fingers come away dry. With each pulse of pain, I see Vasquez's dad's face interchange with Vasquez's. I remember how angry Vasquez's dad got when Dunkin scored a basket for the other team, and I understand where Vasquez gets his meanness. His intolerance. A long time ago, Mom taught me that when someone makes you suffer, it's because his own pain is spilling over. But that glimmer of understanding doesn't make the back of my head feel any better. It doesn't help me forgive Vasquez's constant cruelty. *And what did he mean by "you people"?*

During my next class, I have a dull, throbbing headache.

But worrying that Dunkin might have told Vasquez my secret makes my heart hurt even worse.

A QUESTION

At lunch, Tim comes up to our table. He stands right behind me. I want to push him away, send him back to the safety of his table with Dare, who is watching the scene unfold with wide eyes, and some other girl, who's sitting close to Dare.

"Can I talk to you?" Tim asks.

My stomach is clenched. My mouth frozen midchew. I can't believe Tim came over here; it's so dangerous.

"Yeah, Dorfman," Vasquez says. "Why don't you talk to your girlfriend?"

I try to think of something smart to say to Vasquez, but I can't, so I grab my tray and get up. As I walk away, my tray gripped tightly in my fingers, I feel something hit me in the back. But I don't turn and look. I'm sure it's just somebody's orange or something. Vasquez is unoriginal in his meanness.

I think we're going to the table with Dare and the other girl, but Tim keeps walking. So I keep following. I can't believe I'm doing this—walking away from Vasquez and the guys on the team.

We stop at the farthest table in the cafeteria when Tim turns and says, "You told him. Didn't you?"

"What?"

"You told Vasquez what I told you Friday night in the tree."

I slam my tray down, feeling people watching us. "Are you serious?" I whisper-shout. "You pulled me away from the table for that?" I wish Tim trusted me, but apparently he doesn't. "Of course I didn't tell him." I get right in his face, which requires me to bend way down. "I didn't tell anybody. Why would I?"

"Are you absolutely sure?"

"Of course I'm sure. Why?"

"Vasquez said some stuff to me in the locker room."

"What kind of stuff?"

"Stupid stuff." Tim shakes his head. "I guess it wasn't anything nastier than usual. I'm probably just being paranoid."

I glance over. Vasquez is watching us. He looks pissed. "He's an idiot," I say.

"Hey," Tim says, tilting his head. "Since he's such an idiot, do you want to sit with me and Dare and Amy?"

"Yes," I say honestly. A part of me has wanted to sit with them since after the first few days of the school year. "But I'd better go back." I feel like a traitor. "Just for now," I say. "Till basketball season is over."

Tim nods. "Thanks for not telling." And he goes back to his table.

I'd better get this over with.

When I return, Vasquez says, "What did *she* want?"

I shrug, like it's nothing. "To borrow money."

"Did you lend it to him?" Birch asks.

"Course not," I say, and stuff a roll in my mouth so I stop talking.

"Well, I can't stand that kid," Vasquez says. "Total freak. Stay away from *her*."

"Sure," I say, but don't mean it.

Tim is the only *real* friend I've made since moving to Beckford Palms.

The only *real* friend I've ever had.

HE'S BACK

It's a home game.

I've gotten a total of six and half minutes of playing time this entire season. Coach had better play me tonight.

Besides . . .

I.

Can't.

Sit.

Still.

Anymore.

The starting five barely do the tip-off and I'm up and pacing.

"Dorfman. Sit!" Coach says.

I sit.

In my race-car mind, all the cars are crashing into each other. Too many cars. Too much noise. I put my hands over my ears and close my eyelids, but it won't stop. The noise. The colliding thoughts.

I pace again and consider bolting out of the gym into the cool night air.

Coach grabs my jersey and sits me down. "I'll play you in a little while," he whispers. "But you've gotta sit."

He's going to play me. I pump my leg.

I look to my left.

"You're back!" I say.

"Who's back?" one of my teammates, Jackson, whispers. "Who are you talking to?"

I ignore him, like he's not even there, and glance over my left shoulder. "It's been hard. I'm glad you're here."

I'm glad I'm here, too, Dunkin.

"How'd you . . . know my nickname?"

"Dorfman, get out there!"

I feel so much relief. He's back. He knows my nickname. All will be well.

Get out there! Coach just called your name.

"He did?"

"Who are you talking to?" Jackson slides his chair away from me.

Is everyone crazy? Can't they see?

I charge onto the floor. I wonder which player I'm going in for.

288

Show me your moves, Phineas says.

"Okay." I pretend to dribble in a circle, then down the court. I look up and see Coach at the score table. I forgot to check in. Oops.

That's great. Show me more. Your very best moves.

He's laughing. And I feel fantastic. I run up and down, up and down, talking to Phineas. The other players are so afraid of my moves they get out of my way. There's a clear line to the basket. But which basket?

Shoot! Phineas calls.

And I want to shoot. I want to show off for Phineas.

But I don't even have the ball. And I don't know which basket I'm supposed to aim for. I whip around to look for the ball, to figure out which way I'm supposed to go, to find Phineas, to check in at the score table. There are so many things I have to do. *But where's the ball? Where's Phin?* My hands tremble. I'm walking in tight circles. "What am I doing? What am I doing?"

I'm trying so hard to remember.

How long have I been standing here? Why is everyone looking at me like that? I wish I could perform the ultimate magic trick right now . . . and disappear.

Mom's standing near me, her hand over her mouth. And Bubbie's here, too. *Why are they on the floor with me? They should be up in the bleachers.* Coach Ochoa's near me. And other people I don't know. I'm still walking in circles.

I ask Phin, "What's happening?"

I guess the game stopped. Maybe someone got hurt. *But why is everyone staring at me?* Vasquez. Birch. All the guys on the team. Even the coaches and guys from the other team.

Everyone's.

Staring.

At.

Me.

"What's happening?" I ask Phineas again. I cover my eyes because I can't stand the way everyone is looking at me.

It's okay now, he says, calm and assured.

"Norbert!" Mom says.

I look at her, then do a few wild basketball maneuvers to show her I'm okay. "See? See?" I tell her. "See?"

She's crying and reaching for me, but she's not close enough. Bubbie's strong arm is around her shoulders.

"It's okay," I tell Mom. "I'm okay." Then I smile and look to my left. "Phineas is back. Everything's okay."

I hear a gasp, and then someone is pulling my hands behind me. Snapping something cold and hard around my wrists.

I try to wrench free. "I'm okay!" I scream. "Can't you see?" I thrash about wildly to show everyone, but a couple men are holding me now.

Mom stands watching as they drag me out of the gym, out of the school and into the back of a car. A police car. I'm in the back of a police car!

Mom's face is at the window. She reaches her fingers out to me like you'd see in a bad movie, but this is for real.

"I'm okay," I tell her, tears streaming down my face.

I'm not sure she hears me, though, because her face looks so sad.

As the car speeds away, I'm so glad I'm not alone.

Phineas is beside me.

TRAPPED

I'm taken inside a dull building, and a loud door clangs behind me. I know what this place is. I've been in a place like this once before.

"We're trapped," I tell Phin, my heart thud-thud-thudding.

Don't worry.

They put me in a room. My arms are still cuffed behind me and there's a man standing next to me.

"Hello, Norbert," another man near the door says. "I'm Dr. Carter. I'm here to help you."

You don't know that he's a doctor, Phineas says. *He could be with the FBI. He's probably here to hurt you.*

"Don't hurt me!" I scream. "I won't let you hurt me!"

"I'm not going to hurt you," says the man who doesn't look like a doctor.

I'm afraid he might hurt you, Phineas says. *Get away!*

I charge to the door. But realize I can't open it anyway

because my hands are behind me. The man grabs me and pushes me down on a mattress on the floor.

And sticks a needle in my arm.

"Don't let them do this, Phin! Stop them!"

I'm doing my best here. But you have to help, too. You have to—

"Who's Phineas, Norbert? Are you . . . hearing . . . voices, son?"

Son? Dad?

Don't listen to him, Dunkin! Run! R . . . u . . . n . . .

"Norbert, I'm here to help . . ."

The man's voice gets quieter and then vanishes.

Phineas's words go away, too.

And suddenly I'm so . . . sleepy.

THE ROOM

I wake in a tiny room.

I'm lying on a mattress with no sheet. The mattress is in a wooden box on the floor. There's drool coming out of my mouth. I wipe it away and realize my arms are free. There are red marks on my wrists where the handcuffs were, so I know I'm not crazy. Last night happened.

You awake?

"Yeah, I'm up," I tell Phin, glad he's here.

We've got to get out of here, buddy.

"I know. I know."

There's a door, Phineas says. *But I'll bet the bastards locked us in last night. That was crazy, eh?*

"Yeah," I say, rubbing my wrists. "What happened?"

You were a beast on the basketball court, my friend. I think there were scouts from the NBA. I'd be surprised if they didn't want to draft you.

This makes me smile.

You're a superstar.

Phineas always makes me feel good. Well, almost always. I look down and see something different about my sneakers. "Why are my laces missing?"

You know why.

And I do.

Suddenly, I remember exactly where I am.

"We have to get out of here," I tell Phineas.

Tell me about it, buddy.

THIS PLACE

I stare at the fluorescent light overhead for a long time.

Finally, someone unlocks the door to my room, and a big guy in green scrubs saunters in. I remember him from last night. He's the man who gave me the needle that made me so tired. I don't want another needle, so I back up on the mattress. Away from him.

"Hello, Norbert," the man says.

"How does he know my name?" I ask Phineas.

Phin doesn't answer, which scares me.

"Okay, then," the man says in a false cheery voice. "Time to see Dr. Carter."

Even though I'm scared, I follow the man out of my room. My feet slip out of the backs of my sneakers a little because there are no laces, but I'm able to keep up with the guy. The hallway smells bad. People here look weird. Too thin or too heavy. Vacant, glassy eyes.

"Why am I here?" I ask.

The guy doesn't answer. He takes me to a room and opens the door. "Dr. Carter, your patient is here."

"Sit down, Norbert," he says.

The green-scrubs guy closes the door, but stays in the room, with his arms crossed.

I sit.

"Norbert, you had an incident last night. Can you tell me what happened?"

I remember showing off a little on the court for Phineas. I remember the worried look in Mom's eyes. I remember being put in that small room, and Phineas warning me that this guy might not be a real doctor.

I don't share any of these thoughts with the possibly/probably fake doctor.

"Norbert, are you hearing voices?"

I shake my head no.

He marks something on a piece of paper.

I can't hold back something that's been on my mind since they took me to this place. "Can I ask you a question?"

The possibly/probably fake doctor folds his hands. "Of course."

I clear my sore throat. "Could you check to see if my father's in here?"

The pseudo doctor looks through a file in front of him, and I notice his eyebrows arch. "Your father?"

"Yes," I say. "My dad's in a psychiatric facility, too. That's why we moved here."

"Is he?" This guy is doing a good job of pretending to be a real doctor. He even asks questions instead of answering them, like real doctors often do. Maybe Phin was wrong. Maybe this guy actually is a doctor. I kind of hope he is, because then he'll be able to help me find my dad.

"Yes," I say, hopeful. "I was wondering if he's in this one. That's what this place is. Isn't it?"

"Yes, Norbert," the maybe fake, maybe real doctor says. "You are in Beckford Palms Mental Health Center. But I'm wondering why you think your father might be in here."

"Because my mom put him in one."

He's quiet, then says, "Norbert, for right now, I'd like to talk about you. Would that be okay?"

"Okay," I say, but inside I've decided I'm going to find a way to look around. Maybe when that big guy in green scrubs isn't nearby. If my dad is in here, I'll find him. He's probably missing me so much. He's probably dying for some doughnuts.

I'll find him. And Phineas will help. "Won't you, buddy?"

You betcha, Dunkin.

"What was that?" the fake, not fake doctor asks.

I look over my left shoulder.

Say "nothing," Phineas tells me.

"Nothing."

Sleepover

Amy, Dare and I are on the floor in Dare's bedroom.

It's the first time the three of us are having a sleepover.

I'm nervous at first, about how Amy will react to me—the me I get to be at Dare's sleepovers—but when Amy is painting my nails a bright sunflower yellow, I know she's fine with the real me. I should have figured she would be from how cool she was with my mermaid costume at Halloween.

Dare asks, "Did you hear about Dunkin?"

"What about him?" My heart speeds up.

"You didn't hear?" Amy asks, which makes me feel left out.

"What?"

"He got carted off the basketball court in handcuffs."

"Dunkin? What? Why?"

"I heard he went psycho," Amy says.

I want to tell her that's not a nice thing to say, but she's painting my nails and I don't want to make her feel bad since she's being nice to me.

"He was talking to himself and running all over the

court," Dare says, twirling a finger near her head. "They had to call the police."

"No," I say. "That's not possible." I think about Dunkin in the tree with me. I remember when he was talking way too fast in the restaurant the next morning, but I thought that was from all the coffee he drank. "Maybe it's just a rumor."

Amy shakes her head. "Nope. Heard it from too many people. Want me to paint smiley faces on your nails with black polish over the yellow?"

"Sure," I say, distracted, not wanting to talk about nail polish. I want to talk about Dunkin, to find out what's going on. "But it *could* be a rumor," I say. "It's possible. Right?"

"Doubt it," Dare says. "All the lacrosse girls were talking about it. Lots of people saw it happen, Lil."

I pull my hands back from Amy because they're trembling. "Do you know anything else?"

Dare shakes her head.

"I think they put him in the loony bin or something," Amy says.

I cringe. *How can this be happening?*

Tentatively, Amy takes my hand back and focuses on painting a smiley face on my thumbnail.

I try to keep my hand steady while she paints. It's hard because a jumble of questions collide in my mind: *What's happening to Dunkin now? Is he going to be okay? Will he be able to come back to school? Will he be different when he does?*

"What happens to a frog's car when it breaks down?" Amy asks.

I'm not in the mood for stupid jokes right now. Something serious has happened and no one except me seems to really care.

"What?" Dare asks.

"It gets TOAD away," Amy says, dropping my hand and rolling on the floor on her back as though it were the funniest joke ever. She's careful to hold the paintbrush up while she acts like a fool.

Dare shakes her head at Amy, but she's grinning.

I'm glad when Amy is finally done painting my nails. It's too hard to sit still because I'm so worried about Dunkin.

After watching a stupid horror movie, we turn out the lights. I hear Dare and Amy fall into the deep breathing of sleep, but I'm wild awake.

My heart hammers. My breath catches. My thoughts ricochet against each other.

Be okay, Dunkin.

Please be okay.

Please . . .

Exposed

In school, I go to the nurse's office when it's time for PE, but when I get there, the secretary says, "She had to step out. Can I help you with something?"

"No."

I drag myself to the PE locker room. I don't feel like lying to the secretary about being sick. It's not as if she could give me a note to get out of PE anyway. I'll hustle into and out of the locker room as quickly as possible.

The locker room smells particularly bad. I look up at the ceiling and notice more wads of gross toilet paper.

In front of my locker, I change out of my jeans at lightning speed.

Vasquez and the Neanderthals are nearby. I feel them looking at me, and realize it's too quiet. They're usually laughing and horsing around.

I shove my jeans into my locker and turn the combination lock. Then I walk down the row, toward the exit.

Vasquez steps in front of me. "What's the hurry, McGrother?"

I look around—panicked—and think about dashing past, but the Neanderthals are surrounding me. Jason Argo—a non-Neanderthal kid—is watching us, and Vasquez growls, "What are you lookin' at?"

Jason bolts out of the locker room like his feet are on fire.

I wish I could leave with him. My legs tremble, and I will them to still themselves, like a tree trunk. I hope Jason gets help, but I know he won't. I'm on my own.

Vasquez steps closer. He's so tall. I have to look up at him, and I hate looking up at him. "I said, 'What's the hurry, McGrother?'"

I don't answer. There is no answer.

"So," Vasquez says. "Me and the guys were wondering . . ." He looks around. The Neanderthals smile and nod, silently encouraging him.

Alarm bells go off in my head. "I've got to go," I say in my bravest voice. And I step forward.

Vasquez puts both hands on my chest and holds me in place. "Not yet."

"But . . ." It's the only word that chokes past my tight throat.

The Neanderthals draw closer.

"We were wondering . . ." Vasquez locks eyes with me. I see his father's eyes. Hard. Cold.

I consider screaming in hopes someone would hear, but know it's the worst thing I could do. They'd be on me in a second, pounding the life out of me before anyone could get here. Same would happen if I tried to run. And honestly, I'm too terrified to do either of those things. Dunkin's face flashes in my mind, and I wonder what would happen if he were here. Would he defend me? But he's not here. According to Dare and Amy, he's someplace even worse.

"We were wondering," Vasquez says, "what you really have under those shorts."

I gasp, because now I know what they plan to do.

Vasquez grins. "I mean, you're wearing yellow nail polish. With smiley faces. My sister wears nail polish, McGrother. *Girls* wear nail polish."

"Yeah," Birch says. "You a girl, McGrother? 'Cause you sure act like one."

I stand still like a stone statue, barely breathing. Every cell in my body on high alert.

"Well," Vasquez says, looking at the Neanderthals, "there's only one way to find out. Right, guys?"

"Right!" they say in unison.

"Shhh," Vasquez cautions as he nods toward the exit. And they're silent because they don't want Coach Ochoa to see what they're about to do. They don't want to jeopardize their spots on the basketball team.

In one swift, surprising motion, Vasquez bends and yanks down my shorts *and* underwear.

"Well, look at that," he says. "You are a boy. Barely."

They all crack up.

Someone smacks me on my bare rear end.

And they run out of the locker room in hysterics.

I stand there, my underwear and shorts around my ankles.

Exposed.

After

As I yank my underwear and shorts up, I notice my fingernails. Yellow with smiley faces that don't make me happy. They make me feel dirty. I wish I could pull them off.

I open my locker and put my clothes back on.

I walk out of the locker room, out of the gym and out of the school.

No one tries to stop me, which surprises me.

As I walk away from the building, I breathe in short gasps.

Can't go home.

My feet keep moving and before I know it, I'm at the spot where Bob used to stand. Not even his stump remains. The whole area is cordoned off because the playground is being built. I sit on the curb at the edge of the property, feeling sick.

I sit there a long time.

Then I walk.

Later, at home, I don't join my family for dinner.

I go upstairs and take a shower. But I don't feel clean when I'm done. Even though the water is so hot my whole body turns pink.

In bed, I feel uglier than my ugly brown comforter.

Uglier than I ever have in my life.

I can't go back to that school.

I can't face those people.

I bury my face in my pillow. And sob.

And when I'm spent, I think of Dunkin and what he might be going through.

I wish I could help him, but apparently . . . I can't even help myself.

Ever After

I do not go to school Tuesday.

"Don't feel well," I tell Mom.

She places her cool, dry palm on my forehead. "You do feel a little warm. Want me to get the thermometer?"

"No," I say. "It's mostly my stomach. I think I'm going to throw up."

"Want some ginger tea, sweetheart?" she asks, brushing the hair from my forehead.

Her kindness makes me sad. "No thanks."

"Want me to stay home from my class?"

"No, go," I say. "Your yoga people need you."

Mom kisses my cheek. "I like your nail polish color. It's very cheerful."

When she leaves, I get up, find Sarah's nail polish remover and scrub the smiley faces and bright yellow polish from my nails.

I stay in bed the rest of the day.

A GOAL

I'm in bed.

Now that I've been here a few days, they put me in a bigger room with two beds. I have sheets and a pillow with a pillowcase. There's a bathroom in the room, too.

And I have a roommate.

Poor guy doesn't eat. Ever. He's so thin I see his ribs when he pulls off his shirt.

Phin and I try to help him. We let him talk about his problems, but we don't tell him our problems.

When it's time to go to the lounge to watch TV, Phin and I look around as much as we can, but we don't see Dad. It's kids around my age and the people who work at the facility.

They changed my meds when I got here, which mostly just made me sleepy, but the fake doctor says they're going to put me back on what I was taking (or wasn't taking) when I first came in. Except here, they make me take my meds and watch to ensure that I swallow.

The fake doctor also says I'm doing well and being co-operative, so I'll be able to have visitors soon.

Maybe Dad will visit.

Mom has deep, dark circles under her eyes when she comes into the recreation room for our visit.

She puts her palms on my cheeks and touches her fore-head to mine. "Oh, Norbert."

"I'm sorry," I say, even though I'm not sure what I'm sorry for.

"It's not your fault," Mom says, and sits in the chair across from me. "None of this is your fault. Your bubbie and I have been so worried about you, sweetheart. I . . . I should have done more. Should have paid more attention. Watched to make sure you were taking your pills. Something." Mom squeezes her hands into fists. "But I just haven't been myself since . . ." She sniffs hard, then sits tall. "But that's no excuse." She leans forward and pats my knee. "How are you, honey?"

"When can I leave?" I ask.

"As soon as the doctor says."

I lean close. "I'm not even sure he's a real doctor."

"Oh, Norb. I'm pretty sure he's a real doctor."

"Well, Phin and I don't trust him."

Mom closes her eyelids and lets out a breath. Then she looks at me. "Please do what you have to and come home. We want you back."

"Mom?"

"Yes, sweetheart?"

"Did you know there's going to be a dance at school?"

"Really?"

I can tell Mom's not sure whether to believe me or not.

"It's real," I say. "I've been thinking about it. It's a big deal for the eighth graders. Right before the holiday break. I was wondering if I'd be out by then?"

"I don't know," Mom says. "I hope so. Do you want to go to this dance?"

I think of Tim asking me about it when we were out to breakfast. "Yes," I say. "Definitely."

"That would be a good goal, sweetheart. Let's shoot for that."

Suddenly my brain gets fuzzy. I look right at Mom and say, "Shoot for what?"

Mom's face tells me I disappointed her, but I'm not sure how.

Telling

When I refuse to go to school on Wednesday, Mom makes an appointment with Dr. Klemme.

I like her a lot, but I don't tell her what happened. I don't tell anyone. I'm too ashamed.

Mom says I have to go to school Thursday, so I do.

But there's no way—*no way* I'll ever go to PE again.

Vasquez comes up to my locker right away. "Listen, McGrother," he says. "Like, I'm really sorry about what happened."

I'm shocked. I feel like I returned to some alternate universe where Vasquez is a decent human.

"So don't tell anyone. Okay?"

And I get it. Vasquez is afraid he'll get kicked off the basketball team, and he probably would. I have the power to do that to him. If I told, he might even get kicked out of school.

"Okay," I say, looking down.

CARRY ON

I wake feeling better than I have in a long time.

"Phin?" I ask, but he doesn't answer.

"Who are you talking to?" my roommate asks.

"No one." *Sorry, Phin.*

"You wanna play Ping-Pong?"

I can't believe how much fun it is. My roommate actually smiles while we're playing. It's the first time I've seen him smile.

A counselor comes up and knocks on the table with her knuckles. "You two are doing so much better." She nods at each of us. "Carry on, gentlemen."

I know this is a good sign. It means I'll get to go home soon, but I haven't found Dad yet. I figure he's on a different floor since this floor is for kids.

Before bed, Phineas's voice is thin, quiet. *I can't stay much longer.*

"I know," I say. Because somehow I do. "But before you go, can you help me find my dad?"

Yes, he says. *That would be a good idea, Dunkin.*

It's time.

THE TRUTH

Today's the big day. Phineas is going to help me find my dad.

We tiptoe into the room with the Ping-Pong table, except it's folded up against the wall.

I need to talk to you.

His voice is like wind through the leaves of a tree.

You'd better sit for this, pal.

I sit on one of the uncomfortable plastic chairs.

About your dad.

"Yes?" I say, aware that no one else is in the room except the attendant standing at the doorway.

He's not here, Phineas says.

"I can't hear you too well," I tell Phin. "You're . . . fading."

I am fading, Dunkin. This is a good thing.

I smile because somehow I know it's a good thing. "But my dad," I say, trying to hang on to Phineas long enough for him to help me find my dad.

You're not going to find your dad here.

I wonder how Phin knows this.

Or at any other facility.

"What do you mean?" My heart gallops.

Dunkin.

It's almost like I feel his hand on my shoulder.

Your dad's gone.

"Gone?" I say a little too loudly.

"Do you need something?" the attendant asks me.

"No," I say, wishing he'd go away.

I whisper to Phin, "What do you mean?"

You know what I mean.

And just like that, a door swings open in my brain. The door I'd worked so hard to keep closed since that night in New Jersey. Images whoosh out and swirl around. Like movie clips. I squeeze my eyelids tight to shut them off, to stop the images and clips from running. But I can't stop them.

Not anymore.

So I take a deep breath, open my eyes and remember. Mom answering the door. Mom screaming, shrieking. Falling to her knees.

He's not coming back.

Mom wearing the black dress and shiny black shoes.

Mom crying.

Crying.

Nonstop crying.

Ever.

The six pallbearers carrying the coffin.

You know who's in the coffin, Phineas says, his voice almost nothing, a whisper, a wisp, a molecule. Except I think it's actually my own voice, inside my head now.

"I do know who's in the coffin," I say, because suddenly I do.

And a lone sob escapes. Then another. Then I'm wracked. I'm wailing, like Mom did that awful night with the police officers at our door.

"Phineas?" I blubber.

No answer.

"Phineas?"

He's gone.

And the tears won't stop.

I feel a strong hand on my shoulder. "Phin?" I look up into the face of the attendant.

"Do you want me to get someone?" he asks.

I nod. "My mom."

But he takes me to Dr. Carter, who I know now is a real doctor. A psychiatrist.

"He's gone," I say, wiping hot tears from my cheeks.

"Who's gone?" Dr. Carter asks.

"Phineas," I say. "He's gone, and I don't think he's coming back."

Dr. Carter smiles. "That's great, Norbert. You've made incredible progress here in the hospital."

I nod. "And my dad." I sniff hard.

Dr. Carter puts his hands on his desk and leans forward. "Yes?"

I swipe at my eyes. "He's gone, too. Isn't he?"

"That's right," Dr. Carter says in a quiet, kind voice.

Then I admit the one thing I couldn't face until now: "He killed himself. That's the reason Mom and I moved here to Beckford Palms."

Dr. Carter stands and comes around his big, wooden desk. For the first time ever, a psychiatrist eliminates the barrier between us. He comes over to my chair, leans down and puts his arms around me. He holds me fiercely, like my dad would have.

And I let him.

I sob onto Dr. Carter's shoulder, soaking the material of his shirt.

And he lets me.

When I'm done and Dr. Carter lets go, he stands beside me with his strong hand on my shoulder. And I know— for the first time in a long time—I know that everything's going to be okay.

That I'm going to be okay.

Maybe not right now.

But someday soon.

GOING HOME

Mom takes my hand as we walk away from the facility. Her palm is sweaty and warm. It makes me feel safe.

Before we get to the car, she stops and looks up at me. "I'm proud of you, Norbert. This was so, so hard and you did it. You're very brave, you know that?"

I nod.

"Thank you for getting well and coming home to me." Mom lets out a shaky breath. "I couldn't lose you, too."

That's when I squeeze Mom into the tightest hug. "He's gone," I whisper into the top of her hair. "He's really gone for good."

I feel Mom nod into my chest.

I pull back and look at her. "Mom?"

She wipes at her eyes.

"I want you to know I'm going to take my medicine."

Mom smiles.

"Really. I'm not going to stop taking it unless my doctor tells me to."

"That's wonderful, Norbert."

"And I said good-bye to Phineas. For good."

Mom puts her arms around my waist. I feel her body heave. "I'm so proud of you, sweetheart."

In the car on the way home, I say, "You know, I don't think I could have dealt with the truth about Dad before now. It's like my mind knew I couldn't handle it, so it kept that part locked away."

Mom pats my knee. "The doctor told me it was a kind of protection mechanism in your brain, that you'd remember when you were ready."

"Well, now that I remember, I'm really sad. I couldn't stop crying this morning."

"I'm sad, too," Mom says. "But I'm really glad you're okay, Norbert."

I look straight ahead. "Me too."

"Before I left to get you, Bubbie was baking some bran raisin muffins for your big homecoming."

"Oh boy."

"While doing deep knee bends. And mangling the words to some song."

I laugh, eager to get home and spend time with my meshuga—nutty—bubbie, but not to eat her sawdust and raisin muffins. "Mom, I'm not sure I can eat Bubbie's muffins right now. The food in that place was pretty gross. Think we could stop at Dunkin' Donuts on the way home?"

Mom lets out a big breath. "Definitely."

Getting Ready

It's the night of the eighth-grade holiday dance.

I'm in Mom's closet. I pull the lily of the valley dress off the rack. "This one?" I ask.

"Sure," Mom says, and she grabs a pair of sandals and hands them to me. "Go." She gives me a little shove. "Get beautiful."

In my room, I slip into the dress. It feels as good as it did that first day I tried it on when I met Dunkin. I get a pang when I think of him. *Please be okay.*

I go into Sarah's room so she can do my makeup.

"You ready for this?" Sarah asks, her long red hair pulled back in a ponytail. She's wearing one of Dad's reject T-shirts: *Jupiter Academy Chool of Music.*

I give my sister a huge hug. "Thanks for being you."

Sarah shrugs. "Like I could be anyone else."

And, I think it's the same with me. I can't be anyone but exactly who I am, even if John Vasquez and the Neanderthals don't like it.

I look at myself in the mirror. Mom's dress and sandals. Bright red nail polish. My hair long enough to put up in two little clips on each side. I think about what Vasquez did to me in the locker room, how he tried to shame me for being myself. I think of the reaction I'll get when I walk into the dance as me—Lily Jo McGrother—girl. "I'm ready!" I say.

Sarah applies my eye shadow and blush. I do my own eyeliner, mascara and lipstick.

"You need something else," Sarah says, examining me.

I look in the mirror but don't see anything missing. Except for the fact that the dress is still a little baggy in the front, I look pretty good. "What?"

"My black onyx pendant. The one with the teardrop stone."

"You'll let me wear that? It was a birthday gift from Grandpop Bob." I know it's precious to her because she wears it only for special occasions.

"It'll be perfect," Sarah says. "It's in the jewelry box on the shelf in my closet. Go get it, and I'll help you put it on."

I can't believe Sarah is letting me wear that necklace. "I'll take good care of it," I tell her as I open the closet door and turn on the light.

"I know you will," she says. "It'll be nice for you to have something from Grandpop Bob tonight. I only wish he could have met you as Lily. I know he would have—"

"No way!" I shriek.

In the corner of my sister's closet are half a dozen plastic pink flamingos, adorned in various scarves, hats and costumes.

"I should have known!" I turn and see Sarah beaming.

"It wasn't just me," she says. "It's a Knit Wits project. These things are going up in neighborhoods all over the world."

"Really?" I ask. "That's so cool!"

Sarah nods. "Besides, sterile Beckford Palms needed something . . . unexpected."

I look at the hilarious flamingos my sister has been planting all over the neighborhood. I look down at my dress and sandals. "Well, they sure got it from the McGrother house."

We both crack up.

Sarah helps me put on the gorgeous necklace from Grandpop Bob, and I'm ready to make my grand entrance downstairs.

Mom's waiting at the bottom of the steps, camera in hand. She gasps when she sees me, which makes me feel terrific. And she takes about a billion photos—which is a conservative estimate.

Meatball barks his approval. "Thanks, boy." I scratch behind his ears.

When Dare and Amy arrive, Mom takes a bunch more photos of the three of us glamming it up. And she takes a few of Sarah and me.

Then Sarah gives me a big hug and stands in the doorway, waving, as Mom drives me, Dare and Amy to the dance.

We're nearly there when I ask, "Where's Dad?"

"Hmm?" Mom says, as though she hadn't heard me.

"Dad?" I say louder.

"Oh," Mom says. "Your dad needed to take care of something at the shop."

Yeah, sure he did. I touch my sister's pendant and decide I'm not going to let anything ruin this night—even Dad's absence.

The Real Me

The dance is held at a fancy country club.

I don't even know if the administration from my school will let me in dressed like this, so Mom comes up with us to make sure I get in.

Dare, Amy and I walk arm in arm, three across, with Mom behind us.

Mr. Andrews, the vice principal, is at a table checking IDs.

My stomach is in so many knots I can't stand it. My hand trembles as I pull out my ID. Dare lays her warm hand on mine for a second, which is enough to still it.

Mr. Andrews looks at me, then up at Mom.

The moment seems to last years. I'm sure he's going to embarrass me, tell me to go home and change into something more appropriate. And I have no idea what I'll do if that happens. Probably dissolve into a puddle of tears. I think of Sarah and the necklace and the flamingos. I think of Grandpop Bob. And I look at my friends and Mom standing beside me. I pull my shoulders back and look right at Mr. Andrews. Let him try to keep me out!

"Go ahead," he says, waving his hand.

Mom kisses me on the cheek, and I walk into a dark room with Dare and Amy.

It's amazing. There's a sparkly ball on the ceiling that sends bits of rainbow light onto the floor. There's a DJ playing music, and a table with drinks and food. We head over that way.

While Amy and Dare pile little plates with snacks, I stand and survey the scene. The kids look so pretty—the girls dressed up and the guys in suits. I don't see Vasquez or the Neanderthals, and that makes me incredibly happy. I know they can walk in at any moment, but I choose not to focus on that. Tonight is not about them.

Lots of people are staring at me, and I let them. I stand tall, tip my chin up and take a deep breath.

I let them see me.

Lily Jo McGrother.

Girl.

THE DANCE

I'm halfway through my second doughnut when Mom says, "Sweetheart, did you still want to go to that dance?"

I do want to go. I told Tim I would be there. "Nah," I say. "I don't need all the kids staring at the guy who just got out of the loony bin."

"Norbert," Mom says. "This might be the perfect thing to do. Go to the dance. Let everyone see that you're okay. Then enjoy your holiday break. That way, it won't be so hard to go back to school when the break's over."

I imagine walking into the dance with everyone staring at me, whispering to each other behind their hands. "I think it will be too hard."

Mom laughs. "Seriously, Norbert, after all you've been through? Going to a school dance will be too hard? But if you really don't want to go . . ."

I think about Tim there and wonder if maybe Vasquez would bother him, pick on him, embarrass him in front of everyone. Maybe if I were there, too, I could protect Tim—keep that from happening. "Yeah, I'll go."

Mom raises an eyebrow.

"You're right. It'll be easier to let everyone see me tonight than worry about it all during break. I'll need clothes, though. It's fancy."

"Well then," Mom says. "Let's go."

And she takes me to a men's clothing store near the mall that has things for tall guys like me. Mom pays for the clothes, then makes me lean down so she can whisper in my ear. "I got a job."

My eyes go wide.

Mom nods, all proud. "Yup. I'll be making gourmet cupcakes at this place in town called the Cupcakery."

"That's so great," I say, because it is, and not just because I'll probably get to eat way more sweet stuff now. But because Mom used to love her job working at a bakery, when we lived in New Jersey, back before Dad's illness got really bad. Besides, this means that instead of sitting around being sad, Mom's finally moving forward.

I look down at myself, wearing spiffy clothes and dress shoes.

And so am I.

Sharing Secrets

I grab a glass of punch and realize my hands are trembling.

Vasquez and the Neanderthals have come in. They look uncomfortable, tugging at their ill-fitting suits. When Vasquez sees me, his eyes go wide, but I don't move. I hear him call me "fag" to his buddies and point in my direction, but still, I don't move.

They move.

They go to the other side of the room.

Score: Lily—1, Neanderthals—0.

Dare and Amy ask me to join them on the dance floor, but I'm not ready yet, so I don't go. And I'm glad I chose to stay back when I see how silly Amy dances. She looks like a chicken with poor muscle control.

Songs play. Everyone dances under the disco ball. And it's a really nice night.

I don't move from my spot, though, and I keep an eye on the door. *Wishing.*

After a long time, I realize Dunkin's not coming. I'd overheard he was getting out of the hospital and hoped he'd show up.

I look across the room and see Dare and Amy along the far wall. Dare reaches out and takes Amy's hand. And they stand like that, holding hands with each other. Dare and Amy are holding hands. And smiling like crazy.

And suddenly, I get it.

I wasn't the only one keeping a secret. Dare could have told me. I guess if I were paying closer attention, I could have figured it out.

When I look away, I see someone walk in.

"Dunkin!" I rush over to him. "You're here!" I want to throw my arms around him, but refrain.

"Wow," Dunkin says, looking me up and down. "You're . . . you're . . . you."

He couldn't have said anything better.

We go to the table and get a drink together.

"It feels like everyone's staring at me," he says.

I laugh so hard I spit my drink. "You?" I ask. "I walked into the dance wearing a dress and makeup, Dunkin. I'm pretty sure everyone's staring at me!"

He laughs. "Yeah. I didn't think of that. Thanks for deflecting attention from me like that."

"Hey, no problem."

Dunkin clinks his plastic cup with mine. "Seriously, you are really brave to do this."

I nod. "It was time."

"Does this mean I can call you Lily now?"

I feel like all the light in the world has filled me up. "I guess it does."

We go to a deserted corner, and Dunkin tells me where he's been and why.

I can't believe everything he's gone through. Then again, I can't believe what I've endured with Vasquez and the Neanderthals.

Then Dunkin tells me something else. "You know," he says, "my dad died."

"I'm sorry," I say.

"He killed himself."

"Oh."

"That's why we moved here."

I bite my lip. "I'm so sorry that happened." Then I look up into Dunkin's eyes. "But I'm so glad you're here."

MAY I HAVE THIS DANCE?

Her kind blue eyes and just-right words burrow softly into my heart.

The room is dark with sparkly bits of colored light.

The DJ says, "Last song of the night."

And Donna Summer's "Last Dance" remix blares from the speakers.

Kids crowd onto the dance floor.

"May I have this dance?" I ask.

"Are you sure, Dunkin? Everyone's going to stare at us."

"They'll stare anyway," I say. "Remember, I just got out of the loony bin."

This makes Lily smile. "Okay."

We walk onto the crowded dance floor. People make space for us. And we rock out to the music, just like everyone else.

I bend and say into Lily's ear, "This isn't so bad. Is it?"

"Nope," she says, moving from side to side and waving her arms around. "It's actually pretty awesome."

Way #11 to die in South Florida: of happiness.

Perfect

When the lights go on, Dunkin and I back up a couple steps from each other.

I blink, blink, blink.

The spell is broken.

Kids are looking at us.

Teachers are looking at us.

I feel exposed in the bright light and want to run out, like

Cinderella ran from the ball when the clock struck midnight. I'm about to do it, too, when something catches my eye. Some*one,* actually.

"Dad?"

He's standing there looking at me like I'm the only person in the crowded room. His thick arms wide open.

I take a step closer and squint. He's wearing a T-shirt that says: *I love my DAUGHTER!*

I take another step closer, feeling like my legs are going to give out.

That's when Dad moves toward me in sure, strong strides and scoops me into his arms. "I love you," he says.

"I can see that."

Now everyone has turned to stare at us. A teacher is dabbing at her eyes with a tissue. A couple of girls have their hands over their mouths. Some people nod. Mr. Creighton gives me a warm smile. Vasquez and his goons are gone, and I'm so glad they're not here to ruin this moment. Dare and Amy are still holding hands. They wave at me with their free hands, and Dare gives me a thumbs-up, as if to say, *You finally did it, McGrother.*

Dad takes my hand and squeezes. We turn toward the exit.

"Bye, Dunkin," I call.

"Bye, Lily!" he says, and it sounds so good.

* * *

In the car on the ride home, Dad pats my knee. "You're so brave, you know that."

I smile.

"I mean it," he says. "I wouldn't have the guts to go to that dance in a dress, but you ..." He sniffs. "Grandpop Bob would have been so proud of you."

I touch the teardrop pendant and let Dad's words fill me. We're quiet for a while. "Dad?"

"Yes?"

"Can you tell me what Dr. Klemme said that day? When we first went to her? It felt like you ... you changed after that. Everything changed after that."

Dad inhales deeply. *Maybe Mom's having an influence on him after all.* "The doctor said something that completely upended the way I thought about everything." Dad pulls into our driveway and cuts the engine, but doesn't open the car door. He turns to me.

"Lily? That's what you want to be called. Right?"

My name never sounded so wonderful. I blink back tears. "Right."

"She showed me a statistic. Forty-three percent of transgender kids try to kill themselves." Dad sniffs again, hard. "Then she said, 'Would you rather have a dead son or a live daughter?'"

"Oh, Dad." I put a hand over my mouth.

"She explained that kids who get a lot of love and support have a much lower suicide risk."

"I wouldn't do that," I tell him, thinking of what Dunkin

told me about his dad. "I would never hurt you and Mom and Sarah like that. Never."

"I know," Dad says, choking back tears. "I'm glad."

That's when I look at Dad's T-shirt. Really look at it. "You know," I say, "how you sometimes make mistakes on your T-shirts?"

He smiles. "Yes."

"Well, Dad, you got this one just right. It's perfect."

"So are you, Lily." And he squeezes me into the tightest hug. "So are you."

Author's Note

People often ask me, "Where do you get your ideas?"

I don't always have a great answer. But in the case of this book, I know exactly what inspired Lily's and Dunkin's stories.

THE GENESIS OF LILY'S STORY

In 2012, I attended Lunafest (Lunafest.org), a traveling festival of short films by, for and about women, with my friend and neighbor, Pam. One of the films was *I Am a Girl!,* written and directed by Susan Koenen. The film begins with Joppe—a joy-filled girl— riding a bike. Joppe swims, jumps on a trampoline and confides to her friends that she likes a boy, who she hopes likes her, too. Joppe is a girl, born with male anatomy. She speaks eloquently, heartbreakingly, about understanding that she will never be able to carry a child, and hopes her future husband will be okay with that. When the film ended, I looked over at Pam. Tears were streaming down her cheeks.

I knew I had to write about this.

But I also knew I couldn't write about this. Yet. I didn't have the understanding. And I didn't have the experience, which meant I'd have to work incredibly hard to get the research and the heart of the story right.

I put the idea on a back burner and got on with my life, but every time I read an article about a transgender individual, I saved it. I paid attention. I began to educate myself.

Still, even with a growing file of research, I was too scared to write this story. I didn't know enough. And it was too important to get wrong.

So I wrote another novel—*Death by Toilet Paper*—about Benjamin Epstein, a sweepstakes fanatic, who goes to great lengths to keep a promise to his recently deceased dad and save his mom and himself from eviction . . . and about the indignities of cheap toilet paper.

I also took a wonderful job teaching high school students creative writing. All the while, I kept gathering more information, kept paying attention. I poked at beginnings of this new novel about a transgender girl, but I wasn't brave enough to commit.

One day, a student, Isaac Ochoa asked, "Mrs. Gephart, how's that new novel coming?"

How *was* it coming?

Isaac's innocent, thoughtful question reminded me that this novel wouldn't write itself. That maybe it was time. But would I be able to give this subject the weight and respect and quality writing it deserved?

I thought of how bravely my high school students wrote about challenging issues in their lives. The risks they took with their writing inspired me.

I thought of how brave every transgender person is, living an authentic life, or trying to live it, in a world where people are often ignorant and less than accepting.

When my department head invited me to return and teach again the following year, I said no. It was a hard no to say because I loved the students and my colleagues were extraordinary.

But I understood that saying no to teaching meant saying yes to writing this book.

I was ready.

After many failed attempts, I found my way into the story. I created a proposal and sample chapters and sent them to my agent, Tina Wexler. She read and then forwarded them to my editor, who shared it with my publisher.

This new book was different from anything I'd written before. I'm sure they were expecting me to write another funny book, but my publisher could tell this was a book from my heart, and she bought it.

So I got to work.

I pored over a mountain of books and articles. I watched documentaries and videos. I spoke with people and really listened. And I wrote.

Lily, of course, is fictional. But she is a composite of the many stories I read and heard.

It is my hope that her story will open a pathway from heart to heart—a pathway of empathy, compassion and kindness.

THE GENESIS OF DUNKIN'S STORY

Dunkin's story emerged from a promise I made to our older son, Andrew.

Incredibly bright, Andrew stopped doing his homework from about seventh grade on and often skipped class during his last years of high school. His moods were mercurial and volatile. His behavior often upset the people who cared about him. Like Dunkin, our son often self-medicated with caffeine, in the form of copious amounts of sweetened coffee and soda (which ruined his teeth).

Andrew was eventually diagnosed with bipolar disorder.

It took a long time to get Andrew on the right medications that helped modulate his moods and behaviors. It took me even longer to understand that Andrew's illness wasn't hard only on his dad, his brother and me, it was also a daily struggle for him. Things that seemed easy for other kids were impossible for Andrew. Even now, in his early twenties, school and work seem beyond his capabilities. But he has a small group of devoted friends, a caring family and creative hobbies that bring him joy.

Within the difficult reality of dealing with our son's mental illness, we found a beacon, a saving grace: NAMI, the National Alliance on Mental Illness. Liz Downey, the former executive director of our local Palm Beach County chapter, welcomed us with open arms and lots of information. My husband and I took their free Family-to-Family course, and it changed our lives. That course transformed the way we thought about Andrew and his illness. It provided the insight and understanding that allowed us to be compassionate to our son and to ourselves. We met other families struggling with the same and similar situations.

We felt less alone. We felt more empowered.

NAMI not only embraced us, it embraced our son. Smart, charming and witty and completely comfortable with public speaking, Andrew began giving presentations for NAMI to medical professionals, caregivers, teachers and parents about what it's like to live with a mental illness.

After each of Andrew's presentations, people from the audience came up to me and said, "You must be so proud of your son." What a joy to realize they were right. After those presentations, I looked at our son in a different light.

It was after one of those presentations that Andrew and I discussed writing about his mental illness. It was too hard for me to do then. Painful memories of his challenging behaviors were still raw. But I promised Andrew I would write about bipolar disorder. Someday.

I've spent so much of our son's life researching various mental illnesses and learning from families who have loved ones with a mental illness. While there are commonalities and patterns in behaviors, the illness presents uniquely in each individual.

I did additional research and interviewed experts in the field of mental health for Dunkin's story. While his behaviors and symptoms may not be typical of people with bipolar disorder, it is possible for the illness to manifest this way.

I trust Dunkin's story will shine a light on the fact that there's help and hope with good doctors, the right medications and community support. And I back NAMI's mission of ending the stigma often associated with mental illness, which sometimes prevents people from seeking the care and help they need.

Above all, with both Lily's and Dunkin's narratives, I wanted to be as respectful and emotionally truthful as I could while telling a good story.

I hope I have succeeded.

Thank you.

Acknowledgments

A great number of people contributed to this book, even if they may never know it. This work stands on the shoulders of the bravely told stories that came before it—the stories of Jazz Jennings, Janet Mock, Jennifer Finney Boylan and many, many others.

My agent, Tina Wexler, is a wonder. I'm proud of the breadth and scope of the clients and projects she represents. And I'm extraordinarily fortunate to have her on my side, offering support, editorial expertise and guidance in myriad ways.

Beverly Horowitz, publisher at Delacorte Press, Penguin Random House, believed in me and took a chance on this book. Thank you for being open-minded, openhearted and wise.

My editor, Krista Vitola, provided not only extensive editorial feedback but constant and steadfast support.

Editor Kate Sullivan graciously added another set of eyes and a smart editorial voice to the revision process.

Christopher Kye, a Palm Beach County psychiatrist, answered questions for this book and helped our son get on the best medication profile possible. I'm grateful for his expertise and for the time he has taken with our son.

Thanks to Gary Tsai, MD, Medical Director, Substance Abuse Prevention and Control, County of Los Angeles Department of Public Health, for answering my questions and for helping create a must-watch documentary, *Voices,* about the human and untold stories of psychosis (voicesdocumentary.com).

Much gratitude to Liz Downey, former executive director of our local NAMI, who answered questions for this book and provided a lifeline for our family (and *many* families) during a time of crisis.

Friends Marsha and David Martino often provided understanding ears, support and shared experience. As did friends Marcia and Bob Brixius.

With appreciation to author Jeannine Garsee, who graciously answered my questions and shared her knowledge from working at a mental health facility.

Since 2000, I've belonged to the same writing critique group, whose members are my emotional refueling station. Love and gratitude to Sylvia, Jill, Linda, Laura, Ruth, Gail, Becca, Shutta, Dan, Carole, Janeen, Audrey, Lori, Jan, Peter and Stacie. (Special thanks to John for sharing his truth after I read the first chapter; it was then I realized I might have something here.)

So many people work tirelessly to get good books into the hands of young people. Much gratitude to Bobbie Ford and to copy editors Jen Strada and Colleen Fellingham.

For doing vital work connecting young people to the books that might save their lives and will surely shape their lives, thank you to dedicated, creative, compassionate teachers, librarians and parents. It's been a joy to partner with you in our mission to provide windows to the wider world and mirrors to the inner world for young people through reading and writing.

I've been blessed with friends who are like family and family who are like friends. My nieces and nephews make me burst with pride, in particular Nicole, who has shined so much light into my life. And my sister, Ellen, who has been everything you'd hope a big sister would be . . . and more. Love you forever, sis!

My husband, Dan, makes every single day better.

Our sons, Andrew and Jake, have taught me so much about what's important in this life: kindness, compassion, empathy and *love*.

Resources

TRANSGENDER/GENDER VARIANCE ORGANIZATIONS

Gender Diversity (genderdiversity.org): Increases the awareness and understanding of the wide range of gender variations in children, adolescents, and adults by providing family support, building community, increasing societal awareness and improving the well-being for people of all gender identities and expressions.

Gender Spectrum (genderspectrum.org): Provides education, training and support to help create a gender-sensitive and gender-inclusive environment for all children and teens.

GLAAD (glaad.org/transgender/resources): GLAAD rewrites the script for LGBT acceptance. As a dynamic media force, GLAAD tackles tough issues to shape the narrative and provoke dialogue that leads to cultural change. GLAAD protects all that has been accomplished and creates a world where everyone can live the life they love.

PFLAG (community.pflag.org): Parents, Families, Friends and Allies United with LGBTQ People to Move Equality Forward was founded in 1972 with the simple act of a mother publicly supporting her gay son. PFLAG is the nation's largest family and ally organization. Uniting people who are lesbian, gay, bisexual, transgender and queer (LGBTQ) with families, friends and allies, it is committed to advancing equality and full societal affirmation of LGBTQ people through its threefold mission of support, education and advocacy.

Trans Lifeline (translifeline.org): A hotline staffed by transgender people for transgender people.

Trans Youth and Family Allies (imatyfa.org): TYFA empowers young people and their families through support, education and outreach about gender identity and expression.

The Trevor Project (thetrevorproject.org): The leading national organization providing crisis intervention and suicide prevention services to lesbian, gay, bisexual, transgender and questioning youth.

World Professional Association for Transgender Health (wpath.org): As an international multidisciplinary professional association, the mission of the World Professional Association for Transgender Health (WPATH) is to promote evidence-based care, education, research, advocacy, public policy and respect in transgender health.

Videos, Books and Other Materials

Beyond Magenta—Transgender Teens Speak Out, written and photographed by Susan Kuklin, Candlewick Press, 2014.

The Cooperative Children's Book Center School of Education University of Wisconsin–Madison (ccbc.education.wisc.edu /books/detailListBooks.asp?idBookLists=446) lists suggested books for children and teens that provide information about or reflect the lives of gay, lesbian, bisexual, transgender and questioning (GLBTQ) youth and gay- or lesbian-parented families.

I Am a Girl! (lunafest.org/the-films/details/i-am-a-girl): A documentary about a transgender girl, written and directed by Susan Koenen.

Professor Jennifer Finney Boylan (jenniferboylan.net) serves as the national cochair of the Board of Directors of GLAAD, the media advocacy group for LGBT people worldwide. She has written memoirs about her life in two genders and writes about transgender and other issues on her blog.

For a list of books inclusive of LGBT family members and characters, visit welcomingschools.org/pages/books-inclusive-of-gay -family-members-and-characters.

Additional Transgender Resources

neutrois.me/resources: An intimate exploration of identity and finding life wisdom beyond the gender binary.

Trans (transthemovie.com): A feature film documentary about transgender individuals.

Trans Bodies, Trans Selves—A Resource for the Transgender Community edited by Laura Erickson-Schroth, introduction by Jennifer Finney Boylan, Oxford University Press, 2014.

A video in which a mother stands up for her child and all transgender children:
youtube.com/watch?v=mkHx_2dpEbw&feature=youtu.be.

MENTAL HEALTH

Facing Bipolar: The Young Adult's Guide to Dealing with Bipolar Disorder by Russ Federman, PhD, and J. Anderson Thomson, MD, New Harbinger Publications, Inc., 2010.

National Alliance on Mental Illness (nami.org): Support, education and advocacy.

Voices (voicesdocumentary.com): A documentary about the human and untold stories of psychosis.

Welcome to the Jungle: Everything You Wanted to Know About Bipolar, But Were Too Freaked Out to Ask by Hilary T. Smith, Conari Press, 2010.

FOREST CONSERVATION/TREE PLANTING

The Arbor Day Foundation (arborday.org/trees/index.cfm): Information about how to plant a tree and which trees to plant where you live.

The Legacy of Luna: The Story of a Tree, a Woman and the Struggle to Save the Redwoods by Julia Butterfly Hill. HarperOne, 2001.

Plant a Billion effort through the Nature Conservancy (plantabillion.org): They have a goal of planting a billion trees by 2025.

"Up a Tree Without a Paddle" (huffingtonpost.com/david -horton/up-a-tree-without-a-paddl_b_23099.html): An essay by David Horton about the need to not plant single trees, but to save the existing biodiversity in forests.

Discussion Questions

Lily and Dunkin is a powerful, timely story with tremendous potential for meaningful discussion. Below are some questions to consider as you read:

1. A transgender person is someone who does not identify with the biological gender assigned to him or her at birth. Lily, born Tim, associates as a female and wants to start the hormone therapy that will allow her to begin the physical transition to becoming a girl. When did Lily begin to think of herself as a girl? Why is it best that she begin the hormone therapy now? Her mother and sister are very supportive, but her father is not. Discuss why her father is resistant. How is Lily's father finally convinced to support her decision?

2. Throughout the book, members of Lily's family and her close friend tell her how brave she is. How does Lily exhibit this bravery when she stands up to the city in an attempt to save the tree she has named Bob? Why is the tree especially important to her as she takes bigger steps in becoming Lily? What is her ultimate act of bravery?

3. Norbert suffers from bipolar disorder, a mood disorder that causes extreme lows and extreme highs. The proper medication can control his mood swings. Why does he think stopping the medication will help him on the basketball court? Why does his mother suspect that he isn't taking his medication?

Who is Phin? Why is Norbert's mother so concerned when he talks to Phin?

4. Lily is one of the first people Norbert meets when he moves to Florida. Why does Lily nickname Norbert "Dunkin"? Why is Lily so disappointed when Dunkin wants to sit with the basketball team at lunch? Cite evidence that Dunkin is uncomfortable when the basketball players call Lily names like "fag" or bully her in the hallways.

5. Both characters are bullied because they don't fit in with their classmates. Why are they hesitant to report the bullying to school officials? How might schools intervene to help students like Lily and Dunkin?

6. Discuss the enormous courage it takes for Lily and Dunkin to share their secrets. How does their acceptance of one another affect the way they act throughout the rest of the novel? It won't be an easy road for either of them. What are some of the obstacles they are likely to face in the future?

7. How is this book about tolerance and understanding?

Prepared by Pat Scales, Children's Literature Consultant, Greenville, SC.

About the Author

Donna Gephart's award-winning novels are packed with humor and heart. They include *Death by Toilet Paper; Olivia Bean, Trivia Queen; How to Survive Middle School;* and *As If Being 12¾ Isn't Bad Enough, My Mother Is Running for President!* Donna is a popular speaker at schools, conferences, and book festivals. She lives in South Florida with her family, including two shelter dogs, and has no pink plastic flamingos on her lawn (yet). For reading guides, resources, writing tips, and much more, visit donnagephart.com.